There was no denying it. She was attracted to Ian.

She wanted to stay here, close to him. Cementing this chemistry in her mind to go over and over again later. A chemistry she saw reflected in the depths of his dark eyes, heard in the catch of his breath.

Except she couldn't dare linger, not with an audience of her sons and his mother, and when she had a waterlogged cabin to investigate.

Breathless, she stepped back. "Thank you. For stopping the boys. For keeping me from falling on my face. I'm okay now. I need to call the O'Briens before it gets worse."

His chest rose and fell quickly in a way that affirmed yet again that he wasn't unaffected either. "I'll look into turning off the water valve and power from outside."

"Thank you," she said. Was that husky voice hers? "But I hate to keep imposing—"

Quirking an eyebrow, he held up a hand. "I thought we'd moved past that. This is a crisis."

Without another word, he powered toward the side of the house with powerful, take-charge steps. Tall. Broad-shouldered. As steady as the sturdy trees around him.

It would be so easy to count on his help.

Dear Reader,

What would happen to your Christmas plans if all of your decorations were somehow destroyed? Well, that's exactly the dilemma faced by single mom Gwen Bishop in the latest novel of my Top Dog Dude Ranch series! A burst water pipe in her cabin soaks the gifts for her triplet sons as well.

Definitely a catastrophe!

However, as I wrote about Gwen's struggle to "recreate" the perfect holiday with the help of Christmas tree farmer Ian Greer, it became clear that the truly perfect season is not found in the decorations or gifts. The meaningful spirit of Christmas comes through making memories together. I hope that as you read *Their Convenient Christmas Engagement*, Gwen and Ian's story will bring back happy memories of holidays past, while inspiring ideas for creating future traditions.

Happy holidays!

Catherine Mann

PS To learn more about my Top Dog Dude Ranch series and other books in my backlist, visit my website, www.CatherineMann.com.

Their Convenient Christmas Engagement

CATHERINE MANN

HARLEQUIN

SPECIAL
EDITION

HARLEQUIN®
SPECIAL EDITION™

Recycling programs
for this product may
not exist in your area.

ISBN-13: 978-1-335-59435-8

Their Convenient Christmas Engagement

Copyright © 2023 by Catherine Mann

For questions and comments about the quality of this book,
please contact us at CustomerService@Harlequin.com.

Harlequin Enterprises ULC
22 Adelaide St. West, 41st Floor
Toronto, Ontario M5H 4E3, Canada
www.Harlequin.com

Printed in U.S.A.

USA TODAY bestselling author **Catherine Mann** has won numerous awards for her novels, including both a prestigious RITA® Award and an RT Reviewers' Choice Best Book Award. After years of moving around the country bringing up four children, Catherine has settled in her home state of South Carolina, where she's active in animal rescue. For more information, visit her website, catherinemann.com.

Books by Catherine Mann

Harlequin Special Edition

Top Dog Dude Ranch

Last-Chance Marriage Rescue
The Cowboy's Christmas Retreat
Last Chance on Moonlight Ridge
The Little Matchmaker
The Cowgirl and the Country M.D.
The Lawman's Surprise

Harlequin Desire

Texas Cattleman's Club: Houston

Hot Holiday Rancher

Visit the Author Profile page
at Harlequin.com for more titles.

To my sisters, Julie and Beth.

Much love to you both. I treasure the
Christmas memories we made growing up together.

Chapter One

Most people hated the hectic pace of the holidays. But not Gwen Bishop. She embraced the chaos as the perfect tonic for forgetting heartache.

And today? She was busy enough to forget every detail of the world's worst marriage.

Breathless, Gwen spread her arms wide to brace a wobbling shelf of snow globes, only half registering the apology of a teenage shopper who'd pulled one from the very back, nearly upending the entire display. Running the Top Dog Dude Ranch gift shop and chasing after her six-year-old triplets kept her busy enough in normal times. During the Christmas season? That pace went into hyperdrive.

Especially when the credit card machine went on the fritz like today. While the ranch had state-of-the-art Wi-Fi, connectivity could still be iffy in this mountainous area. Just her luck, the place was packed today with ranch guests looking for a last-minute gift and a warm place to thaw out.

Thankfully, even though the dude ranch's childcare was understaffed this week, her three sons were currently occupied. The downside was that they were in the back room of her store. Which made *her* hectic holiday season even more frenzied. All the mayhem was almost enough to make her forget that two years ago today, her husband died in a car accident—along with his mistress, who'd been in the passenger seat.

Once she'd stabilized the shelf again, Gwen reached for the snow globe in question—featuring a dog with a Santa hat—and turned back to the two teenage girls. After forty-five minutes of browsing, she was just grateful that they'd made a selection. With luck, soon Gwen could move on to the other customers before the music piping from the sound system finished another chorus of "The Twelve Days of Christmas."

Pulling a smile, Gwen placed the snow dome on the counter, the flurry of flakes mirroring the ones on the other side of the shop window. "Are you ready to check out?"

"Yes, thanks," one of the girls said, toying with her necklace that sported the initial *K* and motioning to the other teen, who was totally focused on taking selfies in front of the display of nutcracker necklaces. "My big sister will pay."

The other teen paused taking her diva, duck-lip selfies long enough to pass over her leather cross-body bag to her sibling.

Miss K fished out a wallet and plucked free a credit card, one of three peeking from the billfold. "Here you go."

Of course the girls wanted to use a card. "I'm afraid the card machine is down."

Apparently, this sale wasn't going to wrap up quickly after all.

The selfie-diva waved a hand dismissively. "Just charge it to our parents' room. We would text them but, uh, my battery is about to die."

Gwen pulled a tight smile. "I'll give them a quick call to confirm…"

Except she had only one bar of service on her own cell. She started to reach for the landline.

With a dramatic sigh, diva-girl pushed away from the makeup counter. "Never mind. We can pay cash."

Miss K opened the wallet again and pulled out a folded stack of money. She peeled off four twenties as easily as Gwen used a one-dollar bill. The ranch catered to all price points, from massive cabins, to a glamping campground.

These girls did not look like the camping sort, not even glampers.

After scanning the purchase into the machine tucked inside a vintage cash register, Gwen slid the payment into the drawer and bagged the merchandise—the St. Nick ornament, two Top Dog sweatshirts, the snow globe and a block of peppermint fudge. "Thank you so much for your business. Hope you have a wonderful vacation."

The minute the bells chimed on the closing door, she pivoted to check on her boys, just visible behind the half door between the shop and the back room. None of the remaining shoppers seemed close to making a purchase just yet, so she thought she could spare a minute.

Sitting on a blanket with their homework were Gideon,

Caleb and Timothy, each wearing a different color Christmas sweatshirt with a tree made from a painted handprint. Her sons looked just alike to other people, but they were so distinct to her. Caleb was the bookworm with a current obsession for anything related to whales. Gideon was her mischief-maker who'd given himself a haircut last week—a really *bad* haircut even the barber had struggled to fix. Timothy was her tenderhearted child who stuffed his pockets full of flowers, ever ready for anyone who seemed sad.

Even on such a busy day—and a day darkened with unhappy memories—the sight of her boys filled her heart with maternal love, fierce pride and contentment that had gotten her through the toughest times over the past two years.

She leaned over the half door and called, "Everything going okay with your homework?"

"Yep," Timothy piped up, the first to reassure her, as expected.

Gideon rocked back on his heels, running a hand over his new close-cropped cut. "Caleb is hogging the blue crayon and I need it."

"I don't see a timer." Caleb didn't even look up, only colored faster. "Whales are blue."

She started to open the half door to referee and locate the extra box of craft supplies—just as a hand tapped her on the shoulder. So much for breaks. She turned to find…not a stranger, but a local who landed in her shop often lately.

"Hello, Mrs. Greer," Gwen said, looking around the woman to see if she was alone. "What can I help you with today?"

Florence Greer wandered in at least every other day, looking for conversation rather than something to buy. Her attention was usually drawn by the vintage toys Gwen restored. In her sixties, Florence had been diagnosed with Alzheimer's, according to her son, who usually arrived to help steer her back home when she lost her way. Her too-handsome son was a gruff lumberjack sort of man who seemed more comfortable in the woods than with people. He had left his park ranger job and moved with his mother to Moonlight Ridge to run a Christmas tree farm located next to the Top Dog Dude Ranch.

It was not a short walk by any means. The woman's memory might be slipping, but clearly her hiking skills were top-notch.

Florence shrugged out of her wool cape, revealing an oversize cable-knit sweater, jeans and duck boots that were still damp from the snow. A long gray braid trailed down her back. "I'm doing a little last-minute Christmas shopping and just love that metal train set in the window."

The same toy Florence had asked about three times this week.

And the week before that, she'd been fixated on a refinished wooden horse on wheels.

Before that, she'd coveted an old stuffed doll with a fresh gingham dress.

Gwen's heart squeezed with sympathy. She restored the toys to bring people joy and even though she wouldn't be making a sale today, she couldn't help but be pleased that the train had brought a grin to this lady's face.

"Of course, Mrs. Greer, I'll take you over to look at it." Gwen leaned into the play area, calling out to all, even though she really only meant Caleb. "Boys, behave now, share the crayons, and we'll go to the cowboy cook-out after I close up."

Stepping forward, Mrs. Greer waved at Caleb, who was crab walking his way off the blanket. "Well, hello, Ian. Imagine finding you here."

Gwen winced. Ian was Florence's son's name. The hot lumberjack-looking son. Who would need to be called. Soon. But right now, Gwen struggled with how to handle the woman's confusion about Caleb. Before she could speak, her son jumped up on the half door, balancing on his stomach.

"Hi, lady. My name is Caleb and I like whales." As he rocked on the ledge, his feet drummed against the bottom panel. "I got a girlfriend. Her name is Ruthie and she likes piranhas."

"She sounds like a wonderful young lady." Florence stepped forward, taking Caleb's hand as he lunged over and into the shop. "I used to teach science to little children just like you."

"That's cool," Caleb said, still holding her hand. "Maybe you can be *my* teacher. Mine is cranky and is always telling me to sit at my desk."

Now, that was a discussion for another day. Gwen tried to reroute the woman. "Mrs. Greer, would you like to look at the train now?"

"The train? No, I came for… Uh… I'm looking for…" Florence fished through her purse, growing more and more agitated. Finally, she looked up with confused brown eyes. "I seem to have misplaced my list."

Caleb leaned closer and whispered upward, "I misremember things too sometimes. Like how I forgot to brush my teeth last night, but don't tell my mom."

"It's our secret," Florence said before her forehead furrowed. "But I did not forget. People keep moving my things around. Where's my son?"

Gwen recognized the signs of sundowning, an increased sense of confusion and agitation later in the day. More often than not, that was when Mrs. Greer landed in the Top Dog's gift shop. When that happened, she couldn't be trusted to make her way home on her own. Gwen would have to contact Ian.

"Mrs. Greer, your son's not here but we can call him." Gwen rested a light hand on the woman's arm. "I'm sure he's wondering where you are."

And as Gwen reached into her apron pocket for her cell phone, she prayed that one bar of connectivity would be enough to get her message through. As she tapped out the words of the text message, she told herself her speeding heart rate was only a byproduct of her busy day. Not because she would soon be seeing grumpy, hunky Ian Greer.

Because even if she had the time for a relationship—which she did not—today's gut-wrenching anniversary reminded her that she wasn't interested in putting her heart on the line ever again.

Ian Greer was out of ideas for keeping his mother safe.

Exhausted and frustrated from the top of his head all the way down to his muddy boots, he steered his work truck along the snowy mountain road leading to the Top Dog Dude Ranch's main lodge. He'd changed jobs, purchasing the Christmas tree farm in Moonlight Ridge, Tennessee, for more flexibility to care for his mom. And still it wasn't enough to keep track of her, according to the latest text he'd received from Gwen Bishop.

A text sent over an hour ago, when he'd been deep in the woods.

The instant he'd read it, he'd assured Gwen he was on his way and asked her to please, please not let his mother leave until he could get there. Asking for favors didn't come easily, especially when he knew that the single mother already had a full plate herself.

He'd loaded his dog in the crew cab and hit the road. His oversize mutt was tethered in the back seat, but sitting up, Sampson rested his head on Ian's shoulder. The dog looked to be a Great Pyrenees/Labrador retriever mix, with gangly legs and a fluffy white coat, but there was no way to be sure since Ian had gotten him at the shelter as a puppy. A puppy that grew and grew and grew. Thank goodness the Top Dog Dude Ranch was dog friendly throughout. Taking Sampson home first would have delayed him even more in retrieving his mom.

Besides, he enjoyed having Sampson with him.

Throwing his truck into Park, he waited for the sidewalk traffic to clear before stepping out, a crisp breeze whirling the snow around him.

"Come on, buddy." Ian opened the back door and unhooked the mutt's tether before attaching a leash to his collar.

His gentle giant lumbered out of the truck and onto the icy sidewalk, giving himself a massive shake-off before ambling forward. While the Top Dog Dude Ranch covered acres—stables, barns, cabins, a main lodge, even a small arena—this narrow little main street was the hub of activity. As always, there was plenty to see and do.

But today, he focused only on making fast tracks to the gift shop. To his mom. Who was in the care of the too-distracting shop manager. Not that he was in the market for a love life. His fiancée had dumped him because—according to her—he spent too much time taking care of his mother. He'd been glad to uncover her true nature before they'd tied the knot. Good riddance. Still, it would be a long time before he trusted another woman. He'd come to accept that his mother's welfare was his top priority. Anyone who had an issue with that could take a hike.

Sampson padded alongside him, leaving fat paw prints in the freshly fallen snow. Ian charged forward, past the packed ice skating rink with a massive Christmas tree in the middle. He'd delivered the forty-foot-tall specimen himself just yesterday. Decorations had been hung—large red and green paw prints. Tomorrow night, the staff would host a lighting ceremony for the guests, with dinner and music. His mom would love it.

He hoped.

His feet carried him by memory to the shop. Heaven knew he'd been there often enough lately. The window was trimmed in multicolored lights, the larger, old-fashioned kind. With the vintage toys, the picture window resembled a throwback in time.

No wonder his mother was drawn to this place.

Shoving open the door, he stepped into the scent of

cinnamon and Christmas. Cookies and tradition. Carols chimed through the air.

Sampson at his side, Ian searched the store for his mother, scanning past a group wearing matching family reunion sweatshirts, over a couple that looked to be on their honeymoon. But his mother was nowhere in sight. Had she wandered off again? He hated to think that Gwen Bishop would have let his mom walk out, still he knew all too well how adept his mother could be at giving people the slip.

As he scanned for his mom, his gaze stopped short—on Gwen.

Only twenty feet away, she stood behind the vintage cash register, the red highlights in her pale blond hair shining in the overhead fluorescent light. Her blue eyes widened in recognition as they locked with his, a snap of current popping like static. The same awareness he experienced every time their paths crossed.

Did she feel it too? If so, then she'd been doing her level best to ignore it as well, because she hadn't given him so much as a hint of encouragement.

She angled to say something to the customer beside her before starting toward him, winding around a display of carved Santas, past a shelf of snow globes. She sidestepped a young family kneeling to inspect the electric train circling the base of a decorated tree.

And as she moved, he allowed himself a moment to study her before real-world concerns took precedence again. Her apron was patterned with tiny paw prints, her name tag shaped like a bone with the Top Dog Dude Ranch logo and her name. A sprinkle of freckles danced across her nose. She looked like a life-size version of a treetop angel.

Except his thoughts traveled very naughty paths when it came to this particular angel, even though he knew she was too sweet for a jaded guy like him.

Stopping in front of him, Gwen stuffed her hands in the apron pockets. "You're here." She nodded toward Sampson. "Both of you."

Her laugh was soft, husky, like a bedroom voice. He reminded himself the sound was more likely from the cold air and a long day at work, which he and his mother had made even longer. Guilt pinched.

"I came as soon as I got your message. There was no time to run Sampson here back to the house. I hope you don't mind." He pulled off his gloves and swept the snow from the shoulders of his parka.

"The shop is canine friendly as long as they're leashed." She tipped her head to the side. "Do you mind if I give him a dog treat?"

"He would like that. Thanks." Sampson was probably as starving as Ian, both having missed supper. "Sorry it took so long, but I was in the woods."

"I'm just surprised the text came through at all. Connectivity is questionable today." She nodded as she reached into a dog-shaped cookie jar and pulled out a treat. "I understand."

After waiting calmly for the dog to sit, she passed over the biscuit on her palm. Sampson nibbled it up gently, eliciting another one of those low laughs that teased the air.

His eyes could linger on her if he let them. He didn't intend for that to happen. "And my mom is where…?"

"Mrs. Greer is in the back." Her eyebrows pinched

together, looking a hint offended. "Did you think I would let her leave?"

"She can be slippery." He knew that all too well. Just this week, she'd gathered everything to work in her little greenhouse patio and take in the sun, only to disappear out the back door in her slippers. "Lately, she's gotten better at pretending to understand what's going on around her. Like a last defense against the disease."

Gwen's face relaxed, her blue eyes sympathetic. "Well, rest assured, I wouldn't have let her wander off, especially late in the day with the whole sundowning effect. I figured if you hadn't responded by closing time, I would drive her over."

It took him by surprise that she knew the phrase *sundowning*—that she understood the increased confusion that came more often near the end of the day.

"I'm glad you didn't have to do that." He adjusted his hold on Sampson's leash. "Mom and I have imposed enough."

"Nothing to worry about. It's been a roll-with-the-punches kind of day." She was always so polite, so gentle-natured. So much so it would be easy for others to take advantage. "My boys' day care had to cancel today, so I've had them here since they got off the school bus."

He felt even worse for putting her out, and her boys too. If they'd had to delay their supper as well... Time to let her move forward with her day instead of holding things up for her. He wasn't even sure why he'd talked so much. He wasn't usually a chatty sort. "You've gone above and beyond on my mother's behalf, and I'm grateful. So if you'll just point me toward her, we'll be on our way."

"She's in back helping the boys with their homework. If you look right over there…" She motioned to the doorway leading to a back office or storeroom-type area, the bottom panel closed, the top half open. Sounds wafted out. Childish giggles mingled with words from his mother, something to do with whales. His mother sounded happy.

Peaceful even.

A state of mind he had not seen in her that often lately.

He missed his mom. Or, rather, missed how she used to be, before the disease started stealing bits and pieces of her. Seeing her now, so totally herself for the moment, made him happy and squeezed his heart all at once.

Memories rushed over him of all the times he and his mother had sat at the kitchen table, with her teaching him multiplication. Or sitting in front of the fireplace listening to the sound of her voice as she read his favorites… *The Call of the Wild, White Fang, Watership Down.* Even then he'd had a love for anything to do with the outdoors. His mom's life must feel so isolated now with him at work all day.

No wonder she wandered over here, between the draw of the vintage toys and young boys to tutor.

"Thank you," he said, meaning more than just an afternoon of keeping her from leaving. Wishing he could properly thank her for this momentary glimpse of who his mom used to be.

"My grandmother had Alzheimer's," she said, her blue eyes full of empathy and sadness. "She lived next door to us. I understand the worry, the need to know that she's safe."

"It gets tougher and tougher to ensure every day."

Exhaling, he instinctively reached for the comfort of his dog, threading his fingers through the long fur. "At least let me do something to show my thanks."

"Truly, no—"

He held up a hand to stop her from protesting. "Would you and the boys like to come with us to the ranch's tree lighting party tomorrow night?"

The invitation fell out of his mouth even though he had no idea where the idea had come from. But it felt like the right thing to do.

"Thank you," she said, already shaking her head, "but I'm supposed to work the event."

"And there's no chance of getting the evening off?" Why was he pushing? Still, he couldn't make himself let up.

She worried at her bottom lip with her teeth. "My assistant has been asking for extra hours and the boys have been spending a lot of time here…"

Victory was in sight. "And it'll be Friday, so the boys don't have school the next day."

She hesitated for a moment before smiling. "Sounds like you've thought of everything."

"Apparently not," he said wryly, "or my mother wouldn't keep slipping out and wandering over to your shop."

From the look on her face, the slow nibble of her lip, he could see she was about to say no. He should be relieved. She tempted him in a way that no other woman had in a long time. He didn't need that kind of complication right now. Not after the number his last relationship had done on him. But he then heard his mother's happy laughter, thought of how rare that sound had become.

How long had it been since he'd felt a moment like this one—normal and good?

Just when he'd given up hope of finding a way to persuade her, Gwen nodded tightly and said, "Sure, thank you."

Victory pulsed through him, even as he didn't have a clue why this win was so important to him. He clapped his hands together and called out, "Boys, would you like to see Santa tomorrow night at the tree lighting party? I've got an inside track that will get you to the front of the line."

Chapter Two

Gwen may have said yes, but she'd felt pressured knowing that her boys would love the outing. She still couldn't decide whether to be pleased or irritated by Ian Greer's pushiness.

The two emotions shuffled back and forth within her through the evening and well into the next morning as she helped her boss—Hollie O'Brien—prepare for the tree lighting ceremony. A festivity she would be attending with Ian Greer, thanks to his offer that had her boys squealing and jumping up and down with excitement. How could she say no? She couldn't. And he had to have known that.

Irritation edged in for the win.

But she would hide it for the sake of not ruining the event for her sons. She was good at tamping down emotions after a loveless marriage. Her boys' happiness mattered most to her.

Bundled up in a parka and leather gloves, she unloaded an assortment of her restored toys, placing them along the vendor table—wooden nesting Santas, a reindeer jack-in-the-box, a carousel music box with gleaming new paint and an extra coat of varnish. Some days she fantasized about making a living off her refurbished toys. But that dream would have to wait until her boys were grown. As a single mom, she didn't have the time and couldn't afford the financial risk of leaving her steady, dependable job to try to start up a new business. Her job was fine for now—especially since her focus was on her family, anyway.

This evening's event would launch the wonder of the holiday for Caleb, Gideon and Timothy. And there was no doubt this festival promised to be a memorable, top-notch night. The tree lighting ceremony would include crafts and food. A sleigh was even parked by the tree with baskets of ornaments for the guests to add to the towering pine. A bright red ladder gleamed, perfect for reaching higher branches although most of the upper boughs had been pre-decorated. Picnic tables with red checkered cloths were lined up under open-air wooden shelters, infrared heaters attached to their ceilings. Centerpieces made of fresh garland boughs stretched along the length of each table, with pine cone wreaths in the middle sporting wooden dog bones. A large doghouse filled a corner, covered in blinking lights, with three LED dog statues in front.

She couldn't deny that the outing was a good idea for them. So she'd agreed to go with him. For her boys, of course. Not because thinking of seeing Ian again launched butterflies in her stomach.

For now, though, she had a full workday ahead of her while two of the ranch's interns manned the gift shop.

Her boss called from the opposite end of the table, her voice puffing a cloud into the cold air, "Can you grab the other end of the tablecloth and even it out?"

"Of course," she said, adjusting it carefully so as not to upset the items already on display. Then she spread fresh greenery strategically. "I can't thank you enough for giving me the evening off."

She had the best bosses in the world. Hollie and Jacob O'Brien extended the family friendly vacation atmosphere into a family friendly work environment as well—something that was crucial for a single mom. She couldn't imagine working anywhere else, which was all the more reason to tackle any extra tasks Hollie requested.

"You work overtime at the store, even pulling shifts with children's events." Hollie opened a box with fat red bows and attached one at either corner of the table. "There are plenty of staff looking for extra hours for the holidays. You deserve to enjoy the evening...all of you. It's our pleasure for our Top Dog family to join in the events we offer."

Staff were welcome to use everything that was on offer for the guests, from the childcare to dining hall to recreational events. Even things that weren't completely gratis were still accessible through vouchers whenever there were openings. It was quite a perk on top of a generous paycheck with benefits. She even lived in one of the cabins.

Schedule permitting, she frequently signed the boys up for children's events at the ranch. Riding lessons, fishing, cookouts and crafts. Right now, though, the ranch calendar was booked with guests, with not a single cabin left unoccupied. Gwen had no problem taking on as much work as the ranch needed from her, after all that she got in return. Going above and beyond was just how things worked at Top Dog.

So she was treading water here as fast as she could.

Stepping back from the table, Gwen felt the weight of Hollie's gaze and asked, "Is there something between my teeth?"

"No, not at all. I'm just curious," she said with a gleam in her eyes, which matched the blue of her fleece-lined jean jacket. "The grapevine is fruitful around this place. I heard you're going to the event with Ian Greer."

Gwen didn't even bother asking how she'd learned that. It could have been from any number of employees walking through the gift shop on break. "And with his mother. And with my boys. It's not a date."

"Sounds like quite the outing," Hollie said with a grin.

"It's *not* a date," Gwen repeated—for Hollie's benefit as well as her own. "He's thanking me for the times I've helped look after his mother when she wandered into the store."

Hollie tutted sympathetically as she unloaded craft supplies onto the next table. "Sounds like he's thanking you with a date."

"She's a sweet lady," Gwen said, ignoring the "date" comment. Florence's help with Caleb's homework had been precious to watch. Her boys didn't have grandparents or older relatives and she felt that loss for them—

among others. "But Ian has a lot on his plate with her struggles."

"As do you," Hollie reminded, arranging plastic bags with makings for homemade ornaments. "I just wish you could find time for yourself. If you need me to watch the boys, our kids would be thrilled for extra time with their buddies."

The offer sounded idyllic but impractical. "You're very generous, but I wouldn't want to impose."

Hollie rested a hand on her arm. "It's not imposing to help a friend."

Given regular circumstances Gwen believed she and Hollie could have been the best of friends.

However, Gwen couldn't allow herself to forget for a moment that the O'Briens were her employers. Keeping this job was too important to her boys' well-being in ways that went far beyond the income. With no family to lean on for even emotional support, her boys needed the healing peace this place offered. All the more reason to double down, work hard and push back distracting thoughts about what she would wear tonight. "What do you need me to do next?"

Hollie hitched her hands on her hips, scanning the setup in progress. "We're in the homestretch. Let's finish up here so you can get ready for tonight…and your non-date with Moonlight Ridge's most eligible bachelor."

Ian had barely had time to shower after a full day prepping the farm. The tree lighting ceremony at the dude ranch would offer the best press possible for his burgeoning business, and he was expecting a massive influx of customers after the event.

His farm's location, right next to the Top Dog Dude Ranch, was perfect for growing the operation. He'd bought the place for a song because the previous owners were unable to sustain the upkeep any longer. He'd hated having to move his mom from the familiarity of the home in Gatlinburg where she'd lived for over twenty years, but the opportunity had been too good to pass up.

Sitting beside him in the front seat of the truck, his mother hummed "The Little Drummer Boy," tapping out the rhythm on the armrest as she stared out the window. Those familiar tunes from decades past seemed to soothe her.

The heat blasted through the cab, dash lights just starting to glow as the day waned. He guided the vehicle over the covered wooden bridge leading to the ranch's main entrance. Wreaths and lights broadcast the holiday vibe. Cars were already parked along the side of the road, clusters of people walking the rest of the way. He'd hoped the event would be a success, but this went beyond his expectations.

Thank goodness he had a reserved parking spot near the lodge once he picked up Gwen and her boys. His heart slugged against his rib cage at the thought of seeing her again.

His mother's singing dwindled into gasps of wonder. "Everything is so pretty here. All the lights in the trees." She pointed, waggling a finger excitedly. "Look at that one over there. They have those lit-up deer. I always wanted those."

He didn't bother reminding her they had two of them in their front yard now right under her favorite apple tree. The minute she'd mentioned wanting them last week, he'd picked up a pair after work.

Given how late it was in the day, he questioned his decision to bring her along. Evenings could be...challenging. But it was too late to change his mind now. He couldn't cancel on Gwen and the boys. At least his mom wasn't agitated. Forgetful, yes, but she seemed content commenting on the holiday trim all around them, linking to older memories which were clearer than something that happened last week.

Lights twinkled in the trees lining the narrow road winding through the ranch's cabins. He guided the truck slowly past snowmen in plaid scarves. Luminaries. A wooden crèche. His mother delighted in all of it. Maybe he would be best served taking her on more drives in the evening. Heaven knew the Top Dog Dude Ranch made for miles of scenic viewing.

And at the end of the road waited Gwen's cabin, a log structure tucked in the woods. His heart kicked up a beat against his ribs again. He wasn't sure why, but he couldn't deny the pulse, pulse, pulse.

Parking alongside Gwen's minivan that sported a wreath on the grill, he turned to his mom. "Would you like to wait in the truck or come up with me to get Gwen and the boys?"

He tried to offer her choices whenever possible. Simple ones, but enough to still give her a semblance of control over her world. She'd lost so much.

His mom popped the seat belt free. "I'd like to stretch my legs and get a closer look at those pretty decorations. Perhaps we could even walk to the lodge—it's not far from here."

"Yes, ma'am," he said, jumping out of the truck and circling over to her side to open the door.

Extending a hand, he made sure she was steady on her feet, although it appeared the snowy path had been well salted. He guided her up the front steps to the massive porch—a signature space for any of the ranch's buildings. Everything had been designed to encourage appreciation of the outdoors, a feature he respected. A wreath adorned her door. Two wooden nutcracker statues welcomed guests from either side of the door.

Vintage, fat multicolored Christmas lights lined the porch and glowed from the bushes, matching the ones blinking on the Christmas tree in the picture window. He could see Gwen's crafty hand in every bow and drape of greenery. He thought of his own house, devoid of decorations other than those two fake deer. There wasn't even a decorated tree. How ironic considering his job.

He pulled his hands from his pockets and knocked on the door. Before he could pull his arm back, the door swung wide, two of the three boys perched in the opening like the nutcrackers on the porch.

Gwen stood just behind them, and the sight of her in holiday red leggings and black boots stole his breath. She was like a beacon standing just inside the door, the living area scattered with toys behind her.

His mother knelt, her flowing wool cape pooling around her. "Hello, little man." She reached under her cape and pulled out her mammoth bag. "I have something for you to take to your friend Ruthie."

And what do you know, his mother reached right for the boy who'd spoken to her the previous day. At least

Ian thought it was Caleb. The boy next to him must be Gideon, given the shorn hair. Timothy usually stuck close to Gwen.

Funny how he was getting to know them so well, each one's personality shining through. They were not just triplets but individuals.

Caleb bounced up and down in his bare socks. "For me and Ruthie? Really?"

"Yes, I brought this little book on fish. You said she likes piranhas." She reached into her bag and pulled out three Little Golden Books with faded covers. "I brought one for each of your brothers too, although I wasn't as sure of what they would like."

Gwen reached to touch the book gently. "Oh my, those look like family treasures. Are you sure?"

"Of course," his mother said, rising. "My little boy is in junior high now, so he won't be reading them anymore."

Sighing, he gave a gentle nod to Gwen, giving the okay.

How ironic she could remember the name and interests of this child's friend, but couldn't recall the age of her adult son. Ian noticed how more and more, his mother found different ways to address people that didn't include a name. Little man. Not Caleb. Yet, she remembered speaking to him, and Ian hung on to that.

Today, his mom was having a good day. He hoped it lasted. Christmas had always been her favorite holiday and he wanted her to be able to savor as much as possible... Who knew what next year would hold for her.

Gwen placed the books reverently inside, calling out, "Come on, boys. It's time to go. Gideon, do you have your gloves? Caleb, let's leave the book here. Timothy, I've got your letter for Mrs. Claus in my purse. Alright," she said breathlessly, shrugging into her plaid coat. "Lead the way."

His mom spread her arms, the cape swooping the boys into motion. The boys squealed and barreled down the steps in that gravity-defying way of children. His mom followed behind them. Ian waited for Gwen.

She closed the door and turned the key. "That was really thoughtful of your mom to bring the books."

"She misses teaching." He checked his mom's progress and found her flanked by the boys, beaming at their animated chatter. "To be frank, she plain misses being busy."

"That's understandable." Gwen joined him at the bottom step. "Is that why she keeps wandering away? Because she's looking for something to do?"

An insightful thought, but it didn't take into account the full picture.

He tucked into step with Gwen as they picked their way along the well-lit path toward the main lodge. The echo of laughter and live music—holiday carols—carried on the early evening breeze. "I wish it was that simple. But she disappeared the other day while we were cooking supper together. I thought she would enjoy making her favorite cornbread in a cast-iron skillet—maybe even be reassured by the familiarity."

Her sleek ponytail swished over her shoulder as she tipped her face to look up at him. "What does her doctor say?"

"That this is the expected progression of her condition." He scrubbed a hand along the back of his neck, weary from discussing the disease when no amount of conversation would change things. "Let's talk about something else. Sell anything interesting at the shop today?"

With a quick nod, she smiled and said, "The sweetest young couple came in looking for a gift for her sister's new baby." She chuckled, her blue eyes reflecting the twinkling holiday lights draping the bowers overhead. "They just about cleared out my window display—two rag dolls, a set of hand-painted blocks, a miniature cradle, a set of wooden rattles and a spinning top."

"Wow." He whistled long and slow. "That's quite a haul. I'm impressed."

"I'll be up late tonight finishing some other projects to restock the window displays." She rushed to add, "But I love it."

"Do you ever sleep? A full-time job managing the shop…" He counted off on his fingers. "Skillful restorer of toys. Mom of triplets. Rescuer of the lost."

"I'll sleep after the holidays," she said wryly. "I imagine you understand feeling pulled in many directions as well given this is your big season."

"Sure, it's a busy time of year, but the tree farm gives me more flexibility to look after Mom, so I'm not complaining." Back before his mother's diagnosis, being in the woods all the time brought him peace. That was not the case anymore as he worried about his mom every moment he was away.

Fast footsteps echoed behind them just before a half dozen teens raced by, laughing and throwing snowballs on their way toward the party.

Gwen fell silent until they passed in a flurry of crunching footsteps. "Do you have other family to help you?"

"I'm an only child. My parents are divorced." The last thing he wanted was to talk about his dad. Some of the worst days were when his mom thought she was still married, before the divorce.

"You're a good son, Ian." Her encouraging words warmed the air.

"She's an incredible mother," he said, then added, "like you are."

"I don't know about that, but thank you all the same."

"My mom had it rough with just me." He exhaled a long white cloud into the cold air. "I can't imagine juggling triplets."

"At least they keep each other entertained." She motioned to her sons, squealing as they fake-skated on their boots. She reached forward as if to caution them, only to stop short at the sound of his mom's soft voice and sight of her gentle hand on their shoulders.

"They're cute little rascals." He and his former fiancée had talked about having kids, but he and Becky never could come to an agreement. Now he was glad they had never taken the plunge—on marriage or babies. The breakup would have been so much messier. Thoughts of her, while unhappy, reminded him why it wasn't a good idea to get involved again. "And Mom sure has taken a liking to little Caleb there."

He pointed toward the boy holding his mom's hand, kicking chunks of ice out of the way.

"Did you know that one is Caleb," she asked skeptically, "or was it a lucky guess? Most people can't tell them apart."

He clapped a hand to his chest and stumbled as if wounded. "I can't believe you doubt me." Righting his steps, he continued seriously. "Caleb is the one who's always taking everything in, like he's cataloging the world. Gideon has the shorn hair. And Timothy is the one who usually sticks closest to you."

"Wow, I'm even more impressed." And she looked it, her eyes wide, her cheeks flushed.

Her smile was so pretty it made his teeth ache.

"Well." He cleared his throat. "I've had a lot of time to get to know them lately with how often my mom has been wandering into your shop."

"I thought we'd cleared up that I'm glad to help." She elbowed him lightly as they sidestepped a family taking photos in front of a decorated covered wagon. "I do understand that Christmas can be a time of loneliness. Your mom seems drawn to the toys I restore."

"The older memories are stronger for her than the present." Like how his mom seemed drawn to young children the age of her former students, falling into those past routines and old sources of joy.

"If you think it would be okay, she's welcome to come sit with me while I restore a dollhouse."

Tonight had been about helping Gwen after all she'd done for him, not piling more onto the list of what he owed. Although he had to admit her offer was tempting—for his mother, of course. Nothing more. "That's generous of you, but we're okay."

"I would enjoy the company," she insisted. "And it would be my way of saying thanks for getting my boys those front row seats with Santa."

He searched for the right words as they stepped onto the main street sideway, nearing the main lodge and center of activity. How easy it would be to table this discussion altogether, but for some reason he couldn't define, he felt compelled to explain more, reveal more.

"I wish you could have known my mother before. She was so organized. She really kept her students in line. I spent a lot of time with my grandmother when I was little. My mom worked overtime as an elder sitter and went to night school to get her teaching degree. She finished by the time I was in second grade." He remembered well sitting in the bleachers at her graduation, convinced he would be in her classroom and finally get to see more of her. "After that, I was able to ride with her to school."

"What about your father? You mentioned they were divorced, but did you get time with him?"

Her genuine interest in others was admirable.

And a little intoxicating.

"You mean did my mom get a break other than when my grandmother pitched in? Not really." His father wasn't a bad man, just not present. "Dad was a truck driver, gone long hours, then they divorced."

"Thank goodness your grandmother could be there for your mom—but for you too," she said as they waited to cross at a street corner, his mom and her boys only an arm's reach away. "My grandmother always made me feel like the most important person in the world. She used to give me cheese toast for breakfast, with the good cheese, not the processed stuff. No matter what cheese I buy, though, I've never been able to replicate the taste."

"Memories have a flavor all their own."

"I like that." Her smile edged at all the chaos around them.

Lighting the air between them with more of that electricity, like static crackling and snapping. Stinging even.

But exciting. Then her grin faded, her pupils widening with awareness.

Gideon's shout cut the air. "Hurry up, everybody. We're gonna miss Santa."

Gwen blinked. The connection broke and she looked away, turning toward her sons.

"Gideon," she called, her hands gravitating to hold her son's hood, "slow down or you'll slip and fall."

Caleb bounced on his boot toes. "If you're hurt, we'll have to go home. And this night is too great to be over."

The child's words sent a whisper of alarm through Ian. As much as his mom would enjoy sitting with Gwen, he needed to put an end to the favors between them before he started looking forward to evenings like this. Because life had taught him many times over that great times often came to an abrupt end.

Chapter Three

"Now, aren't y'all a cute family," called out a lady wearing a knit cap with tiny reindeer antlers. "Boys, are you having fun with your grandma?"

Family?

The word froze Gwen from the inside and out until her breath felt like shards of ice lodged in her chest. Luckily, her sons didn't seem to hear. They were engrossed in waving to a couple walking their dachshunds, the pups decked out in Christmas tree sweaters with booties.

She pulled a tight smile. "We're having a lovely time."

Ian touched Gwen's elbow, leaning to whisper, "Sorry about that woman's comment. Let's just move along."

Scrunching her nose, Gwen glanced up at him, their faces so close she could see the masculine bristle along his jaw. "No need to correct a stranger."

She'd told herself a million times that this evening

with Ian wasn't a date. And even with her breath hitching in her throat, she knew it wasn't.

In fact, it resembled something far scarier—a family outing.

Because they truly did look like a family, and on the walk toward the Christmas tree, the people they walked past made that appearance evident. Compliments flowed, congratulating the two of them on their cute kids as if they belonged to Ian as well. An older gentleman shared a grandparent story with Florence. A newlywed couple said how they hoped they would be as happy after a decade.

Gwen would have put the brakes on the whole evening, but her boys were so excited about the event. Plus, Florence's face absolutely shone as they walked under an icy bower of trees. So Gwen resolved to tamp back her own insecurities and ghosts. She would make the most of the night for those who needed the holiday celebration: her kids and Florence.

And Gwen absolutely would not let herself be tempted by the man next to her, who smelled of fresh air and tangy soap.

Stepping away from Ian's enticing, towering self, she hooked arms with Florence as they waded into the crowd gathered for the tree lighting ceremony. Even having been a part of decorating that afternoon, she had to admit, the finished product was next level. Perhaps because of the energy buzzing all around them. Or the glistening wonder on the faces. Even the sunset was cooperating, refracting just the perfect amount of light off the snow.

And finally, she was in the Christmas spirit.

Up until now, she hadn't realized how little she'd been able to enjoy the season, too busy making sure it happened for others, from her customers to her children. Tonight, however, she let the festive air saturate her senses and soothe away the stress.

Florence smiled over her shoulder at her son, clapping her gloved hands together, her oversize cape fluttering. "What a wonderful party. This reminds me of when I would take you to the zoo to see the lights. They had live music, remember?"

"Definitely a good memory, Mom." He angled past a family tugging a garland-covered wagon full of children. "I suspect we're going to make plenty more this evening."

"With Gwen and the boys," his mother said, "it's all the more special."

Gulping, Gwen tore her gaze off those broad shoulders and focused on the celebration in front of them. On a flatbed wagon, Raise the Woof, the ranch staff's pickup band, were dressed in caroler's garb. The lead singer crooned familiar Christmas tunes, encouraging the guests in a sing-along. Children shook sleigh bells, while stable manager Eliza sang from behind a keyboard.

In spite of the cold evening, the space was arranged perfectly with designated areas to warm up. Three bonfires blazed, flames licking skyward. Baskets with the makings for s'mores were strategically placed nearby. Infrared heaters were mounted along the rafters of the open-air picnic shelters that sported stations with cocoa and cookies, cider and pastries from Hollie's bakery, including treats for both people and pups.

"Mama," Caleb called, pointing excitedly at the live

nativity petting zoo, with a camel, donkeys, sheep and goats. "They even have a llama."

Gideon spun in circles, arms airplane wide. "I wanna ride the donkey."

Timothy tugged the edge of her jacket gently with his mittened hand. "Can I feed the sheep, pretty please?"

"Yes, yes and yes, to all of it," she agreed with a laugh. "We have the whole evening. And don't forget there will be even more activities at the ranch before Christmas."

"Thanks, Mommy." Timothy gave her a quick, tight hug. "The kids at school say we live on vacation. I think they're right."

"That's a good way to think of it." Certainly this place offered fun activities for her sons on a regular basis that she could have never afforded on her own. The triplets were thriving here. "We are all very lucky to live here. Especially during the holidays."

"Mr. Ian, Mr. Ian, Mr. Ian…" Gideon rocked from foot to foot, his navy blue snow boots crunching as he seesawed. "If we come to your farm, will you take us out to cut down a *real* tree? We just have a fake one. I really want one that I can pick out and that smells like Christmas. Then we can decorate it with strings of popcorn and candy canes."

Thank goodness Ian hadn't heard as he was engrossed in getting a cup of cider for his mother.

"Gideon—" she rested her hands on his shoulders in her never-ending quest to ground her restless boy "—I'm sure he's too busy to have time to help just us. It's kind of him to bring us here tonight. We can't make a habit of taking advantage, though."

Besides, they already had a perfectly sufficient artificial tree and she didn't have the money to buy a live one.

"But Mr. Ian is having fun," Gideon insisted. "He's been smiling at you ever since we left home."

Gwen felt the heat climb to her cheeks and forced a logical answer up her tight throat. "That's because we *are* having a good time. And tomorrow the grown-ups have to go to work. As much as it may seem like we live on vacation, Mr. Ian and I both still have to work. Do you understand what I mean?"

"Yeah, I guess so," he said, batting at a low-hanging branch, knocking loose a shower of snow. Then his face lit with inspiration. "Maybe you could ask Santa Claus for more time off?"

This conversation was going nowhere fast. She knew the best way to distract Gideon was to keep him busy. The second his feet slowed, his mind would go into overdrive. "Look up there. Mr. and Mrs. O'Brien are about to start the event. You don't want to miss anything."

Jacob and Hollie O'Brien made their way slowly through the crowd, greeting guests. They moved in sync in their matching jeans, Stetsons, thick flannel shirts and suede jackets with fringe. To ring in the festive season, Hollie wore forest green boots and Jacob carried a sack over his shoulder that Gwen knew was full of gifts and party favors.

Their smiles genuine, they took the time to make all gathered feel special. That warm, sincere welcome was a trademark of the Top Dog Dude Ranch brand. The place was more than a resort. It offered a family friendly retreat with activities designed to heal hearts and strengthen bonds. She appreciated it all for her kids' sake, but for herself, Gwen wasn't counting on any relationship magic beyond affording gifts for the boys.

Jacob eased the fat red bag to the ground and took a microphone from the band's lead singer. "Welcome to the Top Dog Dude Ranch's annual tree lighting ceremony. Can you believe it's only four weeks until Christmas?"

Cheers rippled through the crowd, punctuated by applause and the enthusiastic ringing of jingle bells.

Jacob continued, "This year is all the more special since we've partnered up with the Greer Family Tree Farm."

Hollie leaned toward the mic, her dark braid swinging forward. "Wouldn't you all agree this is the most gorgeous tree ever?"

After the boisterous countdown, multicolored lights flickered on along the branches of the mammoth fir, eliciting first a big gasp, then oohs and cheers through the onlookers, followed by a deafening round of applause. The glow shone in the dusky end of day. Her boys' eyes went wide. All three stood side by side, silent and still. Ian slung an arm around his mom's shoulders and gave her a quick hug.

Gwen's heart squeezed at the beauty of the moment, of the joy so much brighter than any holiday decor.

After waiting for the applause to die down, Hollie continued, "Help us out by placing ornaments on the lower part of the tree. Staff are on hand at each ornament making station. And it's not just for the children."

The top boughs already glistened with pre-hung decorations, each one representing an animal that could be found in the manger, a nice way to incorporate the holiday with the ranch's vibe.

Hollie leaned forward conspiratorially. "There are also pens for you to write your Christmas wish on the back of the ornament before placing it on the tree. Afterward, we have a table where you can write a letter to Santa. The elves will help."

Jacob tipped the microphone back to himself. "We won't keep you any longer. Enjoy your dinner. Or s'mores by the campfire while we wait for Santa's arrival. Let the festival begin."

All three of her boys moved forward at once, in that triplet wave of synergy she'd long ago learned not to question, but still found mesmerizing. They charged toward the ornament table, ready to craft. Mrs. Greer trailed them, sipping her cider and leaning a hip on the table beside them.

Leaving Gwen alone with Ian.

Ian braced a boot on the bottom rail of the fence, drinking coffee as the triplets made their way through the petting zoo set up around the living nativity. Gwen snapped photos of Caleb with a donkey, Timothy threading his fingers through a lamb's wool, Gideon perching an angel's halo on his head. Meanwhile, Ian wondered how long he and Gwen could ignore each other.

His mother sat with two other ladies eating cookies and sipping cider. She looked relaxed, a rarity this late in the day. Perhaps it was because of the timeless nature of holiday traditions. She didn't have to rely on recent memories or wonder what year it was.

It was Christmas. And he should be happy.

Tonight's gathering brought back so many memories of holidays growing up. His mom had always done her best to make the most of any free event in town. Parades. Church plays. Town lights. On and on, she'd packed their December calendar. He wished he had more time to give her Christmas memories like this. Certainly the opportunities were available here at the ranch.

And yet, he wasn't able to focus on making new happy memories because one woman had him so on edge he couldn't think straight.

Backing as she snapped photos, Gwen stopped against the rail and lowered her cell phone. Sighing, she angled a look over her shoulder at him, her eyes wary. "Thanks for inviting us to come here with you. It really is easier to keep track of the boys with your extra set of eyes, which has made it more fun for them."

He folded his arms over the top of the fence, closer to her. Maybe if he acted at ease long enough the tension between them would fade. Life would return to normal. "Having the boys here with us made the evening more enjoyable for my mom too. She loves being around people—especially kids. I probably don't do enough to make sure she has the chance to socialize. Christmas is her favorite time of year and I'm working all the time. That's probably why she's even more restless lately."

"She looks like she's having a wonderful time now with Patsy and her sister." Gwen nodded toward the trio of ladies gabbing while watching the children write letters to Santa. "Patsy used to work here as a massage therapist, then moved to the other ranch location. They're here visiting family."

An awkward silence settled between them, cut only by the echo of people laughing, animals chuffing and bleating. Of their own volition, his eyes skimmed from hers down to her mouth. Her throat moved in a slow swallow before she licked her lips nervously.

He cleared his throat, then held up his napkin. "Cookie? The shortbread ones are top-notch."

"Thank you, yes, I didn't have time to eat earlier." She smiled, taking the treat, their fingers brushing, sparking with awareness even through gloves. Her eyes went wide for a startled moment before she took the cookie from him and stuffed it in her mouth, her gaze darting away.

Clearing his throat—yet again—he shuffled back a step, searching for a diversion, something, *anything* else to talk about.

His mom's laughter on the night breeze offered the perfect distraction. "She's missed her friends since we moved here. I really wish I could have found somewhere closer to where I grew up."

"I know what you mean," she said, her words tumbling out in a nervous rush. "I imagine you miss all those familiar places too, and the memories they hold. Tell me one of those memories. Bring it here. Metaphorically."

Something about this woman just got to him. Maybe it was the way she cared—genuinely cared—about what others were dealing with.

Scratching the back of his neck, he slid his boot off the bottom rung. "One year on Christmas Eve, I was lying in my bed, not having any luck willing myself to sleep. And then this thudding sound echoed from the roof. And then again. My grandma ran in the room and said Santa's reindeer had landed on our house and that Santa had dropped the gifts down the chimney in a hurry because he was running late."

She clapped her gloved hands together, the tip of her nose red from the cold. "I can see where your mom gets her sense of fun from."

"I hadn't thought of it that way." But it fit. Gwen was insightful. "Since it was after midnight, my grandma said I could go ahead and open my presents and stay up for as long as I wanted. I played with my new train set until sunrise. At that point, I was too exhausted to stay awake anymore and ended up sleeping until midafternoon."

"Your mom has been drawn to one of the train sets in my shop," she said softly, insightfully. She touched his wrist, smiling her encouragement. "Tell me more."

And he would. He knew that. He wondered how much else he would do to see that smile on her face again. "When I was older, I realized that my grandmother had done that so I would sleep all morning and my mother wouldn't have to wake up early after working so much overtime to make ends meet while she was getting her college degree. My grandmother always said Mom regretted not furthering her education. She wanted to be a geologist. She loved—loves—the outdoors."

The air filled with childish squeals as Gideon chased Caleb in a raucous game of tag. Other kids joined the triplets as they darted around Santa's sleigh.

"Like you," she said astutely. "My grandma—"

"The cheese toast one?"

"Right. She watched my cousins too. One year during summer break, she bought each of us our own baby chick. We built the coop ourselves." Her pretty blue eyes lit with nostalgia. "It was such a beautiful way to grow up."

"Much like your boys are enjoying at the ranch, out

here with nature and other kids they're close to. I've heard it said that the Top Dog Dude Ranch staff is like a family."

At the word *family*, she straightened, her neck and spine going ramrod straight. As if seeing her reaction triggered his own, he found himself itching with memories of his ex. It had been too easy to fall into the ease of talking with her, of sharing the evening with her.

He needed space before he did something reckless, like stroke her hair back from her face. He pointed toward a craft table near Santa's sleigh, where Hollie O'Brien was frantically passing out paper packets for crafts. "And speaking of family, I think yours needs your help."

All three of Gwen's boys were jostling to get closer to the ranch owner for one of the marker sets.

Gwen blinked fast. "Oh, that's right. Letters to Santa. I should go help them."

The speed with which she walked away shouldn't have felt like a personal rejection. He understood that she wasn't in the market for romance any more than he was. But still…he hoped she'd enjoyed their time together as much as he had.

He watched her walk away. How could he not? She drew his thoughts even when she wasn't around. And taking in the sight of her when she wasn't looking was safer. She truly was a stunning woman, in such a natural way. Sleek blond hair swishing as she walked. Long legs in holiday leggings. The whole package drew him.

Tempted him.

A hand clapped him on the shoulder, jarring him back into reason. He pivoted to find his buddy, Moonlight Ridge's sheriff. It was no surprise to see him there. Declan Winslow was married to the ranch's landscape architect, who'd played a large part in integrating the tree farm's greenery into the ranch decor. She was the one who had introduced the two men, and they had quickly hit it off.

In full uniform, Declan grinned. "How are you enjoying the limelight? Everyone's talking about the stunning trees you supplied around the ranch. And of course, particularly that towering one in the main street square."

"I'm thankful to your wife for the extra work." He'd been socking away every spare penny to save for the day his mother needed round-the-clock care. He feared that day was coming faster than his bank balance could accommodate. He'd even taken on extra duties at the dude ranch. A decision that had nothing to do with a certain single mom.

Or so he told himself.

"And I'm glad you're pulling overtime here while Charlotte's on maternity leave," Declan said, hitching a hand on his belt, just above his police radio. "She was worried if they hired a temp, she would be out of a job."

Not a chance of that. Charlotte was excellent at her job. Her gifted horticultural fingerprint could be seen on this event, even when she was absent. From the strategic placement and health of the trees, to the preservation of a natural, mountain forest.

"I doubt she's in any danger of being replaced. I'm just glad she and the baby…" a girl, but Ian couldn't remember the name "…are alright."

"Me too," Declan said with a huge but proud sigh. "We're not getting much sleep these days, but little

Heather is worth it. You and Gwen should bring the boys by to meet her."

Ian tipped his head to the side, sighing as, once again, someone assumed…

Before he could speak, another man pulled up alongside them—Micah Fuller, the ranch's lead contractor.

Grateful for the interruption, Ian nodded. "Good to see you, I've been meaning to reach out about the lumber project you mentioned."

"Let's meet tomorrow morning at the ranch café for coffee. If you're free, that is?" Micah grinned knowingly. "I hear you've been making friends with one of our other team members and her family."

Ian looked back and forth between the two guys, not fooled for a moment by their seemingly innocent comments. They were curious and looking for the scoop on gossip. Not gonna happen. "Definitely, let's have a work breakfast tomorrow. Don't let me keep you from enjoying the festivities this evening."

Micah shook his head, his work boots firmly planted. "I'm in no rush—I'm waiting for Susanna to lead the story time."

The excuse sounded likely enough. Susanna and Micah had become a couple when he oversaw his first construction project. She tutored his young nephew when Micah gained custody of him. Now they were married and expecting a baby. The guy had marital bliss written all over him and Ian didn't begrudge the fella a second of it.

But Ian wasn't interested in joining the club.

He started to turn away only to realize his mother was joining Susanna Fuller to assist with story time.

His mom took her place beside the elementary librarian. Ian flinched, hoping when he guided his mom away, she wouldn't become confused or upset.

Micah put a hand on Ian's arm. "Don't worry, man. Susanna's got this."

Sure enough, the librarian included his mom, and Gwen sat with her boys in front of Florence, as if looking out for her as well. "You're just in time for the next round of our Christmas story corner," Susanna announced to the triplets. Dressed in a Victorian costume, Susanna passed out sleigh bells, finger cymbals and wood blocks with tiny mallets. Her scruffy dog stayed close to her side, dressed as an elf. "Kids, I need your help with the sound effects. Are you up for that?"

The cheers and squeals of excitement swelled along with the jingling, clanging and drumming. Then story time began, his mother syncing into a director's rhythm with the sound effects as if the old teacher skills were ingrained in her muscle memory.

Micah leaned against a pillar on the picnic shelter. "Enough beating around the bush. Are you two an item?"

These guys were tenacious. But so was he when it came to his privacy, even if the dude ranch's gossip mill could make that tough.

"Gwen and me?" Ian shook his head. He needed to nip this in the bud. "No, we're just helping each other out."

Micah chuckled softly. "Looked like more than that to me. But whatever."

He didn't have time for "whatever," and neither did she. Ian clapped a hand on Micah's back good-naturedly. "Don't you have your own life to look after?"

"You're right," Micah conceded. "My beautiful wife asked me to have some of those cookies ready for her after she finishes. Pregnancy cravings and all. We make a good team—always have. Funny how when you're focused on working together romance just sneaks right up on you."

His gaze tracked directly to Gwen, her face lit up with laughter. Her hair swished forward, glistening like an angel.

And her legs. Man, those legs…

Time to put an end to this talk. "Just because you two hit the marital jackpot, doesn't mean I intend to play in that lottery. Thanks all the same."

He planned to keep his head down. Focus on work and his mom. And if that meant he and Gwen crossed paths on occasion? He would go in with eyes wide-open so as not to be sideswiped by a sneak attack from the wayward attraction.

Caleb liked that he got two chances to make sure Santa heard his wishes. First, when he wrote it on the back of an ornament for Santa to check later. And the second time, when he wrote a letter. He was really glad to have Mrs. Florence's help with all the words since he was only in the first grade. Timothy was doing better on his own. Gideon was happy just scribbling pictures.

Except his brother—younger by five minutes—kept hogging all the best crayons and coloring them down to a nub. He would've gotten his mom to make Gideon share, but Mom was getting refills for everyone on cocoa. There were grown-ups all around but nobody seemed to see what Gideon was doing.

Caleb leaned across the table. "You should give some-body else a turn with the red."

Gideon pushed harder, getting every corner of Santa's suit. "I don't see a timer."

Having his own words turned around on him, Caleb huffed back into his seat.

Timothy looked up from his long, long letter and said softly, "We're supposed to share. If you don't, Santa won't give you anything for Christmas."

Caleb panicked for a minute at the thought of Gideon not getting any presents, because even when he was mad, he didn't want his brother to be sad. His mom would be really upset too.

Then he realized, "You're wrong, Timothy. Santa doesn't play favorites. Santa likes me too, even when I forget to do my chores because I'm reading a book."

His mom read books on her tablet, but he liked the feel of paper in his hands. He had a big list of books that he wanted from the book fair, but he wasn't going to have enough money saved to get them all—because he kept getting lost in a book and forgetting to do his chores, which meant his weekly allowance was less.

He hated that chore chart. He wanted a chart for how many books he'd read.

Gideon tossed the crayon his way. "Take the red. I'm done anyhow. Mrs. Greer, will you take me to get a cookie?"

The sweet old lady nodded, holding out a hand that he knew was soft and smelled like flowery lotion. "We'll get some for your brothers too. Because sharing is car-ing. And you can call me Mrs. Florence, if you'd like."

Caleb watched her walk away and his stomach went

tight. Since she was gone, he was on his own with his letter. But he figured Santa would be good at making out all the words. He'd had lots of practice reading little kids' notes.

Across the table, a girl with pigtails was sitting on her knees, all focused on cutting out shapes for her letter, but the round safety scissors made for slow going. "I bet Santa can't even tell you apart from your brothers. So if they're bad then you're not gonna get anything either."

He went all panicky again, but worse. What if he was wrong about Santa not skipping bad kids and mixing him up with his brother? Still, he said, "He can so see that it's me. My brother's got a haircut."

The little girl pointed to Gideon. "So that's your brother over there right now. Santa's sure not gonna be happy with him."

Gideon was at the snack station, biting the heads off the gingerbread men then putting them back. Mrs. Florence knelt to talk to him, but Caleb saw his brother still had a cookie behind his back just waiting to be maimed.

The little girl pushed the scissors away and grabbed the green glitter. "You probably shouldn't eat the peppermint sticks either," she said in a know-it-all voice. "I thought I saw him licking them."

Great. Just great. Pretty soon there wouldn't be anything left to eat. This night had been really fun so far, especially since his mom had help. Now Gideon was wrecking everything. Mr. Ian probably wouldn't want to come with them anyplace anymore. This might be the last chance to talk to Santa Claus. So he'd better make sure his letter was perfect in case he and St. Nick didn't get another chance to talk.

Caleb chewed the end of his marker, trying to decide what to write on the back of his ornament. He had a lot of things he wanted—some simple stuff and some tougher. Simple stuff, like the next three books in the "Super Duper Scientist" series. But the tougher stuff? The stuff that he was even willing to give up his books for? That was hard to even think about because he probably couldn't get it.

He wanted more time with his mom without his brothers around.

That felt really not nice. He loved his brothers. They were triplets and that was special. But he also wondered what it would be like not to share everything—his room, his clothes, his toys.

Not to have to share his mom.

Was that a bad thing to wish for?

He knew Santa didn't play favorites, just like his mom didn't. So he wasn't going to waste his wish on something that wouldn't happen anyway. And he really didn't want his brothers to go away, not forever, anyway. Maybe just for a day to be the only child.

He scrunched his face up as he wrote on the ornament, worried because the space was small and his letters were big and he didn't know how to spell all the words. Still, he was gonna try to sound-spell the tough words because he couldn't take a chance asking somebody to write this part for him. This was just between him and Santa Claus.

Caleb held up his ornament to check it over. Not too bad.

Then he got a strange feeling, the kind he had when one of his brothers was hurt. He looked fast and saw that Timothy was breathing hard. Hyper-venting, or something like that.

"Timothy?" Worried, Caleb hopped off the bench seat. "Are you okay? Do you need your inhaler?"

His brother shook his head fast, pointing to where Gideon was pulling the bratty girl's pigtail. "Santa's gonna skip Gideon for sure," he said between gasps. "And if Santa keeps getting bad reports on our brother…"

Caleb sighed, putting his ornament back on the table. "I'll get him before Mom sees."

"Wait!" Timothy's eyes went wide. His breathing got slower. Almost normal. "I've got an idea."

Caleb waited, curious. Timothy might be the quiet one, but when he had something to say, it was usually worth listening to. "Yeah? What?"

Timothy tapped a glue stick on the table while he thought. "Maybe if Gideon isn't the one to get in trouble *all the time*, then it'll be okay. We can share the bad, so it's not just his. Like if Santa can't tell if it's me or Gideon. I never get in trouble, so if Santa thinks some of it is my fault…"

Lickety-split, before Caleb could figure out what his brother meant, Timothy grabbed the scissors and started cutting his own hair.

Chapter Four

Standing at the base of the stage waiting for Santa, Gwen crinkled her toes in her boots, the chill starting to leach through both pairs of socks after four hours at the festival. She scanned to check that her boys were still bundled up and saw all three had their stocking caps firmly in place as they formed a line for St. Nick. Her boys looked happy in this moment. A moment so precious, thanks to Ian.

Having him at her side to share in the holiday joy made the tree lighting festival all the sweeter. She savored the rumble of his laughter as Gideon raced around the ice skating rink in a fat bumper car. Soaked in his affectionate smile as Timothy won the snowman contest. Reveled in his cheers of encouragement as Caleb participated in the snowball bowling tournament.

Now, as she and Ian stood with his mother, waiting for her boys to share their letters to Santa, Gwen fought the urge to slip her gloved hand in his. Instead, she hitched the canvas bag higher onto her shoulder. The sack, sporting a Top Dog Christmas logo, bulged with the treats and stocking stuffer toys the boys had accumulated tonight.

Santa and Mrs. Claus rode in on horses, him on Goliath, a large Tennessee walking horse, and her on Nutmeg, a blood bay Thoroughbred. Both horses sported a wreath around the neck and plaid ribbons braided through their tails. This year, the jolly couple was being played by two former guests who'd returned to the dude ranch as an anniversary celebration. Constance and Thomas had planned a fairy-tale wedding at the ranch a couple of years ago, having found their happily-ever-after later in life.

Thomas dismounted first, then extended his hands for his wife. They both carried the sweetest romantic glow that made Gwen ache inside. From the corner of her eye, she saw Ian's shoulders slump and she wondered…why would seeing a happy couple seem to make him so sad? He seemed such a confirmed bachelor. Maybe he was just tired. The season was demanding—for both of them.

Santa tucked his wife's hand into the crook of his arm and climbed the stage decorated in wreaths and buffalo plaid ribbons. The Claus couple waved to the cheering crowd, pausing at the microphone.

"Ho-ho-ho," Thomas chanted, his nose bright from the cold. "Has everyone been on their best behavior this year?"

Constance leaned in, her fur trimmed cape fluttering in the breeze. "Or at least did you try your very best to be good?"

Children squealed and shouted, the yeses echoing all around. A few snowflakes drifted down, giving a glistening snow globe effect.

"Outstanding," Constance applauded. "Now, we can't wait to hear what you each wrote in your letter. So let's get started."

Pausing only to adjust the microphone to a child's level, Constance joined her husband on a massive bench made of logs. A basket of candy canes waited on either side. Children bounced up and down on their toes as they lined up, letters clutched in hand. Somehow, Gwen's triplets had made it to the front of the line.

Ian angled his head toward hers, the tree lights reflected in his deep brown eyes. "I bet this will be interesting."

"You never know with my boys," she answered with a laugh, keeping her hands stuffed in her pockets. "I'm just amazed that all three of them have kept their stocking caps on this long."

Smiling, Florence raised a finger to her lips. "Shhh. It's the boys' turn."

The triplets moved up in tandem, their boots and puffy jackets giving them a waddling walk up the steps. Gwen's heart clenched with pride and a hint of apprehension. What if she couldn't fulfill their wishes? They'd already lost so much in their young lives. Their father may have been unfaithful, but he'd been a loving dad and her sons had felt his loss deeply at the time. They still did, especially at night when they read a book before bed.

Gideon took the mic first, his paper clutched in two mittened fists. The paper clearly was covered in pictures, even if it was torn a bit on the side. But he pretended to read with such earnest enthusiasm, how could people help but be enchanted? "Dear Santa, I want a new sled. One that goes really, really fast like my friend Benji has. Then Mr. Ian and I can go sledding with Benji and his uncle. Thank you. From Gideon. PS I didn't eat all the cookies out of the jar at home. Just three. They were good. I saved some for you."

A light wave of chuckles rippled through the gathered throng.

Timothy walked up next, her careful son taking his time to adjust his stocking hat with one hand before lifting his letter with the other. "Dear Santa, I want a puppy—or a grown-up dog—from the shelter. 'Cause wouldn't it be nice to give it a home for Christmas?"

The audience swelled with a big collective "awwwww."

She should have seen this coming. The boys had all been lobbying for a pet for ages now. Actually, they wanted three pets—one for each of them. If anything, she should be surprised Gideon hadn't included that in his letter as well.

Inhaling deeply, Timothy read solemnly, "But I want to pick out the dog myself. Then I can be sure he likes me so we can be friends forever. 'Cause family is forever. Your friend, Timothy."

Her sweet boy. How she wanted to make that wish come true. If only she didn't already feel so overwhelmed.

Up next, Caleb approached the microphone, his red cap lopsided, with the pom-pom on top listing left. "Dear Santa, I want a magic trick kit so I can earn extra money to help my mom."

She felt the weight of Ian's gaze, others' as well. Her eyes burned with unshed tears that had nothing to do with the crisp wind. She glanced at Florence, who'd helped her sons pen their notes. The older woman pressed a hand to her chest over her bright red scarf, her lips moving in time with Caleb's words.

Continuing, he read haltingly, "I'll put on shows and people will pay me to come to their birthday parties. I love my mom very much and she works hard. You should come buy her toys. They are the best. Merry Christmas. From, Caleb. PS Could you give Sampson some extra dog biscuits? He's been a very good dog."

A strong hand came to rest between her shoulder blades. Ian. She leaned into his comfort, not daring to look at him. She didn't need the temptation when her emotions were so very raw and vulnerable. If she didn't pull herself together, she would be crying all over Ian's broad chest, breathing in the yummy smell of him. How long had it been since she'd allowed herself a moment to enjoy a man's touch?

Enough of this insanity. She needed to put an end to this evening and cut short the wishful thinking that had no place in real life. They'd already been at the tree lighting festivities for four hours, so it wasn't like she was cutting out early. "I should gather up the boys and head home. Thank you again for the invitation."

His palm fell away. The warmth on her back lingered.

Florence took both of them by the hand. "This has been a magical evening. I'm the one who should be thanking you both."

"Mom," he said, "I'm so very glad you enjoyed yourself."

Gwen understood Ian's bittersweet smile all too well. Life was sure a mixed bag of blessings this holiday season.

The triplets bounded back down the steps, their waddle walk faster than before, as if already hyped on the sugar from the candy canes clutched in each fist.

"Mommy, Mommy, Mommy, did you hear me?" Gideon asked. "Mr. Ian? Mrs. Florence?"

Florence knelt to pat his face. "You were A-plus spectacular, young man."

"I'll clean up after a puppy," Timothy said, words tumbling over each other. "I promise."

"I love you, Mommy," Caleb said quietly.

She might have thought the last words came from Timothy, they looked so similar in their hats, but Timothy had already chimed in about the puppy. So that vulnerable comment must have come from Caleb. Something to investigate further after they returned home.

For now, she pulled him in for a hug. "I love you too, my sweet boy."

As he burrowed closer, she opened her other arm for Timothy and Gideon, drawing them. Without a doubt, this was the very best part of her day. She would do anything for her sons. Anything. Their happiness and well-being had to be her number one priority.

All too soon, they began squirming, stepping away.

Gwen reached for their candy canes to add to the canvas tote. "Alrighty, kiddos. It's time for us to head back."

"Moooooooom," Timothy said, "we don't have school tomorrow. Can we please stay a little longer? I'll do all my homework and extra chores."

Gideon smirked. "You do that anyway."

"Shhh," Timothy retorted. "Don't make her mad or she won't let us stay."

Gwen rested a hand on Timothy's and Gideon's shoulders as a gentle reminder enough was enough. "We've imposed too much on Mr. Ian. Tell him thank you for letting us tag along tonight."

The boys sighed in unison, then chirped a layered chorus of, "Alright. Thank you, Mr. Ian. This really was a fun night. You're the best."

"My pleasure," he said.

And in that moment, with those two simple words, she realized how reticent, how increasingly distant, he'd been for the past hour. But then plenty of people thought it would be fun to spend an evening with "cute" little triplets, only to find it overwhelming when it actually happened. She just hated the disappointment she felt over him being one of those people.

It was definitely time to end this evening. Just a little while longer and she could soak in a bubble bath to regain her equilibrium. "Do you all have your gloves? Both of them?"

The boys held up their hands in unison.

She tugged the zipper on Caleb's coat, easing it the rest of the way up. She dusted the cookie crumbs off Gideon's jacket, then pulled his mittens into a snugger fit. Finally, she reached to adjust Timothy's knit cap, finally realizing it was inside out. She swept it off…

And did a double take at the chopped off hair. Wait. What? Confusion set in, along with a sneaking suspicion… "Gideon?"

Were the boys trying to play tricks on her?

To her left, her boy stopped dusting crumbs off his mittens. "Yeah, Mom?"

Gideon?

She looked back at the child with the cropped hair in front of her, then at the other again. She pulled the hat off the one she now suspected was really Gideon...

Another shorn head.

Florence gasped. Ian chuckled softly, then scratched a hand along his jaw to cover his mouth. Gwen ground her teeth in frustration.

Before she could reach out to check, Caleb—at least she thought it was Caleb—whipped his hat off to show a full head of hair. "I didn't do it, Mom."

Realization dawned. Timothy, usually her best-behaved child, had cut his own hair.

Walking Gwen and her boys back to her cabin, Ian couldn't stop grinning over the boys' antics. The sight of Timothy's hacked hair and memory of Gwen's look of horror punched another laugh right out of him.

Gwen glanced his way. "What's so funny?"

"His hair," he said, sidestepping a patch of ice. "Man, he really butchered it good. And to think he was hiding that under his hat the whole time he read his letter to Santa."

A fresh round of laughter tore through him. It felt good after all the tension and worry of late. Sure, he knew this evening had to come to an end and he would need to keep his distance from Gwen. But in this moment, thanks to that little boy's fresh crew cut, Ian felt the Christmas spirit creep over him.

Elbowing him, Gwen sighed. "It's not funny. I'm

going to have to take an entire afternoon off work to take him to the barber. I just pray they'll be able to fit him in. Appointments are scarce this time of year."

Only a couple of steps ahead beside Florence, Caleb kicked a snowball, grumbling, "Timothy gets to have lunch with Mom all by himself. That's not fair."

Gwen pressed her lips tight then called out, "Don't worry about fair. He will also have extra chores. Just like Gideon did when he cut his hair. Although if you want to come with us, I can have the barber give you a trim. Okay?"

"Nah, never mind. Thanks anyway," he mumbled before punching fast steps through the snow to catch up with his brothers. Florence kept pace behind him, humming "Silver Bells" softly.

Ian held a snowy branch aside for Gwen as they entered a forested area of the path, the night sounds growing more muffled as they drew farther from the tree lighting ceremony. Her furrowed brow made him want to smooth away the worry.

"Hey, he's probably just tired."

She shook her head, hugging herself. "It's more than just tonight. It seems lately the only people he opens up to are your mom and Santa Claus. Listening to him this evening, talking about why he wants a magic kit, made me wonder if he's keeping things bottled up to protect me. *I'm* supposed to be the one who protects *him*."

"And you're doing that, admirably well—"

She continued as if he hadn't spoken, her words tumbling out faster, launching bursts of white clouds into the evening air. "Then there's Timothy and his butchered hair. I can't imagine what made him act out like that. I've always worried because he was too good, as if he was scared of messing up. But now this…"

Ian measured his steps to hers, not too fast or slow. If only his own emotions were as easy to regulate. He was quickly losing his objectivity around this woman. "Are you okay?"

"Not really," she said ruefully. "But I will be—because that's the only option I have. It's been quite a day, that's for sure. I just wish I knew why he did it. Maybe I should pen a letter to Santa asking for some answers as my Christmas gift."

Ian reached to brush a strand of her hair over her shoulder. "I suspect Timothy did it because his brother did."

That simple? "But I've always worked so hard to help them be independent, to develop their own personalities."

"From where I stand, you're succeeding. They're great kids." With a great mom. This family was getting under his skin in the worst possible way.

She scrunched her nose. "Maybe they both cut their hair to get back at me. They've been upset with me for a week now because they each want their own puppy, and I keep saying no. I can barely handle the three of them. I suggested one adult dog…"

He could already see the surrender in her eyes. "When do you plan to pick one out?"

"They're still lobbying for three dogs, even if they're not puppies, and that can't happen."

"Can you imagine if you had three Sampsons running around?"

Her eyes went wide just before she clapped a hand

over her mouth. Laughter trilled from between her fingertips, lighting all the way to her pretty—tired—blue eyes. He wanted to keep that light in place, to keep her here beside him a little longer before they said goodbye and moved on to their far-too-busy lives.

"I got him from the shelter when he was eight months old. His people bought him, but didn't have time to teach him manners or give him an outlet for his puppy energy. I don't think he'd ever been walked on a leash."

"Clearly, he listens beautifully now. You've done a great job with his training." She walked over a fallen branch, her feet shifting along an icy patch.

Hooking arms with her to brace her, he welcomed the excuse to touch her. "We sure do get our steps in every day out here in the woods. But yeah, Sampson did great with training once he had someone who cared enough to put the time in. He's good with Mom too. I never have to worry about him pulling her over on walks."

He paused at the edge of Gwen's yard, knowing he should say good-night and send her straight inside, but now hesitant to end the evening. "I've heard it said there's magic in Moonlight Ridge that traces all the way back to a lost puppy found in Sulis Cave. After meeting all the wonderful animals around this place, I'm beginning to believe in that mystical connection."

Her eyes met his, held, the night air glimmering with hints of puffy flakes until he felt like they were encased in their own private snow globe.

A tug on the edge of his jacket popped the bubble of privacy. He glanced down to find Caleb—it had to be Caleb since he held a hat in one hand, baring his full head of hair. "Mr. Ian? Mom? The cabin's flooded."

Gwen jolted, looking around, confused. "Flooded? Honey, that's impossible. It's not raining. It's just snow around the yard."

At least the kid's active imagination had stopped what was fast turning into an embarrassing scenario.

Caleb pointed toward the cabin, the porch light gleaming. "Then why is there water coming under the door?"

Gasping, Gwen looked past her sons and Florence to the porch. Sure enough a thin sheet of water flowed through the narrow gap, slowly, but undeniably trickling out onto the porch's wood planks. Had she left a faucet on?

Had one of the boys?

Not out of the realm of possibility. Regardless, for water to be flowing that steadily, the damage must be bad. Very bad.

She'd been so wrapped up in talking to Ian, she hadn't noticed. She'd been so thankful to have a listening ear and too heartsore to hold back. So much for her resolution to keep her distance.

Florence pressed a hand to her chest. "What should we do? This looks quite serious."

Gideon scooted around the slick walkway leading toward the steps. "I bet it'll make the front porch into our very own ice skating rink."

The boys starting clambering up the steps. Toward the water.

Caleb jumped up and down to get a peek in the window. "Everything's soggy. The floor." He gasped. "Even the book I left on the floor."

Ian bolted forward. "Boys, stop," he called out. "Standing water can be dangerous. We need to make sure the power is off."

At the sound of his firm authority, the boys halted in their tracks outside the front door with no arguing.

A welcome miracle.

Solemnly, they ambled down the steps again, eyes wide.

Gwen's knees went weak at the thought of the crisis averted, and she flatted a palm against a tree trunk, the cold piercing through her glove. She didn't even want to consider anyone getting shocked or worse. Sagging against the rough bark, she grasped her knees, hanging her head to will away the nausea.

Ian braced a hand low on her back, comforting, exciting. "Careful there. Are you okay?"

Not hardly. But it had more to do with his "comforting" proximity than anything else. He was so much closer now than when he'd kept her from slipping earlier in the woods. They stood body pressed to body, his muscular chest a wall against her. A masculine wall.

She wanted to attribute her reaction to how long she'd been alone, without a man. But she hadn't reacted this way to any other man who'd crossed her path since her husband Dale's death. Not even the one time she'd dated.

There was no denying it. She was attracted to Ian, very much so. She wanted to stay here, close to him, cementing this chemistry in her mind. A chemistry she saw reflected in the depths of his dark eyes, heard in the catch of his breath.

Except she couldn't dare linger, not with an audience

of her sons and his mother when she had a waterlogged cabin to investigate.

Breathless, she stepped back. "Thank you. For stopping the boys. For keeping me from falling on my face. I'm okay now. I need to call the O'Briens before it gets worse."

His chest rose and fell quickly in a way that affirmed yet again that he wasn't unaffected either. "I'll look into turning off the water valve and power from outside."

"Thank you," she said. Was that husky voice hers? "But I hate to keep imposing—"

Quirking an eyebrow, he held up a hand. "I thought we'd moved past that. This is a crisis. You've been there for me through plenty of mine with my mom. This is my chance to return the favor."

Without another word, he powered toward the side of the house with powerful, take-charge steps. Tall. Broad shouldered. As steady as the sturdy trees around him.

It would be so easy to count on his help. So dangerous too.

Caleb trailed him, his cap in hand. "Mr. Ian, can I watch, please?"

"Sure, I'll show you how it works." Ian motioned for the child to follow, then hesitated. "If that's okay with your mother."

What choice did she have? She'd been worried about Caleb and here he was smiling. "Of course. Just keep out of his way, Caleb."

With a cheer, her son punched the air and raced alongside Ian, taking two steps for every one of the man's. Her worries for her son tugged at her again, seeing him so happy at the male attention. Keeping her distance became more complicated by the moment.

Gideon flopped on the ground in front of Florence and started making a snow angel. "Do you think our presents got wet?"

Very probably. Gwen shuddered at the thought of the mess, the loss, the cost and time to replace. "If they are, we'll get new ones. Don't you worry for a minute. Christmas will still come right on schedule."

When had she gotten to be such a good liar?

Florence smiled down at him, her furry hat covered in a light sprinkling of snow. "Your mother has an inside scoop on the best toys."

Gwen smiled her thanks, so grateful for this dear woman's presence in her children's lives, like a surrogate grandmother. Florence's thoughtful heart and quirky humor shone through the damage of the Alzheimer's.

Timothy slid his hand into hers. "Mommy, where are we gonna sleep?"

Exhaustion and defeat crashed down on Gwen because she didn't have an answer. She knew the ranch was booked solid. Probably everything in Moonlight Ridge was as well. If she had to drive all the way into Gatlinburg, she shuddered to think of how late it would be before she could tuck the boys into bed.

Or how early she would have to rise to get to work in the morning. She was already weary and overwhelmed.

Florence slid a comforting arm around her shoulders. "You should stay with us in our big, roomy farmhouse." She smiled warmly in a way that suggested she had no idea what a complicated solution she'd just offered. To make things worse, she turned her grandmotherly eyes on the boys and added an irresistible lure. "You can all play with Sampson."

Chapter Five

His mother's words—her shocking invitation that Gwen and the boys temporarily move in with them—drifted on the night wind and smacked Ian like an arctic blast. He stopped short in his tracks at the corner of the house, pivoting to look back.

He thought he was used to his mom's diminishing filter lately, but this took things to a whole new level. Especially given that she seemed completely aware of what she'd offered. Sure, he wanted to help Gwen and he had a soft spot for her boys. But the thought of her tempting presence under his roof unsettled him. Deeply.

And he didn't have a clue how to handle it.

At least Caleb hadn't heard. The boy was squatting to inspect a paw print in the snow.

Luckily, Gwen was already shaking her head. "Thank you, but that's not necessary."

Her soft words were barely distinguishable as Timothy and Gideon squealed with excitement, jumping up and down until their caps fell off into the snow. Unlike their brother, they'd heard the invitation just fine and clearly liked the idea. Their jumble of words peppered the air with plans of playing with Sampson and tromping through the tree farm.

The situation was spiraling out of control quickly.

He took a moment to gather his thoughts by making fast work of shutting off the water and flipping the breaker. Solve one crisis at a time. Then he picked his way back toward his mom.

Caleb stood to follow. "Did that fix it, Mr. Ian?"

Ian squelched a quick stab of regret that there hadn't been more time to narrate what he'd done for Caleb's sake. But he needed to get back to his mom.

"Mom..." He stopped beside her, choosing his words with care. "I heard what you suggested to Gwen about staying with us. But there are plenty of cabins here on the ranch. I'm sure Gwen will want to stay closer to work."

Wincing, Gwen pulled a tight smile. A forced smile, which set off alarms in his mind even before she changed the subject. "I've already texted Jacob and Hollie about the problem here so they can address it before there's any more damage."

His mother drew the triplets closer to her. "How about I entertain the boys for a little bit so the two of you can talk. Come on, kids. I have a story to tell you."

Her teacher voice corralled them in no time flat, leaving him free to talk to Gwen. Something about what Gwen had said—or rather what she hadn't said—niggled at him. "There *are* plenty of cabins, right?"

He'd toured the Top Dog property before. It was a huge facility.

"Don't worry about it." She waved aside his concern even as the worry lingered in her eyes, pushing his own uneasiness higher. "It was sweet of your mother to offer, but we're not your responsibility. I can take care of my family."

"I don't doubt that for a moment." He stared past her to organize his thoughts, drawing in an icy breath. His mother was entertaining the boys with animated gestures as they all sat together on a garden bench under the lamppost. He didn't have to hear her voice to imagine the wonderful storytelling that had kept him riveted as a child. Was she telling the old familiar tales or concocting new ones?

Either way, the boys clearly brought out the best in her. He thought of how happy his mother had been this evening, how clear. He didn't assume for a moment that it would last, but he wondered if somehow his mom also knew that this family could give her a Christmas to remember.

Which meant it was within his power to make the weeks leading up to Christmas special for his mother. He only had to push past his own hang-ups. For his mom? Yeah, he knew what had to happen.

Now he just needed to persuade Gwen. Given the defeated stoop to her shoulders, he could see she needed help. He couldn't deny that it made him feel good to think he could lighten her burden.

Ian gestured toward the gate leading out of the split rail fence. "Let's move over here away from listening ears and talk for a moment."

"About what?" Her forehead furrowed, her eyebrows pinching together. "I really need to keep an eye out for Hollie and Jacob. They should be here any moment now."

"We won't miss them when they arrive. There's a good line of sight." He took her by the elbow and guided her out of earshot of his mom and the triplets. "Do you think there are any cabins available?"

Her shoulders slumped a little. "Probably not," she admitted. "It's pretty booked." She toyed nervously with the zipper on her parka. "If there's nothing free, we'll get a room downtown."

That sounded like a nightmare for an already maxed out single mom. And he wasn't all that hopeful that she'd be able to find anything downtown anyway. "Juggling the commute into work, along with the boys' school schedule? Plus, paying for a hotel room will get expensive. There's no telling how long it will take to fix the problem."

"I don't need you to remind me how complicated this will be. I get it." Her mouth went tight, her spine straight—which accentuated her curves under the coat. "But it's temporary. A week maybe. I can handle it."

A week? Hopefully it *would* be that fast, for her sake and his. He wanted to lighten his load, but not drive himself to the brink of insanity with her tempting presence.

"What if you didn't have to handle it on your own?" He braced a gloved hand on the tree trunk near her shoulder. "My mother's offer was a good one. A reasonable one."

"I thought we both agreed not to exchange favors anymore," she reminded him in a prissy schoolmarm voice that made him want to tease her into softening, into laughter.

But she had a point. Not that he intended to let that stop him. Now that he'd decided on a course of action, he would follow it through. "True, but this little crisis reminded me of just how tenuous things can be when someone doesn't have a safety net." He tapped her nose lightly before she could interrupt. "Hear me out."

She drew her bottom lip in between her teeth, making him want to do more than tease her into laughter. He wanted to kiss her until she melted against him. The air between them charged with awareness. His hand dropped away.

Clearing his throat, he continued, "I agree it's difficult accepting help, but it's easier when it's not one-sided." He dragged in a weary breath. "We both need support through this holiday season. Me with my mom. You with your boys. So why not be that person for each other?"

"Hollie and Jacob may be able to work something out for me to stay on the ranch…" she said, although her tone didn't sound overly hopeful.

"But if they don't, just promise me you'll think about it."

She chewed the thumb of her glove, watching him for so long he thought she might cave. Giving him far too much time to admire the swing of her silky hair and graceful line of her neck.

Until she shook her head. "You can't be serious."

Not a resounding endorsement at all. But while he should just give up, he found himself doubling down. Winning her acceptance became all the more important. For his mother, of course.

"Why not, Gwen? I have the space." He waved his hand toward her boys and his mom. Caleb had moved on to rolling a snowball that looked like it might be the base of a snowman. "And if you're worried about appearances, we'll have a houseful of chaperones who moonlight as barbers."

She stared at him, unimpressed.

He quirked a brow. "What? Too soon?"

She hitched her hands on the gentle curve of her hips. "Do you know what it's like having six-year-old triplet boys underfoot? It's noisy and messy."

"Do you know what it's like living with an Alzheimer's patient?" he responded quickly. "It's a, uh, challenge."

Her stubborn jaw softened with compassion. "I imagine it must be."

Even as he chafed at the sympathy—his mother was the one who deserved it, not him—he still didn't intend to give up ground. "I'm thinking we can help each other. The holiday season is crazy. So stay with me until your place is repaired—or until a cabin becomes available for you and the boys."

She looked over at her sons and his mom, currently drawing pictures with sticks in the snow, then back at him. "You make it sound so simple."

"It can be." He hoped.

Hesitating, she studied his face as if mulling over his offer, then shook her head, waving her hand. "I don't know why we're discussing this. Jacob and Hollie will find someplace for us while repairs are being made."

"Even if they can scrounge together another option, we both know it would be somewhere small at best. I have a rambling big house with a huge yard and a dog to play with. Your kids will have plenty of space. You'll have privacy—and you'll be close to your work and the kids' school. We are doing what's best for our families, helping each other out. Like we've done in the past."

Her helping occupy his mom. Him helping out the boys with the occasional homework and sport.

"This is different and you know it." Her shoulders dropped again, weariness radiating off her, an exhaustion he understood well, the kind that couldn't be fixed with a simple night's sleep. "And even if I said yes, what about your mom's issues…afterward? Won't she be all the more confused if we're there and then leave again?"

A valid point that cut him clean through. His mother's memory loss was getting worse and bad days were becoming increasingly unpredictable. He used to be able to foresee an upcoming episode, recognize triggers. Lately, there were times he couldn't even tell what had set her off.

The doctor had warned him, spelling out her prognosis. He wasn't delusional about where things were headed for her, or even the heartbreaking timeline. He just didn't like to talk about it.

Right now, it appeared he didn't have a choice. "I realize I will have to come up with answers on how to care for my mother—a long-term solution that keeps her safe." That was the heartbreaking part for him. "But I can't bring myself to make that change at Christmastime."

Her hand floated to his arm, resting in sympathy for a moment, before she went back to worrying that bottom lip again. "So what you're suggesting, with the boys and me moving in temporarily, is a business arrangement of sorts?"

He drew his riveted gaze off her tempting mouth, a welcome distraction compared to the darker thoughts that circled in the back of his mind. "What else could I mean?"

Angling in, she said softly, her voice low enough not to carry on the wind. "It's no secret there's chemistry between us. I'm worried that almost-kiss earlier may have given you the wrong idea."

That memory filled the air between them. However, as much as he wanted this woman, as much as he would welcome the respite of a fling, he knew full well she wasn't the hookup sort—and a real relationship wasn't an option, of course. She deserved better than a guy with a bruised heart and too many responsibilities.

He braced a boot on the bottom rung of the fence. "I won't deny that I'm attracted to you, and like you said, the chemistry is mutual. However, it's very clear neither of us is in the market for a relationship."

Was that a flicker of regret on her face? And did he feel an echo inside himself? If so, well, he was used to living with regrets.

Sighing, Gwen backed a step away from him. "Let's find out what Hollie and Jacob have to say first."

He didn't need to hear anything more. He knew he'd won.

What a very long night.

Gritty-eyed, Gwen steered her minivan through the arched entrance to the Greer Family Tree Farm and guided the vehicle toward Ian's sprawling farmhouse.

The taillights on Ian's truck glowed in the dark, leading her to park in front of the white picket fence.

Throwing the car in Park, she tried not to second-guess herself. So, she and her sons were moving in with Ian Greer and his mother. Just temporarily, though. Until her home was habitable again. The boys were certainly undaunted by all the drama. Gideon had fallen asleep. Timothy and Caleb were chatting quietly in a language all their own. They seemed unfazed.

She, on the other hand, was frustrated, exhausted. Scared. She had surrendered to the inevitable the moment Jacob and Hollie had walked with her into the cabin, getting a first glimpse of the terrible mess created by a very leaky kitchen pipe. The ruined gifts. The soggy rugs and furniture. If it was just a matter of drying things out, she would be back in place within a few days—but what if it wasn't?

If the problem was bigger than just a kitchen pipe, if there were major plumbing problems, she couldn't bear to think about how long she and the boys would be homeless. Vagabonds with barely anything to call their own, since most of their stuff was ruined.

The ranch was packed until after the New Year. Hollie and Jacob had offered a sofa for her and air mattresses in their boys' room for her triplets in their own quarters, a beyond generous offer, especially over the holidays—but she couldn't bear the thought of putting them out, especially when there was another offer on the table. As much as she worried about moving in with Ian, she knew it was the practical choice for her, for her boys and, yes, for Ian and his mother as well. Ian had more room, and at least she could tell herself there would be an exchange of sorts. She would be happy to spend some time with his mom over the holidays. Plus, her sons deserved the room and comfort they would have at the tree farm.

Saying no would have been selfish. She would simply resist the attraction, for his sake and hers. More importantly, for her kids and for his mother, none of whom needed more disruption in their lives.

So now, here she was, with a minivan full of clothes and children. She angled to look in the back of the vehicle. "Boys, we're here. Boys? Gideon?" she called until he stirred then bolted wide-awake. Gideon woke much like he fell asleep. Quickly and fully. And even with his butchered haircut, he certainly looked like he had the worst case of bedhead ever. "Grab your backpacks. We can unload the rest of our gear in the morning."

Once she'd unbuckled their booster seats, the triplets tumbled out like Keystone Kops, barreling into the snowy night. Porch lamps glowed, along with two motion-activated lights streaming across the expansive yard.

After Ian parked the truck, he and his mom headed toward them. Florence had a pep in her step that Gwen had never seen before. Ian took those long, measured strides she was used to seeing, the kind that spoke of determination and an ease in his own skin. He was the kind of man who could down a tree into exactly the right spot. A man who inspired confidence.

And, wow, she must be tired to be thinking such fanciful thoughts.

Hefting one, then two duffel bags onto her shoulders, she thumbed the back hatch closed. Turning, she slammed straight into Ian's chest.

The fresh scent of him filled her cold gasp.

"Excuse me," she said, stepping back, stopping short against the bumper.

"Let me help with those." He slid the bags away from her, his fingers grazing along her arm.

As much as she wanted her independence, she recognized it was silly to argue. She really needed to get unpacked and turn in before she did something reckless, like cry all over that fresh-smelling chest of his. "Thank you. For everything. Your home is lovely."

A wry grin spread over his handsome face. "It's a lot of *lovely*, far more than my mother and I need. You and the boys are welcome to the whole second floor." He nodded toward the spacious yard. "Once I let Sampson out for a quick run, I'll come back in and help you get settled."

The two-story clapboard farmhouse sprawled like a big white beacon tucked in the landscape of evergreen. She'd driven by the place in the past, but had never been up close. Ian hadn't been kidding when he'd said there was plenty of room.

A white picket fence wrapped all the way around the house, front and back. On the side yard, a stone firepit was tucked in a clearing encircled with benches. Pine trees dominated, most in lines of orchestrated planting that flowed into the horizon. Others, closer to the home, shared the yard with oak trees.

The porch wrapped all the way around, but on one side, it was glassed in. She could see rockers lined up inside, perfect for watching the sunset on a snowy evening. White lights outlined the windows. Lighted metal deer were perched near the porch. This was a family dream-home.

"Wow," Timothy whispered, his chopped hair standing up like a rooster tail in the back. "This place is awesome."

Gideon hopped off the walkway and onto the lawn, jumping into the light dusting of pristine snow. "Can we go ice skating on the pond?"

Gwen rested a hand on his shoulder, knowing she needed to keep their expectations in line. "No, it's not safe. But we can go to the ranch's rink."

"Promise?" Gideon paused on the bottom step, holding the white rail.

"Promise." Her boys knew she only gave her word when she could keep it.

She followed their host up the steps and through the large oak door. The foyer soared upward. A staircase led to the second floor. The furniture was a lively mix of antiques and vintage seventies—warm honeyed woods accented by a mustard yellow sofa created a look that was retro and fun. The scent of fresh pine hung in the air. An eight-foot Christmas tree—undecorated—filled one corner of the room.

Florence grabbed the banister, the finish worn from the stroke of many hands. "I'll just go check to be sure everything's cozy upstairs and that you have plenty of towels."

Sampson came bounding down the hall, his hundred pounds of momentum thundering. She started to step in front of her boys… The shaggy white dog stopped short and dropped into a pretty sit, his tongue lolling out the side of his mouth. Drool gathered and dripped.

Gideon giggled, then knelt to wipe it up with his glove. While he might be her most active child, on good days, he also channeled that energy into being her most helpful.

Gwen marveled at the dog's self-control. "He's so good with kids."

Ian gripped the duffels in both hands, kicking the door closed behind him. "Back at my old place when he still had puppy energy, there were kids next door."

"Well, I'm thankful," she said as her sons took turns petting Sampson with careful little hands. "He should help stem the requests for a trio of puppies for a while longer."

A half smile kicked a dimple into his cheek as his gaze stayed trained on the dog and children, monitoring. "I'll do my best to get him to chew up something while you're here just to make a point about how much work a dog can be."

"And lots of late night and early morning walks…" she added, nodding toward the leash on a hook by the front door.

"Wait until you see him shred a roll of paper towels."

Her laughter and his twined, easy, intimate.

She forced herself to slow her breaths, suddenly very aware of being in his home with him. At night. After a fun evening spent together. If she wasn't careful, her thoughts could turn in a very dangerous direction. Instead, she focused on her sons. "Come on, boys. Let's head upstairs so Mr. Ian and Mrs. Florence can go about their evening."

Each child said good-night to Sampson—twice—before climbing the steps ahead of her, their backpacks low-slung.

Ian trailed her, carrying her luggage.

She smiled over her shoulder. "Thank you again for letting us crash here. You've been more than generous."

Was that prim voice hers? Ugh.

"As you can see, we have more house here than we can use." His booted feet thudded on the landing. "But it came with the business and it seemed wasteful to level it just to put up a new tract house."

She shuddered at the top of the steps as the boys ran up and down the hall, peeking in different bedrooms. "Heaven forbid anyone put a cookie-cutter-style home on this beautiful piece of land." She liked the charm in this old home. Like the toys she restored, it carried nostalgia and character, qualities that spoke to her. "I'm glad you didn't take a wrecking ball to the place. Right now, we're very thankful for all that extra space."

"It feels good to be able to help you for a change after all you've done for my mother." He ducked into the first doorway, leading into a room with a large four-poster bed.

A pastel pink-and-blue pinwheel quilt covered the mattress. Ruffled curtains were parted enough to show the moon perched just above the tree line. A porcelain pitcher and washbowl were positioned on an antique dressing table.

She felt as if she could sleep in this peaceful space without moving for days. "I just placed a few calls and made sure she didn't leave before you arrived," she pointed out. This felt like way too much in recompense for the little she'd done.

"That's a lot." His voice came from only a few inches away, so close the warmth of his breath brushed her cheek. "Knowing she's safe with you until I can pick her up has been a huge weight off my shoulders."

She resisted the urge to rub his arm in comfort. They were already on dangerous ground sharing the same roof. Not to mention that her big bed loomed two feet away. She didn't want to give him the wrong idea. Or herself. "Trust me, I understand how tough it is asking for help."

"Well," Florence called from the doorway. "It's usually those who are already doing the most who volunteer to do more."

How much had the woman heard? How aware was she of her fading memory? Either way, the answer would be heartbreaking. "Mrs. Florence, from what I've heard, you're a lady who has always done more than her fair share."

The older woman clapped her hands together. "I enjoy being busy. There are towels and soap in the bathroom. Extra blankets are in the hall closet. Ian? Put down the luggage so she can get ready for bed." His mom patted his cheek. "And no sneaking up the stairs tonight to pay a visit to this pretty lady's room. Do you hear me?"

Waking up to a houseful of childish laughter was surreal, even if it was something he'd once dreamed of. A dream he'd abandoned.

Yet he couldn't help but enjoy having them here, in his house, making the Christmas season come alive.

Leaning against the kitchen doorframe, he took in the sight of Gwen and his mother making pancakes for breakfast. Gideon, Timothy and Caleb were lined up, standing on chairs at the Formica counter, firing rapid questions and editorials as his mother poured batter into the pan, the liquid sizzling in the melted butter.

His mother hadn't been able to indulge in her love of cooking lately—not since she'd almost burned the house down with a grease fire. Watching her make pancakes with Gwen and the boys, seeing her smile, warmed his heart.

The soaring kitchen echoed with their voices. The appliances had seen better days, back when their avocado green had actually been popular decades ago. Dark wood cabinets and wallpaper bore the stamp of wear. The linoleum floor was probably three layers thick.

But it all worked, and in a strange twist of fate, his mother seemed to feel at home in a place with the vintage decor that resembled houses from her past.

This piece of property and the business attached had been a find, an answer to his prayers when the hours and lack of flexibility at his park ranger job made it impossible to be there for his mother. The past year here had been good for her. She'd been happy.

The rambling farmhouse was bigger than they needed, but the land and the tree farm business made a good fit for him. And on a morning like today, it was nice to just relax and enjoy the homey, comfortable morning. Childish laughter echoed up to the high ceilings, barely dissipating before a fresh round of peals launched as the kids helped "supervise" the pancake making. Gwen stood at the other end of the counter slicing oranges and making freshly squeezed juice. Even Sampson was content, sleeping on his dog bed under a window, soaking in the morning sun streaming between two snowcapped mountain peaks.

The scene was everything he'd dreamed of a year ago before his breakup. It couldn't last, of course. But maybe it wouldn't be such a bad thing to enjoy it, just for now. Ian refocused his attention on placing silverware at each place on the round oak table.

Standing on his chair at the counter, Timothy leaned his shoulder closer to Florence's arm. Gwen had trimmed up his hair, evening it out as best she could, but the boy would still need a more professional approach soon. "That one looks just like a teddy bear."

"Because it is a teddy bear. I used to make all sorts of shapes for my son. Cats. Hearts. A pig and butterfly. I'd decorate their faces with blueberries and chocolate chips."

"That sounds yummy." Timothy licked his lips. "Will you make me a piggy pancake tomorrow?"

Caleb hitched up to sit on the counter. "We probably won't be here tomorrow."

Timothy's face fell. "But I want to stay here. There's a tire swing and my room is so big."

Gwen rested a hand on her son's arm lightly. "Sweetie, remember it's just your room for now. We'll be back in our own place before you know it."

Timothy hung his head and Ian's heart squeezed in his chest. He set aside the rest of the silverware and crossed to tenderhearted Timothy. "Wherever you stay, I'll figure out a way to rig a tire swing. Three of them, one for each of you."

Timothy's lip quivered. "What if there aren't any trees left?"

Ian cupped his shoulder. "There are trees everywhere around here. And wherever there aren't any, I can plant them."

Gwen lifted Caleb off the counter, then turned to the other two, lifting them down to the floor one at a time and nudging the seats back toward the table. "Boys, we need to eat up. Mr. Ian and I both have to leave for work soon. And Mrs. Florence told me she's having lunch with Mrs. Patsy and Mrs. Constance."

Gideon scrubbed his sleeve under his nose. "Does that mean we have to stay in the back room at the shop?"

"Thank goodness, no. The ranch's childcare has room for you. Today, they're riding ponies in the arena and doing crafts at Santa's workshop."

Gideon shook out his napkin and tucked it in the collar of his plaid pj's. "Good. My presents got all soggy."

Ian sidestepped her, reaching for the rest of the flatware, so close to her that he could see how her nails were chewed down. Unable to resist, he rested his hand on hers, for only a moment, but long enough that his heart sped.

Had the room gone silent or had the focus of his world just narrowed to this woman? Why had he spent half the night tossing and turning thinking of her? Gwen had been in his house for less than twelve hours and she was already taking up far more room in his thoughts than in his home.

Then she blinked fast, her hand trembling beneath his. "Ian?"

Her voice carried a question he couldn't come close to answering. Instead, he backed up two steps and pivoted on the heel of his boots toward the refrigerator, needing a distraction, a way to bring the focus of this meal back to a group gathering.

Tearing his gaze away from her, he stuck his head inside, and withdrew two cans. "Who wants whipped cream on their pancakes?"

Chapter Six

Only two days living under the same roof and the last thing Gwen needed was more time alone in Ian's tempting presence. His outdoorsy, fresh scent permeated the confined space of his truck cab, teasing her every breath. "Jingle Bell Rock" played softly. The brown leather interior was surprisingly clean for a work truck. There was just a small cooler, a thermos of coffee and a plastic bin full of business cards, blank invoices and a credit card reader for off-site sales. Oh, and a tiny old-timey tractor ornament dangling from his rearview mirror.

When he'd offered to drive her to inspect the cabin on her lunch break, she'd started to refuse. But then she couldn't get a haircut appointment for Timothy until later in the week and when she'd mentioned going to assess the damage and get more things from the cabin, Ian had reminded her that she might not be able to fit everything she wanted to bring back into the minivan.

Yet, if he brought her in his truck… The boys would be in childcare at the ranch and his mother would be occupied with her needlework group. So here they were. Pulling up to her cabin to inspect the damage and repairs.

Alone.

The work crew was pulling out of the driveway as they parked. Just her luck. Ian turned off the ignition, the music silencing. It felt childish to refuse his offer of help today. She couldn't deny, though, that staying in the house with Ian had her on edge. She hadn't shared a house with a man in so long the intimacy of it felt… odd. Unsettling.

Exciting.

She had too many concerns right now. She couldn't afford to be distracted by a "too hot for his own good" lumberjack-looking tree farmer. Instead, she forced her focus on the present, on the depressing sight of her home. The once pristine snow on her lawn was now a swatch of sludge with deep trenches from utility vehicle tires. A dumpster took up the space under the sprawling oak where she and the boys loved to picnic in warmer weather.

Tears clogged her throat. This place had been such a haven for her. A home. A nurturing environment for her grieving children. And now it was a wasteland. Seeing the ruined yard felt like losing her world all over again.

She drew in a shaky breath and helped Ian unload the flattened boxes and tape they'd brought along. She didn't have time to tarry. While the shop had a part-time cashier, her assistant's hours were limited each month.

At the bottom of the steps, Ian rested a palm between her shoulder blades. "Are you okay?"

"Of course." She pushed the words past the lump in her throat. "Why would you ask?"

"You're weaving on your feet." His eyes filled with concern.

This man had a way of taking the cares of the world on his broad shoulders. She hated adding anything more to the weight he carried. She'd seen up close and personal these last two days how much time he invested in his mom in addition to his own business.

"I'm just a little overwhelmed by it all, I guess. Thank goodness for renter's insurance." She didn't want to think about how long it would take for a payment to come through or how little her things were worth. Any delay and she would have to dip into her small stash of savings to make ends meet. Worst of all, her sewing machine—resting on the floor in its case—had been destroyed. There was only so much she could do by hand. She'd planned to use some of her savings to make up the difference when trading her old one in. But now, she couldn't even consider that.

Yet another reason to be thankful for Ian's generosity, saving her the additional expense of a hotel room. Sighing, she clapped her hands together. "Let's get cracking. The sooner I walk in, the sooner I'll know where we stand with damages."

As she pushed through the front door, she was all too aware of him four steps behind her. His boots thudded along the planked porch. One look at the inside stole her breath. And not in a good way at all.

Downstairs, rugs and furniture had already been removed. Large fans had been set up throughout along with dehumidifiers, all hooked up to a generator outside.

But despite the machines and all that had been cleared away, the place was cold and damp and an utter mess. It bore no resemblance to the home she had crafted for her sons.

Kneeling, she scooped up a waterlogged paper with a trembling hand, a math worksheet adding three Santas and five snowmen. The ink from the markers Timothy had used bled together. She'd known it was bad, but the musty smell and water stains leaching up the walls brought the reality crashing all around her in full force.

Ian whistled low and slow, scratching behind his neck before turning his attention to opening a flattened box and taping the bottom. She'd made the right decision in not bringing the boys. This was tough enough for her. At least since they slept in the second-story loft, their clothes and toys should be alright.

She picked down the hall toward her bedroom, only to find it empty as well. "When Hollie told me the contents of the cabin were being dried out, I somehow thought she meant just the rugs and anything on the floor. I didn't realize she meant everything… I would have packed more." She tugged open the closet, relieved to find the higher shelves still full and clothes still hanging from the rack.

The roll of tape made a ripping sound as he assembled another box. "I can take you to the store to pick up whatever you're missing."

And deplete her tiny savings account before they even knew how long in the future she needed to plan? "No, thank you. We'll be fine."

"Do you want to drive by wherever the O'Briens had the furniture taken?"

"I'll reach out to Hollie later." She hated needing so many people. One stack at a time, she pulled folded sweaters from the highest shelf. "I'll just pack what I can and figure out the rest later."

After she cried in the shower.

"This looks…"

"Like I won't be moving back in here," she said on a long sigh, hefting off the hanger items and draping them into the second box. "Like I'm going to end up in a new place, whenever one becomes available—probably after the New Year."

He stretched the tape across the top, his broad shoulders flexing as he moved. "I'm so very sorry this has happened to you, especially around the holidays. I meant it when I said you could stay until then."

The obvious response would be to say yes. The practical answer. But practical felt a little bit scary when she couldn't peel her attention away from him.

Even as the thought formed, she realized she was being selfish. Her boys deserved stability and space. And they deserved a Christmas to remember. "I know you said you need help with your mom, but I wonder sometimes if you were just trying to save my pride. I hate to take advantage."

She grabbed a wicker bin of treasured keepsakes that she kept in her closet—mementos of the triplets' babyhood—and tucked that into the next box Ian had prepared for her.

"I hope that's not a no. Because my mom's been happier these past two days than I've seen her in a very long time."

Despite his words, she knew her pride would sting

a little less if she could offer more in return. "If you don't mind my asking, what do the doctors say about your mom's outlook?"

"It's tough to predict. Everyone's body chemistry is different. There are some new meds out there which have helped slow the progression of the disease. And I'm profoundly thankful for every extra day." He looked up quickly. "Maybe I should have explained that better to make sure you were fully aware—"

She shook her head. "I've known your mother for months. I understand." She admired how he cared for his mom, making sacrifices for her. "I have to admit that remaining at the farm would be the right thing for my sons. The boys have been through so much change— so much loss in their short lives. Somehow, they still manage to be happy at a time most other kids would be crying their eyes out."

Ian glanced up from his work assembling boxes. "They take after their mother."

"Whatever." She waved aside the compliment as she stacked T-shirts and underwear into a box. She was just being a mom. She would do anything for her boys. "Just know I won't forget what you've done for us."

He fidgeted with the roll of tape, his gaze skating between her and the pink flowered panties she'd just tossed on top of the T-shirts. "About what happened…"

That moment in the kitchen, that connection, made even worse by his playfulness with the whipped cream. Somber Ian was enticing. Playful Ian was downright irresistible.

"I won't pretend not to know what you're talking about." But she didn't know what would be accomplished by discussing it. "Are you trying to make me blush?"

"Maybe. Maybe not. Either way, blushing looks pretty on you," he said softly, earnestly.

The simple compliment warmed her. Dangerously so. She needed to set some ground rules. "You know I'm not in the market for a relationship, right?"

He nodded. "Yeah, same here. The timing is off..."

"We have to consider the welfare of our families..."

"Holidays make people sentimental."

Wasn't that the truth? And sentimentality could lead to impulsive decisions when she didn't have any more room for regrets in her life. "Well then, that's settled. Now I just need to pack a couple of boxes for the boys."

She was relieved to have that issue decided...wasn't she? Gwen tried to tell herself that relief was what she was feeling and not the tiniest twinge of disappointment that she wouldn't ever feel the thrill of Ian's strong arms around her.

Gideon loved sugar.

Hiding in the big pantry, he tipped back the can of whipped cream and filled his mouth. The creamy sweetness melted on his tongue. He sagged against the shelf of cans with a happy sigh.

Caleb, sitting across from him, stuck out his arm and waggled his fingers. "Share, please."

"Sure," Gideon said, shooting one last blast into his mouth before passing it over.

A long string hung from the single lightbulb on the ceiling. It was just bright enough to make this feel like a clubhouse. It was a lot larger than his mom's pantry, which was just a bunch of shelves in a closet—no room for anyone to sit inside.

In fact, this farmhouse was full of great things that were bigger and better than the cabin. This week had been the best. He got to play with Sampson in the yard and help brush his soft white fur. The dog followed him all the time ever since he dropped bits of pancake on the floor. They could have pancakes—with extra syrup— every morning if he wanted. It was nice sitting around that table together with lots of talking and noise like the other kids at school.

At lunch, his friends didn't believe him when he told them he'd moved into a Christmas tree farm. But then Mr. Ian had shown up in his big truck to pick them up after school. It said "Greer Family Tree Farm" right on the door.

Their mom had finally gotten a haircut appointment for Timothy, so she'd picked him up early. Mrs. Florence had gone with his mom and Timothy, which was kinda nice for them.

Then they were going to go to work with her for a while. Borrrrrring. So Gideon was glad he got to stay home.

Caleb passed the can back. Gideon filled his mouth extra full, then wiped the corners of his mouth with his sleeve. They probably didn't have much longer before Mr. Ian figured out that they'd ditched doing homework. They'd made their escape when he sat down to do some work on the computer.

Gideon rolled the canister between his palms. Chewing his bottom lip, he scanned the shelves for a snack to tuck underneath his bed for later. There were so many.

Chocolate-covered pretzels. Peanut butter cookies. Graham crackers. "I like it here."

"Because it's a great place." Caleb hugged his knees. "I want to stay."

"So do I, but we don't get a say in that." Caleb pulled the Velcro on his shoes open and closed, over and over again. The *rippp rippp rippp* echoed in the small space. "That's up to Mom and I don't think she's gonna listen to us."

Inspiration struck and Gideon snapped his fingers. He'd just learned to do that last week. He'd practiced over and over again until he got it loud enough for people to notice. "But I know who she *will* listen to. Santa Claus."

"We already saw Santa and gave him our wishes." Caleb shook his head. "It's too late."

Gideon just scoffed. Sure, Caleb was smart. Book smart. But he didn't know everything.

Gideon leaned in to whisper, "That wasn't the real Santa. That was some guy who's on vacation here. Remember yesterday when we got to brush the ponies? Well, I saw him in the stables."

"You're lying." Caleb snatched the can back, his jaw stuck out all stubborn. "It was too Santa at the tree lighting. He told me."

Gideon had thought so too, at first. But then when he saw the same guy saddling up a horse, Gideon had started thinking it through and then he'd figured out the truth. "Santa can't be everywhere. If you look on TV, someone dressed like him is at a bunch of parades. Ivy O'Brien told us she sat on his lap at the mall. And there was that paper at school that said he was gonna be with Mrs. Susanna in the library. Then he was here. All the same stuff is going on for kids in other towns too. There must be hundreds of 'em."

Caleb's eyes went wide and he sorta looked like he might cry. "So how do we know which Santa is real to make sure he hears our wishes?"

"Here's the thing," Gideon explained as best he could. It was pretty mind-blowing so he didn't want to get it wrong. "*None* of those are the real Santa. He's home at the North Pole, getting ready for Christmas. So he gets other people to pretend to be him. Nice people."

Gideon spread his arms wide, ta-da style.

"Then those people are giving him our messages." Caleb's forehead furrowed in deep thought. "So it's the same difference."

"Not exactly." This was the toughest part to understand. Gideon walked his fingertips over a box of cornflakes. "I mean, yeah, I guess they're supposed to. But they're just people. Miss Beale says everyone makes mistakes—that's why we're s'posed to check over our work before we turn it in. What if they forget to give him the notes? Or they don't tell him the right words? Remember when we played that game at ranch camp where we all had to whisper something and by the time it got around the circle from everybody it didn't even make sense anymore? I think that's what happens when we give these fake Santas our lists."

He hoped Caleb believed him. He didn't like it when people laughed at him or called him a dummy. He stacked the cornflakes box on top of the granola to have something to do to keep his hands busy.

"It explains a lot." Caleb scratched his head. His full

head of hair. Caleb would never cut his hair just for fun. "Like how some kids ask for things and then they don't get it even though they were really, really good. I never thought that was very fair."

Gideon hadn't thought of that, but it made sense. He and his brothers made a good team that way, figuring things out together. "See? That's what I mean."

He looked for something else to stack on his food tower, and then Caleb passed him some cereal bars.

"You're smart to figure all that out." Caleb sounded surprised.

That hurt his feelings. "I'm not a dummy."

"I don't think you're a dummy," Caleb rushed to say. "You're just always moving around so much I don't think you always listen good."

Caleb understood. But that's 'cause they were triplets, which made them have a special connection. He wished other people got it too. "I jump around because my brain is running really fast."

"Okay, smartie." Caleb folded his arms over his chest. "How do we get a message to the real Santa?"

Now came the really good part. "I thought you would never ask." He stood. "First, we're gonna need some cookies."

Tucking his foot on the bottom shelf, he hefted himself up and started to climb.

Thank goodness the ranch's hair salon had finally been able to fit Timothy in. Gwen had finished up in time to go back to work, assisting Hollie in setting up a holiday craft fair. The event was being held in the ranch's small arena, a newly built addition that offered so much more flexibility for winter events.

She'd invited Florence to come along to the hair salon and craft fair setup. Not just as a way to thank Ian for picking up the boys after school, but because she genuinely enjoyed the woman's company. Gwen had noticed that Florence thrived most in events that had a timeless air where she didn't have to worry so much about what year or even what decade she was in. At the salon today, she had shared a story about a former student of hers who'd cut a girl's ponytail off in class. She'd told the story three times, but her delight in the memory was such that Gwen didn't mind hearing it repeated.

Now Florence and Timothy were engrossed in unpacking wood carvings for the fair, while other staff carted tables inside and set up a stage. Tomorrow's festival, open to the public, would feature artisans from all over the area, ranging from candlemakers and quilters to calligraphers and even a pet photographer who would take pictures on-site to make into ornaments, calendars and mugs. The exposure would be fantastic for the gift shop—but also for Gwen's vintage showpieces.

She had to admit that Ian's plan to help each other out was working far better than she could have anticipated, lightening each other's loads during the hectic Christmas season. When Caleb and Gideon had balked at going to day care after school, Ian had stepped right in, stating that he had work he could do at home while keeping an eye on them.

After that first morning, she'd expected there to be more tension, maybe a few accidental intimate moments coming in or out of the shower. But with their conflicting schedules, they rarely crossed paths—and since she used the shower on the second floor while he used the one on the first, no towel-clad encounters seemed forthcoming. Which, oddly enough, created a tension all its own because she wanted to see him more. As she lay in bed at night, she found herself imagining him in his room. What was he wearing? Did he snore or hug his pillow?

Hollie hefted a box of crystal jewelry onto the next table down from Gwen. "How are you holding up staying at Ian's? I'm so sorry about the problems with the plumbing at the cabin."

Gwen pulled her thoughts from Ian, her face a little warm.

"No need to apologize. There's nothing you could have done to prevent it." She pulled back the top off the plastic storage bin. Sadly, she'd had to scale back on restoring new toys recently, thanks to the damage to her sewing machine and some of her other crafting supplies, but the press from this event was too important not to bring everything that she had available. While she hoped to sell all of it tomorrow, she did grieve over the prospect of not being able to display toys in her shop since she couldn't afford to replenish them. "I guess it's a good thing that it didn't happen to one of the guests. I would hate for you to lose the business."

"There will be extra money in your next paycheck since room and board is supposed to be a part of your employment package, plus some extra. I know renter's insurance doesn't always cover everything at replacement cost." She nodded toward Timothy and Florence lining up carved Christmas gnomes. "It's for the boys too."

Gwen had hoped so, but would it be enough? Already this move was costing her. "Thank you. You know I love my position here."

She needed the job, now more than ever. She worked her butt off to impress her bosses. And the last thing she wanted was to rock the boat.

Beside her, Hollie arranged jewelry display trees made of carved wood, the pieces created by a local artisan. She draped necklaces and rings along the branches, crystals refracting prisms. "And we're lucky to have you," Hollie assured her.

Just as Gwen opened her mouth to ask about report time for tomorrow, a shout across the arena caught her attention.

"Yoo-hoo!" called stable manager Eliza as she strode through the double barn doors leading into the arena. She pulled up alongside them with a bin full of horse-themed crafts: a wreath made of horseshoes; small carved stallions made into tree ornaments; and a showcase-quality quilt decorated with an array of cloth horses. "I heard about the flood in the cabin. How are you and the boys holding up? I hope you know you're always welcome at our place."

"Thank you for the offer." Even knowing she couldn't accept, she was still touched by the level of friendship from Eliza and Hollie. The ranch brought out the best in people. "But I wouldn't want to disrupt the newlyweds."

Eliza had recently married the town doctor, who had gained custody of his two young grandchildren after his son and daughter-in-law died. "The invitation is open-ended. I hope the drive in from town wasn't too horrible."

Apparently, the gossip mill hadn't kicked into high gear yet. "We're, uh, not staying in town. Florence Greer offered us full run of the second floor in her farmhouse."

Straightening, Eliza covered her mouth for a moment in surprise before saying, "Florence Greer?" She shot a quick look at the older woman arranging planked Christmas signs with Timothy. "*That* Florence Greer? As in, the mother of that hot Christmas tree farmer Ian Greer? Are you saying you live with Ian Greer?"

Did Eliza have to keep stating the obvious? Gwen's hands moved faster to lay out a series of antique nutcrackers, as if keeping busy could protect her from having to deal with kind-but-nosy questions. "Temporarily. The arrangement is spacious for the boys and uplifting for his mother."

Hollie shot a side-eyed look her way with a hint of a smile. "And how is 'the arrangement' for you?"

"Convenient." Gwen placed a restored carousel music box prominently in the center of the table.

Eliza wriggled her brows as she adjusted the folds on a patchwork quilt. "Just *convenient*?"

Here was the start of the gossip mill she'd been concerned about. She needed to nip this line of speculation in the bud. "I don't have time for anything else between work and caring for my sons. In case you didn't notice, I have triplets. They keep me busy."

She nodded toward Timothy, who was surveying the lineup of signs while scratching his head.

"I'm happy to babysit if you want some *convenient* free time," Eliza pressed with a wink as she arranged ornaments with a family of horsefaces ready to be personalized. "Mavis and Gus would be thrilled to play with their friends."

In another world, another age, that offer would have been perfect. She would have welcomed the free babysitting that would give her a chance for a nice night out. But that era had passed for her with the disillusioning end to her marriage. She just didn't have the will left to put her heart on the line again—even for a temporary fling. "You must be a glutton for punishment," she hedged to avoid giving a fuller answer. "That's five very young children at once."

Eliza tsked. "You deserve time for yourself, even if you don't want to use it to go on a date. If you're not interested in Ian, I understand. Well, I actually don't understand because he's a smokin' hot man."

Hollie fanned her face with her hand. "Those broad working-man shoulders for lifting and chopping down literal *trees*…"

Eliza grabbed the edge of the table as if faint. "And that cute butt in blue jeans."

They weren't wrong. Still, Gwen tried to divert them before they created even more vivid images in her mind. "What would your husbands think of this conversation?"

Hollie hooked arms with her. "They would think that we want you to be as happy as we are. So if you're not interested in Ian, we have a new office manager starting soon. He's cute. Right, Eliza?"

"Absolutely," the stable manager nodded. "But his shoulders just don't compete."

Laughing, Hollie lifted out another box of necklaces

and began sorting by color. "How do the boys feel about staying at Ian's?"

Thrilled. Over the moon. So much so, she worried a bit about how they would adjust when they returned to a regular cabin. "I can't recall when the boys have been this excited about waking up. They love breakfast with Florence. She makes them pancakes shaped like teddy bears and pigs."

Before she could say anything more, her phone vibrated on the edge of the table.

Eliza grinned. "I'm not snooping or anything, but that's clearly an incoming call from Ian Greer."

Butterflies tickled inside her stomach. She forced herself to pick up the cell phone casually, when she really wanted to snatch it up to hear his voice all the faster.

"Hello?" Gwen said, stepping away, all too aware of Hollie's and Eliza's rapt attention.

"Gwen," Ian's deep bass rumbled in her ear, "first I want to assure you everyone is going to be okay."

Going to be okay? Panic lanced through her. She gripped the phone tighter, pressing it closer to her ear to hear every word. "What happened?"

"I thought Caleb and Gideon were doing their homework," Ian said, his words clipped with stress, "but they went into the pantry to get snacks. Gideon climbed the shelves and fell."

Her heart stuttered at the mental image of her wild child plummeting. "How bad?"

"A bump on the forehead that's probably going to bruise. He didn't pass out. His pupils look fine, and I've got ice on it." His voice softened to a whisper. "He's asking for you. Are you able to break away?"

Her hands shook and she tried not to catastrophize. But life had taught her all too well that the worst really could happen in the blink of an eye. "I'm leaving now."

Chapter Seven

As Ian disconnected the call to Gwen, his heart was still lodged in his throat, right where it had been since hearing the thud in the pantry, followed by a childish scream.

He'd bolted up from his desk, sprinting in the direction of the sound, Sampson close on his heels. He'd been stunned to find Gideon sitting on the pantry floor, wailing, a palm pressed to his forehead. Caleb had been holding his own head as well, ratcheting Ian's fear up another notch.

Finally, he'd been able to untangle that Gideon had climbed the shelves and fallen. Even though Caleb hadn't been injured himself, his phantom pain could be traced back to their bond. Had Timothy felt something too from a distance?

Not that it mattered right now. Ian's entire focus was on pressing an ice pack against Gideon's forehead, trying to soothe the boy into staying still and calm as he sat in a chair at the kitchen table. Sampson had parked himself on the floor right beside the boy, resting his head on his paws, woeful brown eyes tracking every movement.

Ian adjusted the rag of crushed ice. "Try not to wriggle, buddy."

Gideon's bottom lip trembled as he hugged his knees tighter. "I want my mommy."

"She's on her way," Caleb said as he leaned a hip against the edge of the table.

Sniffling, Gideon rubbed the sleeve of his sweatshirt under his nose. "I wanna see what it looks like."

Caleb, fidgeting with the whipped cream canisters in the refrigerator, glanced over his shoulder. "No you don't. Trust me."

Tears rolled down Gideon's cheeks faster. "How bad is it?" His voice rose in panic. "Is there blood?"

"Not a drop," Ian reassured him. Thank goodness. "You're going to have such a great story to tell the other kids at school."

Caleb shoved the fridge door closed and crossed to his brother. "You can tell them you were a superhero who got into an accident saving the world."

Gideon shook his head. "A superhero doesn't fall."

"Sometimes he does. Maybe your superpower broke," Caleb answered.

Before Ian could caution him not to move the ice pack, Gwen rushed into the kitchen, breathless, with worry stamped all over her pretty face. His mom and Timothy trailed her more slowly. The boy sported a fresh close-cropped cut, his blond hair appearing darker when short. Timothy hung back, clutching Florence's hand as she draped the coats on a row of hooks.

Gwen raced straight toward her injured son, even stepping over Sampson to pull Gideon into a gentle but secure hug. Ian moved away from the table, feeling guilty and at odds, not sure what to do. Most of all, hating that he'd let her down.

Her eyes closed in obvious relief as she drew in a shaky breath, then arched away. "Let me look at your boo-boo."

Gideon gripped the pack tighter. "Mr. Ian said not to move it."

"It'll be okay for me to peek. I promise I'll put it right back." She eased the ice to the side. The swelling had gone down somewhat—thank goodness—but Gideon still sported quite a bump and a burgeoning bruise. "That doesn't look too bad."

Gideon pressed the pack on his bump again. "Does that mean I don't have to go to the doctor?"

Gwen smoothed his hair away from his face—not that he had much left, only marginally more than Timothy. "Mrs. Hollie has called the ranch's nurse. She's going to stop by and check you over just to be sure. But I think you're going to be alright."

The boy might be, but Ian felt like the mishap had shaved a decade off his own life. "I'm so sorry for not keeping a closer eye on the boys."

Gwen waved aside his concern. "These things happen with kids. Gideon had two sets of stitches before he was eighteen months old. Both times, his father and I were in the room with him. He toddled right between us and tripped onto the edge of a piece of furniture."

The mention of her dead husband caught Ian by surprise. She didn't speak of him often, and until now, Ian had not thought to ask about the man. He didn't even know the guy's name, and Ian found himself more curious than he should have been about her life from before he knew her.

Caleb flopped onto the floor by Sampson and plunged his fingers into the fluffy white dog's fur. "It was mine and Gideon's fault. We told Ian we were doing our homework and then we went into the pantry to—"

"To get a snack," Gideon interrupted. "A healthy snack. That's it."

The rushed explanation sounded suspicious to Ian, and made him think of how dodgy Caleb had been hiding behind the refrigerator door a few moments ago. But Ian didn't have anything concrete to note, and it wasn't his place to push or interfere.

Gwen looked from Gideon to Caleb, then back again. "The 'why' doesn't matter. You know better than to climb on shelves. And this is the reason. Rules are there to keep you safe. Do you understand?"

"Yes, ma'am," Gideon said with a big gulp and sniffle. "I'm sorry."

"That's a good start." Eyebrows raised, Gwen put her hands on her hips. "Now, do you have something to say to Mr. Ian?"

Startled, Ian straightened. What did she mean?

Gideon stared at him with earnest blue eyes, so subdued in comparison to his normal mischievous ways. "I'm sorry for not doing my homework like you said and for sneaking away."

Caleb looked up and echoed, "Me too."

Leaning forward conspiratorially, Florence wrapped an arm around each boy's shoulders. "When Ian was in elementary school, he got into his fair share of trouble too. He loved to climb trees, the higher the better. He said he wanted to see the whole forest."

Gideon leaned against Florence's side. "Are you going to tell Santa?"

Winking, his mom squeezed the boy tighter. "I'll probably forget anyway."

His mother's ability to laugh in the face of such a difficult diagnosis humbled Ian. And it reminded him of his desire to keep life normal for her for as long as possible. Right now, having Gwen and the boys living under his roof gave her a taste of that regular life. He would do whatever it took to protect that peace for his mother's sake.

He needed to keep his focus firmly on providing the best Christmas possible for his mom and the triplets. Even if it killed him.

Gwen was dead-on-her-feet tired, in a way that no amount of coffee would fix. But she still poured herself another cup, even though it was three in the morning. She was too afraid to go to sleep when she knew she had to check on Gideon every two hours. She was afraid to trust that the alarm on her phone would rouse her if she drifted off. He was sleeping on the living room sofa and she'd been keeping watch in the recliner so they didn't disturb the other boys upstairs.

The Top Dog Dude Ranch's nurse had checked Gideon over and deemed it a regular, run-of-the-mill bump. She'd advised that they check him every couple of hours and had given a full list of symptoms to watch out for. The mild prognosis had been a relief. But a mother's worries were tough to quell.

Gwen slid the drip pot into the maker again and lifted her steaming mug of dark roast, breathing in the scent before taking a sip. Today at the craft fair would be rough without sleep, but she'd pulled all-nighters in the past. Especially during those early days when the triplets were babies. Her husband had helped—he'd been a good father, despite being a crummy husband. But when all three boys wouldn't sleep and were hungry at the same time? Those nights had been rough.

The echo of heavy footsteps drew her back to the present just as Ian stepped into the kitchen doorframe. "Is everything alright?"

Plaid sleep pants hung low on his hips, a well-worn T-shirt stretched across his broad chest. His hair stood up, all mussed as if he'd plowed his fingers through again and again.

Or like it would if she had. Gulp.

"Just fine," she assured him, gripping her java. "I hope I didn't wake you? I can take Gideon upstairs…"

"Not at all. I've been pretty amped." He shot a glance through the archway toward the living room where Gideon was curled on the couch under a quilt, hugging his tattered baby blanket he'd yet to give up. Sampson slept on the floor beside him, having stuck like glue to Gideon since the accident. "You should get some rest. I can take the next wake-up shift."

"I'm okay." She lifted her coffee as proof, the mug warm in her hand. "I wouldn't be able to sleep anyway. Besides, you have to work in a few hours."

"So do you."

"But he's *my* son." She cradled the ceramic cup, her palm over the tree farm logo.

Ian approached her warily, reached into the cabinet and withdrew another mug. "Are you angry with me about what happened with Gideon on my watch?"

She blinked in surprise, though she was also touched that he would wonder—worry—rather than getting defensive. "No, not at all. I meant what I said earlier. It was an accident. The same thing could have happened on the stairs or on an icy patch outside. Or he could have fallen in the pantry while I was home too. Please don't blame yourself."

"I still feel bad." He pulled out the pot and poured the steaming brew.

"Well, let yourself off the hook." She leaned her bottom against the edge of the counter, facing him. "Promise?"

"On one condition?" Propping a hip against the Formica, he crossed his socked feet at the ankles.

"What's that?"

"If you won't go to bed, then at least let me keep you company." He motioned toward the kitchen table, where her cell phone rested on the scarred oak. The screen lit with numbers clicking down on the timer.

"Deal," she said, grateful for the company, for the distraction, for someone to share the worry of watching over her child.

And if he stayed with her, there would be less chance that she would drift off. Surely that was the reason why she found herself accepting his offer.

He eyed the ladder-back chairs for a moment as if

trying to decide where to sit. Across from her? Or beside her? As if the distance between them mattered.

Finally, he pulled out a corner seat by her. "I checked Gideon on my way in here, and he woke long enough to ask for pancakes with whipped cream for breakfast before he went back to sleep."

"He has always had a sweet tooth and Christmas certainly amps up those treat cravings." Speaking of Christmas made her curious. "I've been wondering. Why isn't your tree in the living room decorated? I would have thought, given your business, that you would have a showpiece."

"Leaving it bare wasn't a deliberate choice." Ian placed his mug on the table, careful to tuck a napkin underneath it as his mother instructed them at every meal. "I've just been too busy. You know that old saying. 'The cobbler's children have no shoes.'"

"So it's not that you secretly hate the holidays?" she teased. "Because wouldn't that be ironic? A Christmas tree farmer who hates Christmas."

"I'm as sentimental about Christmas as the next guy," he said, grinning. "Especially when it comes to the food."

Laughing, she leaned on her elbows. "What's your favorite holiday dish? The one thing you must have in order for the day to be complete?"

"My mom's sweet potato casserole," he said without hesitation. "It's different from the marshmallow one folks usually serve. Hers has a pecan topping made out of nuts, Rice Krispies, brown sugar and butter."

"Sounds delicious," she said, her mouth watering. "I can't wait to try it."

He scratched his chin. "I need to write down the recipe when she makes it this year…just in case."

She stretched a hand across to rest on top of his. "I think your mother would be very happy to know you're enjoying her sweet potato casserole for years to come."

His throat moved in a slow bob and he flipped his hand to link fingers with her. "Turnabout is fair play. What's the one thing that has to be on the table for your Christmas dinner?"

Sensing his need for level ground—understanding and craving the same—she said, "My grandma used to make this oyster dressing with saltine crackers, chopped up celery and onions. My mom called it 'booger pie' because of how it looked. But man, she would scrape the dish for the last bite."

"Booger pie?" His smile kicked a dimple into his cheek. "I don't know of many kids who'll eat oysters. How adventurous of you."

"Oh, I didn't eat it." She shook her head vigorously. "It made me gag. But the ritual of Grandma offering to skip it and Mom insisting that she should bake it since she liked it… Those family rituals and inside jokes? That's the stardust on top of making memories."

"I like that…stardust."

Silence settled between them. Comfortable. Which carried a danger all its own. "What about dessert?"

"Lemon meringue pie. And you?"

"Pecan pie. With whipped cream, of course." If there was any left after the way her boys were downing it at breakfast every morning.

"Good dessert choice."

Did he know his thumb was rubbing gentle circles against the inside of her wrist?

"Not dessert. For the whole meal," she said, shrugging. "Christmas isn't known for healthy eating. So why not eat pie for breakfast, lunch, dinner?"

The words were barely out of her mouth before a memory blindsided her of the time when she'd done just that for real—after her husband's death—crying her eyes out over every bite of his favorite dessert.

Just after she'd learned he hadn't been alone in the car that night. He hadn't been on a business trip either.

Ian slid his hand free and tucked her hair behind her ear. "What are you thinking that's put such a sad look in your eyes?"

His question caught her off guard, and for a moment she considered fabricating a story. But why lie? The truth was embarrassing, sure, but she hadn't been the one to cheat. And Ian's concern touched a wounded, neglected part of her heart. "I...I actually did that once. Had pecan pie for breakfast, lunch and dinner. It was right after Dale's—my husband's—funeral. I discovered he wasn't alone in the car when it ran off the road. He was with his mistress. After the service, someone brought a pecan pie and I ate the whole thing over the course of a day."

His face filled with sympathy.

"Did that help?" he asked simply, earnestly.

"It didn't make me anything but sick."

His eyes searched her, full of concern and a hint of anger that smoothed more balm to her wounded soul.

"Gwen, I hate that he did that to you. To the boys as well." His palms flattened to the table, pressing, as if restraining himself from reaching for her again. "You deserved better."

His genuine concern and empathy drew her like a magnet.

"Thank you, but it's in the past." Or rather, her love for Dale was gone, left behind. The pain lingered, though. "And without him, I wouldn't have my three amazing boys."

"Well, I, for one, think he must have been an idiot. You're an incredible woman."

The compliment warmed her, more than it should have, so she tried to make light of it. "You're just buttering me up, hoping that I'll share the recipe for booger pie."

"Who could resist a dish called booger pie?" he teased gently. "But when I say you're incredible, I'm only speaking the truth. You can always count on me to be honest."

She wanted to believe that, so very much. His actions certainly spoke of high character. She couldn't help but admire the way he stepped up to take care of his mom. How he'd helped Gwen and her boys. He was a good man. A regular lumberjack in shining armor.

And in her vulnerable, sad state during an already difficult night, she found her walls crumbling right along with her restraint. Before she could second-guess herself, she swayed toward him, the charged air between them tempting her, luring her. She gripped his shoulders, tugging him closer in an unmistakable invitation.

With a low rumble in his throat, Ian tunneled his fingers into her hair, cupping the back of her head. His touch, so gentle, so sure, sent shivers of anticipation up her spine. At his hesitation, she knew he was giving her the chance to say no, to shut down this moment before it even started if that was what she wished.

Instead, she pressed her lips to his without leaving her chair. Just a simple kiss. Maybe she would luck out and the chemistry between them would bomb. Then she and Ian could continue on with the convenient arrangement, focused fully on the holidays for her sons and his mother.

His mouth grazed hers, once, twice. And she knew. The chemistry was far from being a bust.

Sliding from her chair, she glided toward him and he lifted her across his lap. Her hands flattened against his chest and soaked in the muscular expanse, strengthened by hours spent working outdoors.

His arms banded around her, drawing her nearer, deepening the kiss. The fresh scent of him, the bristle along his cheeks, launched a thrill through her. Willpower was waning with each heartbeat, and—

An alarm pierced her foggy senses, confusing at first until she remembered. She had to check on her son.

Equal doses of embarrassment and regret surged through her as she pulled away, reaching for her phone. "It's time for me to wake Gideon."

"Of course." He bracketed her waist and set her on her feet again with a smooth strength. "I don't know what I was thinking."

"The same thing I was?" She pressed a hand to her chest, right over her thundering heart. "That we're crazy attracted to each other and we're alone here late at night?"

"Yeah, that. All of that." He exhaled hard, pushing a hand on the table as he stood. "Let's go check on the boy."

She rested a hand on his arm, trying to ignore the

way that simple touch sent a fresh shiver through her. "He's my son. I've got it."

"Of course." He nodded, backing away. "I'm going to turn in. If you need anything, you know where to find me."

Even though she appreciated the offer, she knew she wouldn't take him up on it.

Ian hadn't slept, and now he faced another breakfast with Gwen. Attracted to her. On fire for her. With his defenses on the ropes due to exhaustion. And the taste he'd had of her just made her that much harder to resist.

Stepping into the mudroom after taking Sampson out for a run in the yard, Ian closed the door behind him, bells on the knob jingling. He was greeted by echoes of the boys' laughter from around the table and the scent of breakfast—buttery pancakes and fragrant bacon. He shrugged out of his jacket and kicked off his boots, wet with snowy sludge from the lawn. Sampson gave a mighty shake, sending droplets of snow flying. Grounded by simple routine, he snagged a well-worn terry cloth towel out of the basket and extended his hand for Sampson's paw.

"Okay, buddy," he said softly. "You need to be my wingman. Feel free to nudge me out of harm's way if you see that I'm weakening."

Sampson flopped one muddy paw after the other into Ian's palm to dry.

"Good boy." Ian tossed aside the towel and plucked a tiny dog bone out of the treat jar. Puffing a hefty exhale, he strode into the kitchen, his wingman keeping pace.

And there she was.

Gwen.

She moved about the kitchen with grace and an over-brightness that hinted she wasn't as unaffected as she tried to appear. The feeling was mutual. He couldn't tear his gaze off her, the lines and look of her all the more alluring after having had her in his arms. The feel of her was imprinted in his memory.

Jeans outlined the gentle curve of her hips, show-casing her slim legs. She wore a red sweatshirt sporting the Top Dog logo in the middle of a Christmas tree, ready for the craft show. The way she avoided his eyes now made it clear she was every bit as on edge as he was after their kiss.

At least his mom was still upstairs getting dressed or she would likely comment on the awkwardness in the air. He couldn't even blame her lack of filter on the disease. His mother had always been outspoken, direct.

Even after Gwen had pulled away and said she would handle the rest of Gideon's wake-ups, Ian hadn't been able to drift off. His mind had still been too full of that moment with her. He'd known having her under his roof would prove tempting. He just hadn't expected a simple kiss to knock his feet right out from underneath him.

By sunrise, he was no closer to an idea on what to do next and that bugged him. Indecision had never been a part of his DNA. But then he'd never encountered any-one quite like Gwen.

Which felt disloyal to his ex-fiancée.

Although they were no longer a couple, he'd loved Becky. He had promised to spend the rest of his days with her. Although she'd betrayed him in the end, his feelings for her hadn't disappeared. He'd planned to spend a lifetime with her, and he hadn't been able to imagine wanting a life with anyone else. Now he had to face the possibility that he hadn't loved her fully after all. Because if he'd felt about her the way he did about Gwen? He wasn't sure he'd have been able to walk away. Not without trying everything imaginable to make things work. Could she have sensed that there was something lacking in his feelings for her, even if he hadn't realized it himself?

That notion shook him. No doubt, her reason for leaving him had hurt, but he hated that he may have wounded her heart too. That was the last thing he'd ever wanted to do to Gwen—

Gwen?

He meant Becky.

Yet the accidental slip mixing up the women's names reminded him of how careful he needed to be around the pretty widow. She'd already been betrayed so deeply by her husband. He wouldn't be a person to disillusion her further. Still, he couldn't keep himself from watching her, admiring the way she juggled the morning routine with ease, bringing calm to what could be a frenetic breakfast.

"Good morning, everybody," he called out, snagging a piece of leftover bacon off a plate on the counter. "Be sure to bundle up. It's a cold one out there today."

"Good morning to you." Avoiding his eyes, Gwen swiped her hands on a small Christmas towel. "Alrighty, boys. Let's finish up. We have family pictures today at the craft fair."

Timothy scraped his chair back, picked up his plate and placed it in the sink. "I'm gonna get my coat."

Gwen called after him, "Be sure to brush your teeth."

Gideon held up a spoon and tried to look at his reflection. "My head looks ugly."

Chewing the last bite of his pancakes, Caleb said, "If you hadn't cut your hair, nobody would be able to see it."

Gwen rested a hand on his shoulder. "Your head looks injured, not ugly. And, Caleb, don't talk with your mouth full."

Gideon dropped his spoon in his empty milk glass. "Maybe I can get a superhero bandage? Then if Santa sees my picture, he won't know I was bad."

Gwen kissed Gideon's forehead. "Santa understands that little boys get into scrapes sometimes. He just wants to know that you say you're sorry and that you'll try your best not to do it again."

Gideon chewed his bottom lip. "What if I had a really good reason?"

The comment sent off an alarm in Ian as he folded another piece of bacon into his mouth. He'd been a mischievous little boy once too. "What might that reason be?"

"Nothing, I was just wondering," Gideon said evasively.

Caleb tugged his mother's hand. "Can I stay with you at the craft show?"

Gwen swiped a napkin along the corner of his mouth. "I'm sorry, sweetie, but I'll be working. I wouldn't be able to watch you."

Caleb slumped in the chair. "Am I being punished because me and Gideon hid in the pantry and ate whipped cream?"

Gideon elbowed Caleb. "She didn't know that part—

until now, you big tattletale." Then added, "Sorry for sneaking food, Mr. Ian."

Well, that explained the evasiveness. "I knew you were getting a snack—you said that much already. I just didn't know it was whipped cream. It's okay by me as long as your mom says it's fine by her."

Gwen gave a resigned and weary nod. "You three boys are going to have a great time at the ranch today—"

Caleb's bottom lip trembled. "I don't want to go to day care."

"It's not day care today," Gwen explained patiently. "It's more like camp. You're going to Santa's workshop to make gifts for your friends. Maybe Saint Nick will even make a surprise appearance."

Gideon and Caleb exchanged a strange look that set off more of those alarms in Ian's mind. He'd need to find out what they were up to. The last thing he wanted was to be caught off guard again and have another kid tumbling off a shelf—or some other such antic.

Gwen stacked their plates, piling the silverware on top. "But you won't find out if you don't get dressed so we can go. I promise you that it will be fun. Now hurry up and get your shoes on."

The boys slid from their seats, put their cups in the sink, before racing toward the mudroom, whispering the whole way in that triplet language of theirs.

Quiet descended, making Ian all too aware that he and Gwen were alone. Completely alone. Standing pretty close to the spot where they'd kissed just a few hours earlier. He hated the awkwardness between them, but didn't have a clue how to dispel it.

He plucked up the wadded napkins from the table and joined her at the sink. "I guess I'll head out now…"

She spun to face him fast, cutting him off. "Before you leave, do you have a minute to talk about last night?"

He should have known she would tackle things head-on. It was the way she approached everything in her life.

"Sure, let's go somewhere away from curious ears." A quick conversation would give him a chance to clear the air. "The enclosed porch is private."

Motioning the way, he was careful not to touch her. He swung open the door leading to the glassed-in area that gave a panoramic view of this property. This space was his favorite, a spot where he could enjoy the feeling of being outside without the freezing weather. The walls were lined with built-in sofas with fat cushions and stuffed ottomans. A woven jute rug stretched across the brick floor.

Gwen dropped to sit on the edge of the sofa, her hands clenched on her knees until her knuckles went white. "I would like to talk about how we're going to navigate these next few weeks until we leave."

"Because of the kiss last night." He eased down onto the opposite side of the sectional, keeping distance between himself and the temptation to touch her again. Especially since he wasn't sure of her state of mind. Did she plan to leave earlier than scheduled? The possibility sent a bolt of regret through him. He hoped that wasn't the case.

Her cheeks pinkened as she nodded. "I suggest that when we're not at work, we take advantage of the holiday celebrations at the ranch. I have a free pass to all of the activities. If you think your mother would enjoy them as well, you're both welcome." Her gaze skirted away for a moment toward the main part of the house, then back to him again. "That way, we won't be alone together in the house quite so much."

She had a point.

"Stay busy doing things together?" An interesting—and surprisingly appealing—notion. "That shouldn't be difficult this time of year."

His brain was already running with the possibilities. Sleigh rides. Horseback riding. Ice skating. He didn't have much in the way of free time this time of year. So when he did, he wanted to make the most of it. The extra activity would be good for his mother. But then, it would also be a welcome diversion for Ian. Especially since he'd be spending time with Gwen.

"So we're in agreement. Good."

"Mom!" a childish shout sounded from the porch doorway.

Ian hadn't even heard the kid approach—it had to be Caleb, since he'd still resisted becoming an amateur barber and therefore had longer hair. The boy looked troubled, scratching at his forehead.

Gwen startled, standing so quickly she almost tripped over an ottoman. "Do you need help finding your shoes?"

She must really be rattled, because the boy already had his sneakers on his feet and his snow boots in his hands. Maybe she was just tired. Ian stood up, ready to offer assistance.

Caleb shook his head. "We can't find Mrs. Florence."

Chapter Eight

Timothy's head hurt.

He slumped against the side of Mr. Ian's truck and traced the lettering with his finger, waiting for everyone else to get ready to go to the craft festival. His mom had said to hurry up and he'd done what she asked like a good boy. He still felt bad about cutting his own hair, but he'd meant well, had been trying to help out Gideon. And he'd been extra good about doing what his mom said ever since—like getting ready to go.

So where was everybody else?

He tucked his fingers up under his stocking hat and scratched his forehead where it still ached. Sure, his brother was the one who fell, but triplets felt each other's pain. Even the doctor had told him so once when they'd gone to the emergency room because Caleb had the stomach flu, and the other two were puking even though they weren't sick.

But Timothy had that shared hurt happen more often than his brothers. He didn't know why. He just knew that's how it was.

Yesterday, he'd realized something was wrong before his mom got the call. His head had been burning and he wasn't sure which brother was in trouble.

So, he understood that Gideon was aching. And that Caleb was sad. But as he stood there tracing the green letters that spelled out "Tree Farm," it felt unfair that he had to be both hurt *and* sad. He was used to it, though. His mom said that's why he was such a "peacemaker" and that it was okay not to worry so much about everybody else. That was a mom's job.

He'd nodded because he'd known that was what she wanted him to do, not because he really agreed. He figured she didn't need to hear he worried about her too, especially about her being alone. He didn't remember much about his dad and sometimes he thought what he did recall came from watching videos instead of really remembering. Like how seeing a family boat trip and picnic in a home movie filled up his mind until he tricked himself into believing it was a real memory. He'd been thinking about it more lately, being at Mr. Ian's house and seeing how his mom had help.

A movement by the new tire swing caught his attention. Mrs. Florence held the rope, swaying, staring off into space. Was she waiting for everyone too? She had on one of those capes she liked and fuzzy snow boots.

Timothy trekked through the light dusting of fresh snow over to Mrs. Florence. "Where is everybody?"

Blinking fast, she looked toward him, then smiled.

"Dear boy, if you're expecting *me* to keep track of everyone, then we're in a sad state."

Timothy frowned. "What does that mean?"

"I'm just teasing." She laid a hand on his short hair and ruffled it. "I only meant that I am forgetful and that I get lost more and more often."

"Oh, okay." He kicked his toe through some sludge by the minivan. "We're supposed to be leaving for the Top Dog Dude Ranch. There's a craft fair today."

"That sounds delightful." She motioned for him to climb into the swing. "Would you like to wait together here? I'll push."

She didn't need to ask him twice. Timothy tucked himself inside the tire right away. Mrs. Florence put her hand in the middle of his back and sent him soaring. She was strong. He stretched his feet out and flew through the air. The wind was cold on his face, the sun bright in his eyes. It was awesome. He didn't feel so sad and his head stopped hurting.

He looked back over his shoulder. "So you really don't know where my brothers are?"

"I'm afraid not, dear." She shoved again, launching him higher.

"Or my mom?"

"The kitchen, maybe?" she said, not sounding too sure. "With my son?"

"Yeah…" He nodded. "She spends a lot of time with Mr. Ian."

"That's what people who like each other do."

Mr. Ian was nice and being here with Mr. Ian was fun. But what would that do to his memories of his dad? It was already tough enough to remember what he was like. If Mr. Ian started doing dad things, would he forget his first dad completely? "Do you think they love each other?"

Florence stepped around until he could see her, her hands stuffed under her swoopy cape. "I'm not sure about that. But they seem as if they are trying to figure it out. Does that bother you?"

He didn't want to hurt her feelings about her son, so he just said, "Should it?"

Florence eased to sit on a metal bench. "When my son was younger, I worried sometimes that he would get jealous if I dated a man. How does it make you feel to think about your mom liking someone?"

He dragged his feet along the ground to slow the swing while he thought about her question. He wasn't sure exactly. "I don't want to be alone. My teacher says it's because I'm a triplet that I get extra sensitive to being by myself. But if that's true, then why does Caleb always want to be all by himself?"

Mrs. Florence tipped her head to the side. "*All* by himself?"

"Well, by himself with Mommy." Timothy's stomach got tight. Maybe he really was worried about sharing his mom with somebody else. He already had to share her with his brothers. But that wasn't very nice of him. "For somebody who says you don't remember much, you sure are smart."

"Dear boy, that is the sweetest thing anyone has said to me in a long time." She smiled, but her eyes were sad.

And that made Timothy sad, even though she wasn't his brother. He knew she got confused sometimes, but he thought she was still really special. He loved her pancakes and the way she always had time to read him a book at night.

He should do something for her. He'd seen a bunch of photo albums on the bookshelf by the fireplace. Maybe if he asked her to show him the pictures that would help her remember stuff. Like how he watched videos of his dad to keep him real in his mind a little longer.

The idea took root, and he didn't feel so blue anymore. Helping people felt good.

The screen door banged open, startling him. It must be time to go. He climbed out of the swing as Mr. Ian and his mom and brothers poured out onto the porch.

Mr. Ian jogged toward them, his face all scrunched up and worried. "There you are, Mom. I wondered where you'd gotten off to."

Caleb ran behind him, arms pumping. "We looked all around the house for you."

Gideon shouted, "Even in the pantry."

Mrs. Florence spread her arms wide, her cape rippling in the cold wind. "I've been right here with this sweet young man."

Mr. Ian hugged his mom hard for a minute. He was good to his mom.

Timothy wanted to help his mom too.

Even though sharing his mom would be tough, he wanted her to be happy. He wanted to be a good son like Mr. Ian. And if that meant sharing his mother, then that's what he would do. Hadn't he already thought about how much happier she'd been here with help?

First chance he could get, he needed to talk to his brothers. They had important work to do.

* * *

Gwen felt like her eyeballs must be floating in coffee, she'd drunk so much of it today. Stifling a yawn, she stepped into the Top Dog Dude Ranch's sprawling main lodge. The space was stately and inviting, with a two-story Christmas tree dominating the lobby. It was no wonder the place stayed booked—not just guest suites in the lodge, but also the cabins and glamping campground with renovated vintage campers. The ranch offered the best in a wholesome, natural environment, with a slew of fun events that catered to the whole family.

The craft festival was well underway. Gwen had already sold most of her inventory, so she'd left the booth in the capable hands of her assistant, Ashlynn, to sell regular inventory brought over from the shop.

Which freed Gwen to lead a crafting party for adults in the lodge's massive dining area. Shrugging out of her parka, she stepped deeper into the soaring space. Concentrating was tough, with her eyes gritty from lack of sleep and her mind full of that toe-curling kiss.

Where was the coffeepot? If she was going to make it, she needed to fully drown her eyeballs, instead of just floating them in java.

Spotting the carafe in a corner cart decked out in pine garland, she made fast tracks to fill a fresh cup for herself. As an afterthought, she added two packets of sugar for an extra boost of energy.

At least her boys had stopped grousing about the day spent apart from her, thank goodness. They'd had some kind of confab in the back of the van on the way over, speaking in their triplet language, heads close together. Still chattering, they'd set off on their way to the Santa's workshop event without a single complaint or even a sullen look. She hated that she didn't have more time to spend with them over the holidays because she was so busy making Christmas happen for others.

Tables were covered with holiday plaid cloths. Piles of crafting supplies littered the center of each surface—precut pieces of fabric, lengths of yarn, stuffing, potpourri. Instructions were provided for DIY gift options—rag dolls, yarn babies, drawer sachets. She would monitor the activities, moving from station to station, offering help as needed.

Peering over the top of her coffee cup, she looked over to check Florence's table, reassuring herself that the woman hadn't gone missing again. Thankfully, she was easy to find in her bright red tracksuit, her plaid shawl draped over the back of her chair. Florence sat with Constance—aka Mrs. Santa Claus—and four sisters from Minnesota. Two were widowed, one divorced and one never married, so they'd decided to spend Christmas at the ranch together. All four siblings had matching bobbed gray hair and sparkly Christmas sweatshirts, each with a different animal theme—a cat, a dog, a moose and a reindeer.

Florence was happy, smiling, her body relaxed.

That moment when they'd thought they'd lost her had been terrifying. Gwen had allowed herself to become complacent because the woman hadn't wandered since they moved into the farmhouse.

Guilt pinched. She and Ian had made an arrangement to share responsibilities and she didn't want to let him down. Even though Florence hadn't wandered any farther than the yard, it had still been a sharp reminder of what could happen.

Setting down her coffee, she addressed the room full of ladies and a couple of men. "Thank you for joining us. The children don't get to have all the fun making Christmas gifts today. We're all in as well. If you'll look at the center of your table, you'll find instructions for various items that can be created from the supplies in front of you."

She gave the participants a moment to pass the papers around before continuing, "Any of these projects are great stocking stuffers or presents for gift exchange parties."

Next, she held up a paisley sample dolly. "This sweet baby can be for a child. Or you can stuff it with potpourri to freshen a dresser drawer or bathroom. Or my personal favorite use—a version with regular stuffing called a 'Dagnabbit Doll.' When you're angry, slam it against a piece of furniture and say…"

The room chanted in unison, "Dagnabbit!"

One of the Minnesota sisters—the one with a moose on her sweatshirt—called out, "I could have certainly used one of these during my divorce. Although I probably would have mangled the toy in the first twenty-four hours after our first court hearing."

Her sister with a holiday tabby cat on her sweater patted her arm. "Honey, put that out of your mind. This trip is supposed to heal your heart."

What might life have looked like if she and Dale had discovered the Top Dog Dude Ranch during those last troubled days of their marriage? But once the babies were born, they hadn't managed a vacation. Well, not one together, anyway. She pushed away thoughts of trips she'd later learned Dale had taken with his girlfriend.

Gwen's chest went tight. She and Dale had planned a getaway when the triplets turned one, a trip to the beach with nothing but umbrella drinks, lovemaking and sleep-ins. But they'd had to cancel at the last minute when his parents backed out on watching the triplets because they'd gotten a great deal on a cruise.

She'd known the triplets weren't their responsibility, but it had still stung that they'd bailed. She and Dale had so desperately needed time as a couple, and since her parents worked double shifts to make ends meet, Dale's folks were the only option for overnight help. And they had helped…but only when it suited them. Being there for her had never been very high on their priority list. Even once they had learned of their son's infidelity after the accident, they'd never said a word about it to her, not a word of sympathy and certainly not any kind of "can we help with the boys and we're sorry our son was such a dagnabbit loser."

All a moot point now. Letting bitterness eat at her would only create more negativity, which would hurt her boys. Time to look forward and count blessings.

And live up to her responsibilities.

Satisfied that everyone was settled into their projects, Gwen topped off her coffee and wove through the crowd, offering encouragement and suggestions. She paused at Florence's station in front of the stone fireplace. A full blaze rolled inside, lights and greenery draped along the mantel. "What are you ladies making?"

Florence held up a rag doll she had halfway finished, and that she was in the process of stuffing with cotton. "I had one almost exactly like this as a little girl. My grandmother made it for me. Constance here tells me they have a foster daughter. I thought perhaps she would like to have it."

Constance angled toward the sisters, swiping her phone open to show a photo of a little girl with a French braid and big hair bow. "Actually, Isabella's adoption is almost complete. She's at Santa's workshop or I would introduce you." She showed the picture to the Minnesota guests. "We were worried the court wouldn't let us have her since we're older, but everything worked out beautifully. As a matter of fact, Thomas and I met Isabella here. When we got married, the ranch was also hosting a camp for children in foster care."

Gwen pulled up a chair, welcoming the opportunity to rest her feet. "That same camp brought the O'Briens' four children into our lives. Freddy, Elliot, Phillip and Ivy lost their birth parents in a car accident."

The oldest sister pressed a hand to her chest over the sequined Santa paws. "How devastating for those little ones. I'm so glad to know the ranch helped them to find a happy future—and what a blessing that they were able to keep all four of them together. I don't know what I would do if I was separated from my sisters."

Gwen straightened the piles of supplies, picking pieces of potpourri out of the yarn. "The ranch has a way of bringing out the best in life for people. This job has been a godsend for me and my triplets."

Florence jabbed her finger into the doll, pressing stuffing deeper into an arm until it took shape. "And let me tell you, those boys are adorable."

Gwen's maternal heart swelled with just a little pride.

It was kind of Florence to be so good to her children. Each of her boys had benefited from the extra attention.

A moment later, the divorced Minnesota sister held her craft up, staring through narrowed eyes. "What if I make mine into a voodoo doll?"

The reindeer sister mumbled, "This party sure turned dark quickly."

Time to redirect this conversation. "Now, that would be a craft night to remember. Perhaps perfect for a Galentine's Day party?"

Florence plucked up another pinch of cotton. "A woman needs her girlfriends for when things get tough. I don't know what I would have done without mine to help me through when Ian's dad drained our bank account."

The table went silent.

Florence's forehead twitched with confusion for a moment before she snatched up her half-stuffed doll and slammed it down twice.

Jaws dropped and eyes went wide all around the table. Gwen started to reach for her phone to call Ian when Florence grinned, setting the craft down more carefully.

"Relax, everyone," Florence said. "Consider that an attempt at humor that didn't go well."

Gwen wasn't so certain it had been a joke. Florence was good at covering her moments of disorientation and confusion. But there was nothing to be gained in pushing the point now. Clearly that would only upset Florence when she was having an otherwise delightful day. The best course of action would be to keep a close eye on her in case there might be another concerning incident.

Gwen scraped back her chair. "I'm going to get a refill of my coffee. Can I bring any of you back a snack or something to drink? I'd like to hang out with you ladies and make a doll of my own."

Ian had logged a record number of tree sales, and the sun was only just setting. Multicolored lights flickered on. Country Christmas tunes echoed softly through his portable sound system.

The stand was set up just outside the Top Dog Dude Ranch's main entrance—a bonus for him. And he liked to think that he was building such a name for his high-quality product that he'd drawn some traffic for the ranch as well.

Through the afternoon, he'd been running on fumes, but as the sun sank lower, he began to hit his second wind.

A young man slung his arm around a woman—likely his wife, given their wedding bands and matching reindeer antler headbands. Humming, they each grabbed an end of a four-foot Fraser fir.

Just as he started to offer to help, a familiar minivan turned into the lot and parked. Sure enough, Gwen stepped out of one side, his mother from the other. The side doors opened and the triplets bounded from their booster seats, all three so hyped on holiday cheer their voices carried.

The young husband said, "Is that your family? What cute little fellas."

Ian didn't bother correcting them. He was beginning to get used to the assumption—maybe even enjoy it a little. He processed their payment and passed the receipt, trying his best not to follow Gwen's movement across the parking area. "Do you need help loading up? Or rope to tie the tree down?"

The husband shook his head. "No, we're good. Thanks, though. You should go rescue the ladies before your boys pull over their mom and grandma."

And there it was again. The world assuming they were a family. It's like the cosmos was shouting at him. Except he wasn't sure what to make of the persistent commotion.

Closing and locking the cashbox with the card reader and receipts inside, Ian strode toward them, his focus still very much on Gwen. "How did everything go with the craft festival today?"

Gideon raced toward him, holding up his mittened hands. "Mr. Ian, Mr. Ian, do *not* peek in the boxes in the van. We've made presents for you and Mrs. Florence and Mommy. They're really cool. When we get home, we get to wrap them up all by ourselves. Mommy's got gift bags and tissue paper and tape. I love tape."

"I'll be on my best behavior," Ian said, clapping a hand over his heart.

Gwen held up a doggie bag. "Don't let us interrupt your work. We just stopped by to bring you food. Things were so hectic this morning, I wasn't sure if you had time to pack a lunch…or supper. It's barbecue."

His mouth watered. "Thanks, that's really thoughtful. I'm starving. I've just been snacking off the cookies and cocoa here when I get a break."

He pointed toward the stand he'd set up with refreshments, a vintage bar cart with sturdy wheels and a generator humming behind it to power the coffeepot and a Crock-Pot of cocoa. He'd hung a garland of miniature pine wreaths along the front, always trying to give his customers a festive experience whenever they bought a tree.

Gwen extended her hand, the scent of warm, tangy barbecue teasing his nose. "Then I'm glad we stopped by."

There was a wariness in her eyes that made him think of how deeply she'd been rejected by her dead husband. Before Ian could second-guess himself, he said, "Would you-all like to hang out here with me for a while? I have cookies and cocoa. There's a small park within eyesight."

Caleb tugged on Gwen's hand. "Can we, Mama? Please, please, pretty please? I'm not ready to go home."

Then Ian remembered how tired she must be. "Maybe you're ready to turn in…"

Gwen rocked back on her bootheels. "I'd love to stay. If I go to bed now, I'll wake up in the middle of the night and won't be able to go back to sleep. Point me toward the chocolate."

The triplets each grabbed a cookie before running toward the wooden playground surrounded by inflatable Christmas decorations—Santa, a herd of reindeer and three snowmen who reminded him of Caleb, Gideon and Timothy.

"You two talk," Florence said, choosing a gingerbread man and disposable cup of cocoa. "I'll be right here on the bench by the swings. Also within your eyesight so you don't have to worry about me either."

Hearing her speak so openly about her symptoms and the necessity of keeping an eye on her made his heart weary. Ian didn't even know how to respond other than to say, "Thanks, Mom. You're the best."

"Well, that's certainly true." Florence patted his cheek before taking her place on the bench.

Leaving him alone with Gwen.

Leaning a hip against the refreshment table, he passed her a Styrofoam cup and dropped two marshmallows on top, the way he'd noticed she preferred. Then turned his attention to the bag of dinner.

"Thanks again," he said, plucking out two fat french fries. "This was really thoughtful of you."

She tapped a basket full of plastic bags filled with candy, graham crackers and tiny frosting packets. "What are these?"

"Mini-gingerbread-house kits for children to take home after they pick their tree. See the little gumdrops that look like an evergreen?" He pointed to a bag on top before stuffing the salty fries into his mouth, chewing fast. "Mom put the packets together. Luckily, her crafting skills are still mostly intact, well, other than quilting. Anyhow, you should take one for each of the boys."

As if on cue, the sound of laughter and squeals echoed from the play area. Florence sat on the bench, her phone out as she tapped along the screen. Her doctor had recommended some games to play on her cell like tangram puzzles and mah-jongg. He shifted his focus back to Gwen.

"Thank you, I will." She tucked three of the house kits into her oversize boho sack. "It'll be nice for them to each have their own. This one year, after the boys waited and waited to eat the gingerbread house they'd made together, Gideon leaned over and licked the whole thing thinking that his brothers wouldn't want it with his germs."

That sounded like Gideon. The kid was a character, with a quick mind and big heart. "I'm guessing he was wrong."

"Very. The other two dug right in. Although I was horribly grossed out," she said before taking a sip of her hot chocolate, sighing, her eyes sliding closed with bliss. "Perfect." Her lashes fluttered open. "I'm running on adrenaline, caffeine and sugar. How about you?"

"Same. How did your event go?" He unwrapped his sandwich and bit off a big bite. Awesome. The food, the thoughtfulness…and Gwen.

"I sold out all of my restored toys," she said, but her eyes didn't match the joy of the statement. "I wish I had more stock to market in the shop, but there are worse problems to have. How are sales here?"

"Not much left except the Charlie Brown Christmas trees. I'll have to cut down a few more this week." Inspiration lit. "You'd mentioned staying busy to avoid… well, you know." He knocked back a swig of cocoa. "Would you and the boys like to come along when I cut the trees? We could go sledding while we're out there, maybe while Mom's at her knitting circle."

"The boys would love that." Her lashes fluttered down for a moment before she looked back up at him, meeting his eyes dead on. "I would too."

"In the interest of staying occupied," he said, his voice dropping.

She bit her bottom lip, then released it, slowly. "Of course."

Yet even as she nodded, he doubted all the sled rides and bonfires in the woods would wear him out enough to sleep through a night without dreams of his tempting temporary tenant.

Chapter Nine

Ian hadn't had this much fun since he was a kid sledding on a snowy day.

But then, that's exactly what he'd been doing—sledding with Gwen and the boys since sunup. It was the perfect way to spend his day off. Well, somewhat of a day off, since he'd downed a couple dozen more trees to add to the sale lot. They'd tromped through the tree farm to the best slope, one out of the way with pristine snow and no crowds or lines. Snow sparkled under the sunshine, the light catching crystals and making the whole place look a bit magical.

Now he carried his power saw and axe while Gwen dragged the sled as they made their way back to his truck. The boys frolicked ahead, flinging snowballs at each other with that endless energy of youth. Sampson galloped alongside, sometimes breaking ahead to run circles around them.

Gwen's nose and cheeks were red from the brisk wind even though they'd taken warm-up breaks in his truck each time he'd dragged a tree over to wrap and load on the trailer.

"Thanks for sharing your day with us." Even through her breathless words, Ian could hear the true pleasure in her voice. It made him want to give her that happiness all the time.

He swallowed back the thought to focus on her words. "Today is tops in my Christmas memories. Holidays are all about kids."

She beamed, her maternal nature in full agreement. "I checked with Constance a few minutes ago to see how your mom's doing in her knitting circle and she's just finishing up a stocking."

The quick switch in subject made him wonder if she was working just as hard to rein in her thoughts as he was to redirect his own. Still, he appreciated her looking out for his mother.

"Do we need to hurry back?" He didn't want to leave yet, but he understood the need for boundaries.

He just kept failing with his own.

Gwen shook her head. "Next, they are stuffing them full of treats and dollar-store toys. Constance will be shipping them to the foster group where her little girl and the O'Brien kids came from."

"That's really awesome. Mom has missed crafting since she stopped quilting. I'm glad, though, that she's been able to continue knitting and needlepoint." He glanced over at her again. "Thank you for checking on her so much throughout the day. That put my mind at ease while I worked."

"And what a great job you have." She breathed in deeply, her boots crunching through the packed snow. "This is such an amazing property. Thanks for the tour and explanation of the process. I had no idea how much went into growing and cultivating a tree farm."

She sounded genuinely interested and certainly listened attentively throughout the day. He tried not to compare her response to Becky's and the way his ex-fiancée's eyes had often glazed over when he talked about work, but he couldn't miss the difference. At the start of his relationship, he'd thought he and Becky had so much in common since she'd grown up on a farm. But she'd been negative about the community of farm life and hated the solitude he embraced.

Although today had been far from isolated—in all the best ways. There was a peace about Gwen that soothed the frayed edges in his mind in a way he'd previously only found on long hikes alone on a mountain trail.

Rustling sounded along the tree line just before an elk stepped into sight fifty yards ahead, eliciting a gasp of wonder from the triplets. Closer to them, a cardinal perched on a branch while an unseen woodpecker added percussion to the music of the mountains.

Gwen stepped into a pile of snow and lost her footing for a moment. He grasped her elbow. "Steady there."

It seemed natural to slide his arm the rest of the way around her waist. He held his breath, waiting for her reaction. Her body stiffened for an instant in awareness before melting against his side. A perfect fit.

She brushed a strand of hair from her face. "What changes do you envision over the next few years?"

He hadn't thought much about the future. Doing so

felt like poking a wound since the days to come were so uncertain for his mom. But he didn't want to drag down the day with thoughts or talk of that. Instead, he focused on ways he could answer her. "As we drive back, I'll point out where I found some apple trees closer to the house. They just needed pruning and fertilizing to revive. And I added some berry vines."

His mother loved to can fruit. Or at least she used to. The last time they'd tried to boil the harvest had been a disaster. She'd lost track of time and the batch had been ruined. He'd tried to reassure her the same thing could happen to anyone, but she'd grown so agitated, he'd dropped the subject altogether. From then on, they'd eaten their berries in pancakes and on oatmeal, not in the form of homemade preserves.

Gwen tipped her face toward his, her blue eyes bright. Lively. Appealing. "It sounds like you plan to put down roots. No pun intended."

The idea drew him. Even more, *she* drew him. But he wouldn't think about that now when they were supposed to be distracting one another from the ever-present attraction.

"Let's just say—" he chose his words with care "—that I've been focused on making it welcoming for Mom. When she…later…needs more care than I can provide, I figure all these upgrades will help me with resale value."

Was it his imagination or had her steps hitched a hint before she resumed her measured pace.

"Where do you plan to go?"

"Back to my previous job as a park ranger, wherever there's an opening." He rolled out his answer without hesitation. It had been his plan all along when he'd made this move. "Staying in that line of work had me away from the house too much to provide Mom with the level of care she needs now."

"I think you've done an admirable job at giving her a life that keeps her happy and occupied. She loves joining in the ranch activities."

"Jacob and Hollie have been very welcoming and accommodating about including her in events. Mom's doctor has been great with guidance about how to keep her mind engaged in ways that—hopefully—minimize frustration."

"Hollie and Jacob are good people. And I also happen to know," she said, slipping her arm around his waist, "that they are very pleased to have the draw of your business next door—especially since the land had been targeted by some land developers looking to put in condos."

He winced, wondering for the first time about who might target his property for purchase when he moved away and how that would affect this community that had welcomed him and his mom. "That would be a shame. Still, they have to know I'm not planning to stick around forever."

"I would guess they're hoping to be in a position to buy the land from you by then. But that's just speculation on my part." Pausing, she shook her head. "That's enough work talk. This is my day off. Let's get in the holiday spirit with some carols."

Ducking out from under his arm, she skipped ahead a few steps, turning to walk backward. She launched into a rousing chorus of "Deck the Halls," her pure voice ringing through the crisp air. The boys joined in the tune, with Sampson letting loose the occasional bark.

Gwen's joy was contagious, her beauty mesmerizing. He respected her positive approach, the knack she had for looking for ways to restore happiness in much the same way she brought new life to old toys. How quickly she had become such an important part of his life. At this point, he woke up smiling just from anticipating seeing her.

And then it hit him. When he needed to take those next steps with his mom, he wouldn't be saying goodbye to just the Top Dog Dude Ranch community. He would be closing the door on days like this with Gwen.

And that brought a surprise blast of regret that stole the air right out of his lungs.

As Gwen tossed movie popcorn into her mouth, she wondered, was this a date? It sure felt like one.

Their plan to go on a sleigh ride at the ranch had been canceled due to icy rain. Ian had suggested they take the boys and his mom into Moonlight Ridge to see a holiday movie on the big screen. The old theater was playing the classic *How the Grinch Stole Christmas!* Given the rain, he'd been able to close down tree sales early, so they'd even gone out for pizza first.

Now she sat next to him in the very last row, the kids and his mother a few rows ahead in the sparsely filled theater.

Ian had certainly taken her at her word this past week, filling every free minute with holiday activities to keep them out of the house. There sure hadn't been much time for sleep. They'd taken the boys on pony rides in the arena, the horses wearing antlers. A holiday hoedown. Cookies and caroling by the campfire. A Santa Paws fair with paw-ty games.

They'd been so busy, she had to confess she was enjoying the slower pace of kicking back in the stadium seats with popcorn, cola and a handsome man.

Gwen sipped her soda, then set the cup on the armrest. "This was a fabulous plan," she whispered, careful to keep her voice low enough not to disturb the others. "I don't remember the last time I went to the movie theater." Juggling the boys, who sometimes struggled with sitting still long enough for a movie, was too difficult on her own.

He tipped the bucket of popcorn toward her. "I have a good idea every now and then."

Their fingers brushed as she reached inside. "You must know this is skating dangerously close to breaking our resolution to keep things strictly platonic."

He dipped his head closer, his words soft and low. "You requested that we stay busy and that's what we're doing."

Except it wasn't working. "Okay, back to focusing on the holidays. Thank you for helping me keep the wonder alive for my boys."

"That's important. Like my grandma throwing those rocks on the roof and telling me it was reindeer," he said nostalgically. "I went along with the stunt long after I knew what it was, just for fun. What age were you when you stopped believing in Santa?"

"Shhh!" She pressed a finger to his lips. "Don't let the boys overhear you."

Wincing, he smiled against her finger and whispered in her ear. "Sorry about that."

His breath was warm against the sensitive skin.

She resisted the urge to lean closer, bringing his mouth against her flesh. She shifted in her seat, nodding toward the boys, who were totally engaged in the movie. "I think we're in the clear. This time."

He settled deeper into his seat. "And the answer? About Saint Nick?"

She blinked fast with overplayed innocence that she knew pushed the boundaries toward flirting. "Who says I don't still believe?"

"Fair enough," he said, so near she could smell the buttery scent on his breath. "Then what did you ask Santa to bring for you this year?"

"More hours in the day?" She hadn't come close to catching up on her toy inventory, due to her ruined sewing machine, her free hours all taken up with Christmas fun with Ian and her sons. Although she could hardly complain given how much her boys were enjoying the season.

Her heart swelled to look at them lined up in a row around Florence. They were happy.

Beside her, Ian chuckled softly. "Next on your list? And don't say that you want a new cabin or anything else that's practical."

Surprised at his question, it took her a moment to line up her thoughts. She was always focused on her sons' needs. She didn't consider herself a martyr, but there just wasn't much time left over to ponder her own wishes. Needs, sure. But wishes? That was a whole different matter. "Be warned, my Christmas request will definitely sound boring."

"You've intrigued me. Now I have to know." He eyed her over the top of his cup as he sipped through the straw.

She chewed her bottom lip before blurting quietly, "I would like a new sewing machine to work on my toy restoration projects. I know that sounds like a work-related gift, but the projects bring me such joy." How many hours had she happily distracted herself from day-to-day worries at her sewing machine? It had been a sanity saver after her husband's death and all the complicated shades of grief that came with it. "I was going to trade in my old machine for an upgraded one, but it got destroyed in the flood."

He set the empty bucket of popcorn on the floor. "You don't have a machine? How are you creating new toy inventory if you sold out at the craft fair?"

"That's on hold for a while." The gift shop had felt strangely bereft of Christmas magic without more of her vintage items on display. She jabbed the straw deeper into the ice of her nearly empty drink. "I remind myself it's only temporary."

"Let me help."

She should have seen his offer coming. He had a rescuer's heart. "No, but thank you. You've already done more than enough by sharing your home. I absolutely can't accept charity and that's what it would be."

Stretching out an arm along the back of her chair, he angled toward her. "Wait until you hear what I have in mind. My mother has a sewing machine that she used to use for quilting. She hasn't been able to complete the projects anymore. Something to do with spatial relations. It's just sitting there, unused—which seems like a real shame to me."

"Still, that's too generous," she said. Things between them were already growing more complicated by the day.

"Before you get too excited, be warned. It's an old machine. It's not computerized and it doesn't have much in the way of specialty features. But it'll do the basics." He paused, his brown eyes searching her in the dim, flickering light of the movie. "If you won't take it as a gift, then at least accept it as a loaner."

She had to admit, he'd found an offer that saved her pride while helping her out of a tight spot—again. It would be silly to refuse, especially when she needed the extra money more projects would bring. "Thank you, I gratefully accept. On one condition."

He toyed with a loose lock of her hair on her shoulder. "What would that be?"

"Let me make your mother's Christmas gift."

"Deal." He pulled his arm from her shoulders and extended his hand.

She gripped it, shaking. The warmth of him launched a tingle through her veins. The sounds of the movie faded. He held on, and when she didn't pull away, he placed their clasped hands on the armrest. Definitely like they were a real couple.

And she didn't have a clue where this would lead from here. She just knew that right now, tonight, she wanted nothing more than to keep savoring the simple pleasure of their pseudo dates.

So much for spending any free time away from home on fake dates.

Picking his way through boxes in the chilly attic in search of his mom's sewing machine, Ian ground his teeth in frustration. He and Gwen were housebound due to an ice storm.

After their movie outing, the temperature had dropped overnight with freezing rain. The already saturated ground and roads iced over so badly schools were closed. Even the ranch had closed all nonessential activities. Only the dining hall had stayed open. Guests were holed up in their cabins with catered meals by the fireplace and gift baskets full of games and puzzles—or so Gwen had told him.

Pretty much how things were here at the farmhouse.

At least the power had stayed on. So far. He'd used the time to catch up on paperwork and then snuck up to the attic to work on locating his mom's old sewing machine. Finally, tucked behind an old trunk and a box marked "extra blankets," he hit pay dirt.

His mom's fifteen-year-old Singer.

Sleet tapped along the roof as Ian pulled off the cover and read through the tattered user's manual for tips on care. A quick plug-in had him mostly convinced that it still worked. After dusting and cleaning, then lubricating the bobbin case with sewing machine oil, he covered it up again before hefting it up.

Glancing at the small window confirmed that the weather wasn't letting up. Ice glistened on bare branches and weighed down thick evergreen boughs. How many would break under the burden? He might as well make the most of this day off, get in some R & R while he could, because the cleanup after would likely be intense. He made a mental note to check the generator in case the power went out so Gwen, his mom and the boys could stay warm while he worked.

He picked his way along the narrow wooden stairs and opened the door into the warmer second floor. Where Gwen slept.

Better not to linger on that thought. He jogged to the ground level.

As he made his way down the long corridor toward the living room and sound of the boys talking, his mother rounded the corner and stopped in front of her bedroom door.

She motioned to the covered machine in his hands. "What do you have there?"

A whisper of concern flickered through him. Would she object? He should have thought to ask her first. He set it on the narrow table. "Would you mind if Gwen borrowed your sewing machine for a while? Hers is broken."

Confusion chased through her eyes as if she was grappling to understand what he meant and whom he was talking about. Then she smiled. "Of course, I'm always happy to share. And the more the machine is used, the better it will run when I make my next quilt."

There was no point in mentioning she'd made her last patchwork blanket over a year ago.

Squinting, she rubbed a hand along her forehead. "I'm going to lie down for a bit. I don't know why I'm so tired."

He searched for the right words to encourage her, but navigating the fraying labyrinth of her thoughts grew tougher as time passed. "You sure worked hard cooking that amazing breakfast for everyone."

Her face brightened. "I did, didn't I? I love seeing folks enjoy my food."

"Love you, Mom." He gave her elbow a light squeeze, the scent of her hand lotion bringing childhood memories of her running a hand through his hair while telling him bedtime stories.

"Love you too, my boy." She patted his cheek before stepping into her bedroom and closing the door behind her.

The click echoed, leaving him feeling helpless. The doctors had tried to warn him about the heartache, but nothing could have prepared him for the sense of constantly paddling upstream. Knowing that even on days when he seemed to make a little progress, the overall trajectory was forever trending downward.

His hand fell on his mother's sewing machine and he thought of how Gwen worked so hard and took such joy in the simplest of secondhand things in life. The last thing he wanted was to add to her burdens. He needed to tread carefully when it came to the growing attraction between them.

Lifting the sewing machine and starting down the hall again, he followed the echoes of conversation between Gwen and her boys. He walked down a hall packed with family photos, hung in an attempt to help anchor his mom's memories for a little while longer.

As he drew closer, he heard Timothy whisper, "Shhh. He's coming. Get ready."

His mood lightened. What were they cooking up? There was never a dull moment with those three cute little rascals around. He shifted the machine into a firmer grip as he crossed the threshold into the living room.

"Ta-da," Caleb said, arms splayed wide. "We decorated your tree for you. We made everything ourselves."

Sure enough, his towering fir was covered in home-made ornaments, fashioned from some kind of dough and then finger-painted. The room looked like a Christmas bomb had exploded with glitter, yarn and holiday cheer scattered on the furniture and floor. A season to remember if ever there was one.

Timothy touched the branches one after the other. "Stars. Snowmen. Stockings. Candy canes. Just in case you couldn't tell since some of our paint got smudged."

"It was too cold to play outside," Gideon added.

The three boys lined up in front of the tree, matching grins on their proud faces. Their sweatshirts were covered in dabs of finger paint and glitter.

"I love it," he declared, a surge of affection making him think how much he would miss having them around. "Thank you—all of you. This is the best Christmas gift anyone has ever given me."

Gwen stood by the heavy farm table in the attached dining room, stacking craft supplies into a bin. "Your mom helped. She had wonderful ideas about using supplies on hand. She led our little class in making salt dough ornaments and paper chains."

Ian fought the urge to put a hand on the small of her back. Just to be close and breathe in the scent of her. They'd been careful around the boys to keep things light. It hadn't gone past holding hands under the cover of a dark theater or walking a distance behind the kids in the snow, arms around each other as if they were doing it only for balance.

Timothy climbed up on a chair to grab fistfuls of crayons and drop them back into a craft caddy. "We wanted to string popcorn, but Mommy said Sampson would probably eat it."

At the sound of his name, the dog snuffled from under the table, lifting his head off his paws then settling back to sleep again. Ian noticed Sampson was parking himself under the table more and more often lately, likely because of the kids dropping unwanted vegetables when they thought their mom wasn't looking. Ian didn't want to rat them out, but he also thought Gwen deserved support and encouragement.

"Your mom is correct about Sampson." Ian strode across the braid rug to the fireplace to be sure the screen was firmly latched as the blaze rolled, launching snapping and popping sparks. "But, in my opinion, the tree doesn't need anything more. It's absolutely perfect."

"Really?" sensitive Timothy asked. "You're not just saying that?"

"Scout's honor." Ian crossed a finger across his heart, keeping his focus on the kids, too aware of their mom's gliding movements. Or her pretty smile of thanks at his support, before she hefted the bin of supplies and disappeared into the kitchen. He let his eyes linger for a moment on the sway of her hips in faded denim before returning his attention to the boys.

Caleb sprinted to the window and pulled a jar off the ledge. "Look at what else we made." He held up a Mason jar full of water with tiny toys and glitter on the bottom. "It's a snow globe, with glitter and some things we found at the bottom of the toy box we brought from home."

Gideon grabbed his from the window and sat under

the tree, shaking the jar. "Mommy said we're helping the planet because we're re—uh, re-bicycling."

"Recycling," Caleb corrected.

"That's what I said." Gideon shook the container harder, distributing the glitter through the water. "Mine has little trees in it, like Mr. Ian's farm."

Caleb lifted his on the palm of his hand. "Mine is an ocean full of fish and whales. They love Christmas too."

Timothy left the table to retrieve his jar, displaying it solemnly. "My house is special because it has a puppy in front of it."

Caleb snorted, dropping to sit under the tree with his jar and reaching for a pad of paper on the floor. "That's a reindeer."

"Nuh-uh." Timothy shook his head. "I broke off the antlers. I was using my 'magination."

In the distance, Ian heard the phone ring, followed by Gwen's soft answer. The boys' back-and-forth debate over snow globe construction continued until Timothy gripped his jar and headed toward his mother in the kitchen.

Ian knelt on one knee beside Caleb, who was still sitting under the tree, chewing on the end of a pencil, a pad of lined school paper in his lap. "What are you doing?"

Caleb gripped the fat pencil, his hair sticking up in the back as if he'd napped at a funny angle. "Writing a new letter to Santa from me and Gideon."

"Didn't you already do that at the ranch's party?" Ian asked.

Gideon tucked in beside his brother. "This one is gonna be a letter to the *real* Santa. Caleb writes better than me so he's the scribe... Isn't that a cool word?

I heard it in a book Mrs. Susanna read to us at school during story time."

"It's a great word." He sure enjoyed the way this boy's mind rocketed through ideas. "Do you need me to mail it for you?"

Caleb shook his head. "Me and Gideon have a plan."

A plan? Well, that should be interesting. The moment felt so normal, so perfect in its simplicity it lifted the pall that sometimes settled in his home.

The sound of light footsteps drew his attention to the framed archway leading to the hall. Gwen stood in her fuzzy socks, Timothy so tight up against her leg the kid looked grafted into her denim.

"Gwen?" A hint of unease teased along the edges of his contentment. Had there been some kind of accident on the treacherous roads?

Gwen held up her cell phone in one hand, her other on Timothy's back. "Boys, it's Grandma and Grandpa Bishop. They want to see you over Christmas break."

Chapter Ten

Caleb wrote better than the others, but he still had to think hard. So he wished his brothers would quit talking to him until he could finish with his new letter to Santa. At least he could press on the kitchen table now, and he didn't have to hide under the tree so his mom or Mr. Ian couldn't peek over his shoulder.

After the call from Grandma and Grandpa Bishop, Mr. Ian had asked Mommy if she wanted to go with him to take Sampson out for a run in the yard. That was grown-up code for getting away so they could say things without him and his brothers listening. Which was okay with Caleb, since it would give him time to finish the letter and package it up with the cookies Gideon found. Caleb's mind was still kinda scrambled after speaking to Grandma and Grandpa Bishop. After their mom talked to them, she passed the phone around to all three brothers real fast like normal.

Gideon opened the junk drawer, in search of tape. "When do you think they're gonna get here? I don't remember them saying exactly."

Because they hadn't. They usually didn't.

Caleb knew he *should* be excited about his grandparents' phone call, but what was the use? "They're nice and all, but half the time they don't show up even when they say they will. So I figure there's no need to think about it until they actually knock on the door. They'll probably just mail really cool presents because they feel bad for not showing up."

Timothy was hanging out in the doorway between the kitchen and the dining room, half in, half out. "I think seeing us makes them sad because we remind them of our daddy."

Gideon looked up from the drawer, a fat roll of packing tape in his hand. "That doesn't feel very fair. It's not our fault Daddy got killed in a car wreck." He slammed the drawer closed and turned to Caleb. "Are you almost done?"

"Yep..." He signed his name to the bottom, careful to make sure it was clear. "I got a little box out of the garage and you've got the tape. Do you still have the cookies or did you eat them all last night?"

Timothy stood up straighter. "Cookies?"

Reaching into his backpack on the floor, Gideon pulled out a bag of gingersnaps. "Remember when I fell? I was trying to get some for Santa. I got 'em on my second try. I ate some, but there are still plenty for Santa."

Timothy frowned, scrubbing the toe of his gym shoe across the floor until it squeaked. "Why are you sending a letter and cookies to Santa? We already did that."

Gideon looked to Caleb. "Should we tell him?"

Caleb thought about it. Timothy got upset pretty easily. What if he didn't understand about the fake Santas? "We just came up with some new stuff to tell Santa Claus, and Gideon thought we should send some cookies for good luck."

Timothy scratched his newly short hair. "Like a bribe?"

A bribe? That didn't sound good at all. "More of a reward. Like when you get a sticker at school."

Timothy didn't look convinced. But then it was tough to sneak things past each other, on account of their special bond.

Caleb tried to distract Timothy by pushing the paper across the table toward him. "Do you want to sign the letter too?"

"Sure, pass me the pencil." Timothy traced his fingers along the words as if reading, then looked up with surprised eyes. "You're asking Santa to make Mommy and Mr. Ian fall in love? You should have talked to me about this first."

Caleb waggled the pencil, hoping he would take it and stop asking stuff. Too bad he and Gideon couldn't shut themselves in the pantry away from Timothy, but Mr. Ian had childproofed the knob. "Don't you like living with Mr. Ian and Mrs. Florence?"

"Of course I do." Timothy nodded. "But if Grandma and Grandpa Bishop get sad about our dad already, don't you think they'll be really sad if Mommy gets us a new forever daddy?"

Would they be sad? For that matter, should Caleb feel sad about replacing his dad? The idea stung, shocking Caleb quiet.

Not Gideon, though. He dropped the gingersnaps and tape on the table. "I think Grandma and Grandpa should want us to be happy."

Timothy didn't look happy at all.

Caleb took the letter back. "Don't sign it, then."

"Hold on a second." Timothy flattened his hand on the paper. "How are you gonna get it to Santa? I don't think he's coming back to the ranch."

Caleb sent Gideon a hard look not to blow the whistle on the fake St. Nick stuff. "We are gonna mail it in the box."

"Wow," Timothy gasped. "Is Mommy going to take you to the post office?"

Nope. She would ask too many questions. "We are gonna take it to the ranch's post office the next time we're there."

"How are you gonna get away? They keep watch." Timothy was such a worrywart, always pointing out the problems.

Sometimes, though, that was a good thing since it helped them make better plans.

Gideon chewed his lip, then snapped his fingers. "I know. We can trick them. Anytime they're looking for me, you can say I'm getting a drink of water or something like that. And sometimes pretend to be me and say Timothy is in the bathroom. That way they will think they saw all of us."

Timothy shook his head. "I'm not gonna pretend to be you. That would be a lie. I only cut my hair to help you stay out of trouble as much, not for you to get in trouble more."

Gideon got that scrunched-up look on his face when

he was figuring something out, then he turned to Caleb with a gleam in his eyes.

Uh-oh. Caleb clapped his hands on top of his head. "Nuh-uh. I'm not cutting my hair."

"Think about it." Gideon moved closer and tugged Caleb's hands down. "If you have short hair too, then it will be easier for people to get all three of us mixed up." He shot a look at Timothy. "And we won't have to count on *him* to help us out."

"But I like my hair." Caleb tried not to whine like a baby.

Gideon grasped him by both shoulders. "Afterward, Mom will take you for a trim. You'll get her to yourself. That's good, right?"

He had a point. And spending time with his mom alone had been Caleb's big Christmas wish all along. Maybe the letter to Santa was already working since it made that part of his request come true early. It must be a sign. "Okay, but I'm gonna do this my way. Got it? Pass me the scissors."

The next day in Hollie's kitchen for sewing and cookie baking, Gwen couldn't remember when she'd been this confused, frustrated and angry.

Confused about her feelings for Ian.

Frustrated sleeping under the same roof as him.

Seeing that Caleb cut his hair too was the final straw. She could have sworn she'd hidden every pair of scissors in the house. Did each of them have to do what the others did?

The mini crisis had taken her mind off the Bishops' last-minute insistence on seeing the boys over the holidays. More power to them if they actually showed up, but she hated to see her sons disappointed if they flaked out—again. And, on top of everything else that had her fired up, it didn't help that a nosy, busybody ranch guest had asked her if Gideon was hyperactive.

At least Ian had offered to take Caleb for a haircut and have the other two boys tag along. She'd felt guilty for not taking Caleb herself...but Ian had insisted, reminding her how much fun his mother was going to have with her at Hollie's. She appreciated the help, and she was glad for the time with her friends now. Elementary school librarian Susanna had joined them for baking Christmas cookies—while Gwen worked on a project for the shop.

Ian had helped her haul the sewing machine and a sack of fabric. Hollie's kitchen was so large, she had the table to herself while Florence, Hollie and Susanna decorated cookies at the center island.

Today's projects? Sewing a new blue polka-dot dress for an old Mrs. Beasley doll and put the finishing touches on Christmas shirts for a litter of Labrador retriever puppies that Eliza and her husband, Dr. Nolan Barnett, were fostering for a local shelter. Eliza had asked for help in getting them suited up for the ranch's Santa Paws Parade scheduled for Christmas Eve. The puppies would ride on a float. Sewing was the perfect antidote for ruminating on an attraction to a helpful, compelling and very hot tree farmer.

Hollie rolled out sugar cookie dough. "Are you and Ian coming to the Ugly Christmas Sweater Party?"

"I believe so." The boys would be attending the Christmas pj party with cartoons and supper scheduled at the same time. She had to confess, she was looking forward to the prospect of an evening out with Ian. "What help do you need getting ready?"

Hollie passed green sugar sprinkles to Susanna. "Just what you're all doing, keeping me company while I bake."

Susanna took the shaker and shuffled to cover the cut wreath and tree shapes while Florence covered stars with yellow frosting.

The older woman paused. "Gwen, dear, don't listen to a stranger's opinion of your child."

Susanna quirked an eyebrow. "What's going on?"

Florence dusted a star with sugar. "Earlier today, one of the guests asked Gwen if Gideon is hyperactive."

Hollie gasped. "How dare she. Who was it? I'll make sure there are no candy canes in her basket."

What a time for Florence to remember every detail. Gwen guided the fabric through the machine, gently depressing the foot pedal. "Gideon *is* very active."

Turning on her barstool, Florence faced Gwen. "He's also *very* smart, which sometimes means he's easily bored. It takes a lot to keep that sharp mind of his engaged. There's nothing wrong with that."

Hearing Florence's words was like balm to her soul. The guest's words had hurt more than she wanted to admit. She eased her foot off the pedal. "Am I being neglectful by not getting him tested? I've been so overwhelmed, but I realize that's no excuse. I don't want to label him. Still, I also wouldn't want him to miss out on help if he needs it."

"He's young yet," Florence said, her eyes clear, looking every bit the teacher she'd once been. "Most doctors don't advise considering an ADHD diagnosis until at least the second grade."

"Really?" Gwen shot a glance at Susanna, who nodded. All eyes returned to Florence.

"Winter is tougher for the more active children. There aren't as many opportunities to run that energy off." She touched Gwen's hand. "If it does turn out he has ADHD, I know you're the kind of mother who will seek out all the best options to help him excel."

Gwen loved her boys, but keeping up with the medical, emotional and academic needs of three very different kids often left her second-guessing herself. "So you really think he's smart? Even though his grades are lower than his brothers'?"

Florence waved aside her concern. "Don't get me started on what I think about all those tests kids are subjected to. And yes, I believe you're going to find you have a very gifted young man on your hands."

For a moment she wondered if Florence knew which child she was referring to after all. Even people without memory challenges struggled to tell them apart, especially with them all hacking their hair off.

"And yes," Florence said with a smile as if reading her mind. "I know which boy is which. Young Gideon is the one who cut his hair first."

Susanna winced. "During story time."

Hollie laughed as she slid a pan of cookies into the oven. "At least he didn't bring frogs to story time like Phillip did once before."

"Yet," Gwen said with a half-joking chuckle.

Florence stroked her hand along the top of the machine. "You're doing beautiful work, dear. With the restored doll *and* with your boys. I'm so happy you and my son decided to get married. When are you picking out the ring?"

"So what's this I hear about you and Gwen getting engaged?" Jacob O'Brien slung an arm around Ian's shoulders at the ranch's Ugly Christmas Sweater Party.

Engaged? Ian choked on his cup of eggnog. It was one thing for total strangers to assume they were a couple. But this guy knew the real reason for their arrangement. Hopefully none of the other staff members crowded into the barn had overheard. "What are you talking about?"

Jacob stepped back and popped a cream cheese pinwheel into his mouth, his sweater sporting a beagle driving a sleigh. "Gwen didn't tell you what happened this afternoon? Your mom announced that you two are getting engaged."

"Engaged? Gwen and me?" Ian didn't know whether to laugh or cry. His gaze skated to his mom across the room at a table of her knitting circle friends. In her sweater with blinking lights, she was hard to miss. He scratched over the tinsel tree Gwen had sewn onto an old red sweatshirt of his for this evening.

"I'm just ribbing you," Jacob said, waving to a young couple arriving dressed in matching green reindeer sweaters. "I know your mom was just joking around with some maternal wishful thinking."

"Jacob, my mom has Alzheimer's disease and it's progressing. I promise you that Gwen and I are not engaged. We're not even dating."

"Ah, man, I'm sorry. I know she has some memory

problems, but I didn't realize… I apologize for making light of what happened."

"I know you didn't mean any harm. I appreciate the heads-up." He just wondered why Gwen hadn't told him before the party.

Not that there had been much in the way of time alone to talk. Once he'd returned with the boys after Caleb's haircut, Gwen and his mom had already been changing for the party. Then Gwen had been preoccupied getting the triplets ready for the ranch's kiddy pajama party.

Or had she been avoiding him?

Regardless, he wanted to clear the air with her. He clapped Jacob on the shoulder. "I'm going to mosey on over to speak with my 'fiancée.'"

End of discussion. He made his way across the barn, in search of Gwen. Last he'd heard from her, she was heading toward the hot chocolate station. Country takes on Christmas classics reverberated through the air in the massive barn full of ranch guests and staff. Large Christmas lights the size of basketballs were strung from the ceiling. A towering Christmas tree took up the far corner of the barn, the triangular top covered in a recycled sweater.

He angled past people registering for the ugly sweater contest while others piled their plates high from the spread of holiday-themed finger food ranging from barbecue meatballs to jalapeño cheese poppers. He sidestepped a woman wearing a sweater depicting a hissing cat, captioned Santa Claws, and a man wearing a Sandy Paws beach-themed getup.

In the far corner of the barn, a line had formed for

Santa Limbo with Santa and Mrs. Claus holding the limbo stick.

He spotted Hollie, whose sweater sported a poodle wearing a holiday hat while skating on an ice pond. He thought about asking her if she'd seen Gwen, but he wasn't ready to field her questions about the engagement mix-up. Pivoting hard, he ran slam into Gwen.

She squeaked, clutching her cocoa cup and balancing a small plate of cookies on top. "Thank goodness I put a lid on it or I would need to change."

Her outfit wasn't ugly at all—especially not with her inside it. She'd paired leggings with a long black sweater patterned with an assortment of toys. Her pale blond hair was swept back with a matching band. She was too pretty for his peace of mind.

"Hey," he angled to say in her ear, clasping her elbow. "Do you mind if we step out of the noise for a moment so I can ask you about something?"

Her smile faded. "Sure. Is everything okay with the boys? Your mom?"

"Everyone's fine." He guided her through the crowd with determined steps that kept questions at bay. Finally, he located a quiet corner away from the band, near a table full of door prizes. "I heard something, uh, confusing from Jacob about your get-together earlier today…"

Gwen set down her refreshments on the edge of the table and pinched the bridge of her nose for a moment before opening her eyes again. "Your mom and the 'engagement' announcement?" When he nodded, she continued, "When I tried to tell her that we're not a couple, she insisted and I didn't want to risk upsetting her. The others seemed to understand. But oh my goodness, she surprised a year off my life with that."

"And that's it?" he asked, still wondering what everyone else had said. More importantly, how had Gwen reacted? Were things getting too awkward for her with his mom's condition? Was Gwen feeling a need to bolt? That possibility bothered him—far too much.

"That's everything. I should have told you." Her face turned pink. "It was rather awkward. I wasn't sure what to say to you, and I really didn't think Hollie or Susanna would bring it up."

"That makes sense." He searched her face, twinkling lights overhead casting a magical glow along her golden hair. "I just want to be sure you're alright."

"I was surprised," she admitted, crinkling her nose. "But I should have guessed our arrangement might be confusing to your mom."

This was as good a time as any to explain about Becky. He didn't much like explaining the mess he'd made of things then, but he found himself needing for Gwen to understand. "It's about more than just us sharing the same roof. She might be confused because…well…I was engaged before I moved here."

Her eyes went wide just as the music shifted to a quieter Christmas tune made for slow dancing. "I didn't know. Is it okay if I ask what happened?"

"I should have mentioned it before now." He scratched his jaw. "Once Mom's diagnosis came through, it put a strain on my relationship with Becky. We had a difference of opinion about Mom's care and my moving here."

"That must have been painful." The compassion in

her voice spoke of empathy born from the pain of being let down by a loved one.

But he didn't want her to misunderstand.

"I was sad, more than anything. I understand her reason for walking." Still, yeah, it had been a low point in his life—one that he preferred not to dwell on. Was that his reason for never mentioning the past to Gwen? Or was there something else at play inside him? Even pondering that had him inwardly flinching. "She wanted Mom to go into a care facility immediately. And while I'm not against that when the time is right, I just don't think we're to that point yet."

"From where I'm standing, you're doing a great job managing her symptoms at home." She rubbed the top of his arm, her touch gentle through his wool sweater. "That can't be easy for you, though."

"One day at a time." He brushed aside her praise. His struggles were nothing compared to what his mom battled. "To be frank, I'm not sure my relationship with Becky would have withstood the strain even if we'd tried to stick it out. We'd already had a difference of opinion over where to live."

Her face went still for a moment as she searched his face, the din of the party fading into a hum of music and laughter. "Do you still have feelings for her?"

"Are you asking if I still love her?" The answer to that question was so simple that it almost made him feel ashamed. "No. I'm not sure I ever did. I think I fell into the relationship because it seemed the right time to settle down, the next step in life, and that was unfair to her—"

A couple pushed past on their way toward the barn's

exit, their sweaters glowing with strings of embedded lights. With to-go boxes stacked, they bantered about a romantic evening in front of the fireplace, so wrapped up in each other they didn't even notice anyone else was there.

Once they'd cleared, Gwen crossed her arms. "All those comments from people about us being a couple have to have been rough for you. Do you regret the decision we made?"

"Not for a minute," he said without hesitation, meaning every word. "Having you and the boys at the house these past weeks has brought Christmas alive again for both my mother and me."

"If you're sure." Gwen's arms relaxed to her sides and she tugged at the hem of her sweater. "So how crazy was it for you this afternoon with all three boys?"

Thankful for the conversation shift, Ian thought back to the best lunch break he could remember in a long time. He'd played video games with Timothy and Gideon while Caleb got a haircut, then snagged nuggets and fries to eat in the car on the way back. Simple. But cool. Those boys were so funny, they had him in stitches.

Smiling at the memory, he said, "I wish you could have seen Caleb's face when the rest of his hair started hitting the floor."

She shook her head in chagrin. "I have to confess I'm surprised he did it. He loves his hair longer and has always been the most resistant to trims."

"It appeared so today." He wished he'd thought to snap a photo.

"Thank you for taking him—for taking all three of

them at once." She tapped his chest with one finger. "You're a brave soul."

Her touch scrambled his brain for an instant and then he remembered to ask, "Did you get much work accomplished while you were at Hollie's?"

"In between cookie sampling—yes." Smiling, she reached over to her plate and plucked up a fat, lumpy cookie. "Try the fruitcake bars. They are surprisingly amazing."

Before he could stop himself, he leaned in to nibble the treat, rather than just taking it from her. There was no mistaking the suggestive intent. And she didn't pull away. Her gaze locked with his and held. He wanted to kiss her, right here in the middle of a party, which would only fuel this afternoon's speculation.

The squawk of the microphone snapped the mood and saved him from himself.

Jacob announced, "It's time to play our variation of 'Ho-Ho, Never Have I Ever.' Hollie here will explain the rules."

Taking the mic, Hollie continued, "Listen close. This is a little different. Partner up, and everybody raise both hands. I'll read a statement and if you've never done it, put down a finger. The first in a couple to have all their fingers down, hug their partner—and pick them a gift off the party favor table. The game continues until the presents are all gone."

Gwen dusted her hands on her leggings, brushing away cookie crumbs. Her blue eyes lit with a playful excitement. "Do you want to play?"

How could he resist her? He couldn't. "Lead the way."

She clasped his hand and tugged him into the partner

lineup, her touch reminding him how often she crept into his thoughts each night. He liked having her to himself for a little while this evening. He enjoyed talking to her, sharing thoughts he normally kept on lockdown. Gwen was special and there was no denying it. And her joy was contagious when she turned to him with a mischievous grin, her enjoyment obvious as the fun of the game began winding up around them.

Hollie called out questions one after the other. "Never have I ever made a snow angel… Stayed up all night to try and catch Santa… Spiked the eggnog… Dressed my dog up as a reindeer… Ruined a family picture…" And on and on the questions went until… "Kissed someone under the mistletoe… If not, look up."

Sure enough, clusters of the greenery hung from the rafters.

Chuckles rippled around them, but Ian wasn't laughing. Instead, his eyes were locked on Gwen, who still held up one hand in front of his. Reaching, he linked his fingers with hers and drew her closer until her chest rested against his.

His face a whisper away from hers, he said, "Are you ready to cross this one off your bucket list?"

Chapter Eleven

Gwen wondered how she'd reached thirty years old and never been kissed under the mistletoe.

Regardless, she was grateful to share this particular milestone with Ian.

His mouth slanted over hers, tasting of apple cider and holiday promises. She knew the kiss couldn't go far, given the party audience. And there was a freedom in that, being able to sink into the embrace with no second-guessing. There was no need to worry about things getting out of hand or her giving him the wrong impression. She could simply enjoy the way he made her feel. Ian's hands were warm on her waist, his muscular chest so broad and appealing against her. His lips gently persuasive, tempting her to think about how good it could be between them.

Then all too soon the kiss was over, and wow, did she ever want more. She swayed on her feet a little in the aftermath. The need to explore this attraction grew so strong she wasn't sure how much longer she could hold out—or even why she should. Did Ian feel the same?

One look at the heat in his molten dark eyes assured her they were one hundred percent on the same page.

Cheers and applause rippled through the crowd, teasing calls for the four couples who'd celebrated the game's end under the mistletoe.

Behind the microphone, Hollie announced, "While that concludes our games for the evening, this party's not even close to over. Are you ready to take to the dance floor?" A roar of agreement swelled all the way to the barn's rafters. "Let's hear it for the ranch's very own pickup band—Raise the Woof."

Eliza led the group members back up onstage, taking her place behind the keyboard as lead singer. The rest of the bandmates followed. The drummer and fiddle player were both stable hands. One of the cooks played the banjo, while the morning-shift receptionist played guitar. A teenage intern played bass.

Ian skimmed a lock of her hair from her face, his fingers impossibly gentle along her cheek. "Would you like to dance?"

While away a few minutes in this beautiful man's arms? Absolutely. "I would love to."

As if the cosmos heard her inner yearnings, the band launched into "All I Want for Christmas Is You." Tucking her hand into his, she followed him to the dance floor.

He palmed the small of her back, his other hand linking fingers with hers. "You never told me how the get-together went at Hollie's."

She wasn't surprised he didn't mention the kiss, even though that was certainly at the forefront of her mind. They'd been tamping down the attraction between them for so long, they'd developed a rhythm for dancing around it, as surely as they two-stepped around the floor.

Redirecting her thoughts, she remembered why they hadn't spoken much about her time at Hollie's. They'd been too distracted talking about his mother. "I sewed a dress for a Mrs. Beasley doll and made seven holiday shirts for the litter of twelve-week-old puppies Doc Barnett and Eliza are fostering."

"Seven puppies? Don't they have their hands full with the two kids and their own dogs?"

She laughed lightly. "Eliza told me it's no more trouble than managing the stables. The pups are already twelve weeks old. They'll have their own float in the holiday parade."

"How are they going to manage that?"

"A pen on the float and little elf handlers making sure they don't get away. I just hope the boys don't see them and get their hopes up about having one for themselves."

"If you change your mind about getting one, I wouldn't mind having another dog at the house." His grip tightened around her hand. "And before you say anything, think about how much easier it will be to house-train the puppy with me and my mom helping."

How kind of him. Gwen couldn't deny a moment's longing to accept, for her sons' sake. But Ian had already done so much for her.

"You're sweet to offer, but I don't want to impose any more than we already have."

"Well, just think it over." He kissed her quiet, just a quick graze, but familiar.

And every bit as toe-curling as before. Their steps synced as they silently swayed, one song fading into another until...

Her cell phone buzzed in her sweater pocket insistently. She willed whomever it was to go away.

Ian drew back. "Your phone."

She pulled him closer again. "Ignore it. It's probably just a telemarketer. See, they've already hung up."

"It could be the kids," he reminded her gently.

Of course, he was right. She eased from his arms and stepped to the edge of the dance floor. With more than a little regret, she pulled her cell from her pocket and glanced at the screen. The device shone with a missed call from a familiar number.

Her in-laws.

The phone vibrated again with a notification of a voice mail.

She tapped the transcription rather than try to hear over the din of the party. *We're sorry we can't make it to see the boys after all. The weather forecast has us concerned. We are sending gifts via overnight mail. We hope to see them over their spring break.*

Sighing, Gwen showed the message to Ian. "How am I going to make this up to them?"

His hand folded over hers on the phone. "You always seem to have the right words for them."

"And yet, here I am in the same spot." How much more sadness and disappointment would her sons have to deal with? "I knew this would happen. I have asked them not to promise if they can't deliver. They swore this time would be different or I wouldn't have handed over the phone to the boys."

"The blame for this is squarely on them." His voice was calm, firm. "Not you."

She longed to believe him but still tears clogged her throat. "I don't want to keep them from the boys. My sons deserve the connection to their father."

"From where I'm standing, you've done all you can to make that happen." Gently, he drew her to his chest, his arms going around her.

For a weak moment, she allowed herself the comfort of resting her head on his shoulder. When Dale had died, his parents had vowed to be a help and yet time and time again, their promises created more chaos than assistance. "My parents—who both work two jobs— make the most of any time off work to spend with the boys."

He stroked low on her spine, his breath caressing her ear. "They sound a lot like their daughter."

"Thank you." Angling back, she looked into his eyes, her arms around his neck. "I hate that our evening took this negative turn. Up to then, it was…"

"Incredible." His voice turned husky, rumbling in his chest and into hers.

"I agree." She arched up on her toes to kiss him, half-surprised at how natural the gesture already felt. Later, she would think through to the next step with Ian, but right now, she had another concern that needed immediate attention. "Let's go find the boys."

Nodding, he clasped her hand in his, steering her toward the door. "You'll know what to say and do for them when the time comes. You always do."

Maybe, maybe not. But with him at her side, at least she didn't have to face the task alone.

Gideon stood on his tiptoes in his blue superhero slippers, trying to see over the tall reception desk. He'd seen people bring packages here before to get mailed. He figured this would be easier than going to the post office.

A few minutes ago, he'd snuck away from the pj party. Caleb was pretending to be him by doing cartwheels and other stuff. Timothy didn't do too good of a job acting like somebody else. Besides, Caleb could do a handstand like Gideon and Timothy couldn't.

"Excuse me," Gideon called out. He heard a rustle behind the desk, so somebody must be there. "Hello?"

The rustling stopped and an old man stood—wearing a Santa suit. His beard was thick and gray. That's probably why he got picked. He could sure trick some people into believing.

But not Gideon. He had this all figured out and this was Mr. Thomas again. "I got a package to mail."

Kneeling, he picked up the shoebox, all taped with the cookies and letter. Caleb had written the address on top. Santa Claus and Mrs. Claus—North Pole. Gideon put a Ziploc bag of change on top to pay for shipping, all the money from his piggy bank. He'd been saving for a new scooter, but this was more important.

The man leaned to read the writing on top and passed the coins back. "Well, lookee here. You don't need any postage after all. I'm right here."

Did this guy think he was dumb? "I think you're gonna end up on Santa's naughty list."

The man's bushy eyebrows lifted. "Why is that?"

Gideon went behind the desk to talk face-to-face so he didn't have to stand on his toes while he explained. "Because you're not telling the truth about who you are and we're not supposed to fib."

Mr. Thomas scratched his beard for a long minute. "I think you're a very smart boy. I'm glad to help you with your package. Would you like to tell me what's inside?"

"A letter and some cookies. It's important that the box get there really fast so the food doesn't get stale."

"Okay, I'll see what I can do." Mr. Thomas nodded. "What about the letter?"

Gideon chewed on his bottom lip, trying to decide what to do. He didn't want this guy to mess up the message if he talked to Santa. But what if the letter didn't explain good enough? Caleb hadn't known how to write some of the words. He was smart for his age, but still. "I want my mom and Mr. Ian to fall in love and get married. Then we can stay in the big house with Sampson. Mrs. Florence will be our new grandma. She's always there to read us a story when we need her."

Mr. Thomas knelt until they were eye to eye the way grown-ups did when they wanted a kid to listen really good. "I can make sure your message is delivered. But you need to know that Santa can only give gifts. He can't make people feel things." He tapped Gideon on the chest. "Only you can control what's in your heart."

Gideon thought about that and tried to find a loophole in that so he could get his wish. But what Mr. Thomas said made sense. Suddenly sad, Gideon scuffed the toe of his shoe on the wood floor.

"Gideon?" a voice called from behind him. It sounded like Mrs. Susanna.

He turned to look. "Yes, ma'am?"

Mrs. Susanna walked closer wearing a funny sweater with a dog wearing big glasses and reading a book. "Your mom is looking for you."

Gulp. Caleb must not have done a good job with his handstand. Or maybe Timothy felt guilty and ratted him out.

"Okay, sorry," Gideon said, taking her hand and following her.

His mom ran across the big hall, looking all worried. Mr. Ian was right behind her with Timothy and Caleb.

Mommy pulled him into a tight hug. "I've been looking all over for you."

Caleb shrugged and mouthed the word *Sorry.*

Gideon wriggled free. "I didn't mean to scare you."

She smoothed back his hair. "I'm just glad we found you. Are you ready to go?"

Relieved she didn't ask him what he'd been up to, he shrugged.

"I guess so." He'd been having fun at the party, but it was probably close to bedtime. "I guess we need to get good sleep before Grandma and Grandpa Bishop come."

Mommy and Mr. Ian looked at each other for a really long time like they were talking without words. And Gideon's stomach knotted remembering the talk with his brothers earlier about their grandparents.

Rocking back on her heels, Mommy said, "I'm not sure they're going to be able to make it. The weather is going to be icy."

Well, that wasn't a surprise. Still it made Gideon sad. Especially if Timothy was right about the real reason they kept changing their mind about visiting. Would they drive away their grandparents if Mr. Ian and his mom were in love? He didn't want to mess things up with this Christmas wish.

Caleb's jaw stuck out. "Mr. Ian drives in the snow."

Sighing all heavy like, his mom gave Mr. Ian another one of those no-words looks. Then Mr. Ian nodded and Mommy stood, holding her arms out. "Who wants to go see the puppies tomorrow? If we see one we like, we can pick it out for Christmas. Just one, though."

Timothy squealed. "Really? I would love one lots and lots."

Caleb jumped up and down. "We will share. We promise."

Gideon just stood still, surprised. Wondering. Timothy had asked for a puppy when he read his letter out loud at one of the parties. And Gideon put a PS on his note in the box with cookies. Sure, he'd drawn it in a picture. But he'd hoped maybe Santa would understand. How had his letter gotten there so fast...?

He looked back to find Mr. Thomas, but he wasn't anywhere around. Instead, there was a teenage girl behind the desk, scrolling through her phone and chewing gum. His box was gone.

Could that have been the real Santa after all?

Visiting the litter of puppies at the Barnetts' home, Ian felt like Santa Claus making the triplets' Christmas dreams come true. The added bonus of seeing Gwen so happy and relaxed was tops on his list.

Well, right after hopes for revisiting the mistletoe kiss they'd shared. That moment still seared through him day and night.

Now, parked in the French doorway of the enclosed back porch, he watched the boys romp with the seven pups—four of them black Labs, two golden color and one chocolate. The echo of laughter and high-pitched yips filled the air. Sampson lay on the floor at his feet, his head on his paws as he watched with calm interest. Ian had clipped on the dog's leash, just in case, but it was clear he didn't have a problem with the hyper furballs.

While Ian enjoyed his own sunroom, this space was a custom-built massive haven. Gwen sipped tea alongside Eliza on an inviting sectional sofa. In one corner, a glowing Fraser fir was protected by a low little picket fence. In another corner, a large puppy pen contained the litter, with a doggy door leading outside to an enclosed dog run. The yard sprawled beyond the glass walls, a winter wonderland of snow frosting the trees and a wooden play set.

Earlier today, Ian had taken his mom and the boys to the tree lot for a clearance sale. Gwen had gone to the shelter on her lunch break to make sure she had all the paperwork in order in case today's meet and greet resulted in the boys picking a puppy to adopt. The manager had assured her since the cabins at the ranch were all pet friendly with fences, they didn't need to see her new place. And she'd brought a letter from Ian confirming the puppy would be welcome at his home until she was settled again. She'd told Ian she didn't want to send a message to her boys that a puppy was a gift. The animal would be a loved member of the family.

Ian respected her measured approach. He had no

doubt any puppy she adopted would be nurtured and loved.

A hand landed on his shoulder. He turned to find Doc Barnett holding two steaming mugs of java. "Would you like coffee? 'Tis the season for caffeine."

"Isn't that the truth," Ian said, taking the cup gratefully. He'd been keeping long hours the past two days, after he'd found his mom doing some wandering around the house at night. "Although for me, most folks have already bought their tree. Not too many last-minute shoppers. How about you?"

Nolan Barnett had recently moved to the area, starting his own small-town medical practice. He'd been an incredible help and support with Florence's care and long-term health plan.

"I expect the office will be overflowing after Christmas when everyone realizes they've caught whatever their relative had at a big family party."

Ian winced, lifting his brew in toast. "Here's to good health from our family to yours."

Nolan clinked mugs. "Cheers."

He soaked in the sight of the boys rolling on the floor with the pups, going from one to the other. He found it interesting how the slower approach to this meeting bore fruit. When a pup ignored them or grew too playful or even nippy, Eliza carefully moved that one to another room or to play with Gus and Mavis, helping steer the process for the right pick for the boys.

Finally, they had a favorite. A black puppy with a tiny white patch on his neck flopped from Caleb to Timothy to Gideon, then started the cycle all over again. The triplets held tug ropes and tossed tennis balls.

Gwen leaned forward, elbows on her knees, looking so pretty in her candy cane tights and jean jumper. "So, is this one your favorite?"

The boys' eyes went wide, three sets of identical blue. They looked from their mom, then back to the puppy, then to her again.

Timothy skimmed his hand along the sleek black coat. "Does that mean we can really get one?"

Gideon sat so very still for once. "For real?"

Caleb teased the rope in front of the little scamp's nose. "No kidding?"

Gwen's smile was as bright as the sun reflecting off the freshly fallen snow. "It means that if you can all agree that we only adopt one—not one for each of you— then yes. This will be your new best friend."

The three boys leaped to their feet, cheering while their "new best friend" danced around their feet. Their squeals of delight rolled free with promises to feed, walk and clean up.

Gwen held her hands out, motioning the triplets toward her. They climbed out of the pen and crossed to her in a tumble of shoelaces and enthusiasm, crowding around her in their little family circle. The vision tugged at him, making him think back to how many times he'd dreamed of having a moment like this with Becky and some kids.

"I need you to listen," she said. "I don't want you to make promises you can't keep. I'm responsible for the grown-up things like making sure the dog has food and a place to live and regular visits to the veterinarian. And of course I'll love it too."

Timothy chewed his bottom lip. "What will we do?"

"I'm glad you asked." She drew them closer. "You will go with me on walks with the dog. And you will help pick up the dog's toys. And promise to be very, very gentle. Always. Rules are important to teach the puppy how to be a good dog."

Florence clapped her hands together. "Just like rules are important at school. And at home, doing chores."

Smiling her thanks, Gwen affirmed. "Exactly."

Gideon scuffed his toe. "What happens if I accidentally break a rule? Are you going to take our puppy away? Like Daddy got taken away in the accident?"

The room went silent. Ian didn't have a clue what to say or how to address such a weighty concern for such a young mind. His heart broke for the kid, for Gwen too.

She smoothed a hand over her son's forehead even though his hair was too short to need smoothing. "I would never take your puppy away. Once he's a part of our family, that's forever." She paused, her throat moving in a slow swallow before she continued, "And your father died in a very sad accident. It was nobody's fault."

Ian couldn't help but think of what Gwen had shared with him about that awful car wreck. Speaking about it must be painful for her on so many levels. A surge of protectiveness amped through him, a need to do his best to make sure nothing and no one hurt her ever again.

Gideon nodded, scrubbing his wrist over his eyes, then smiling again. "Are we going to take the puppy home today?"

Eliza set her mug aside. "Well, buddy, the shelter prefers to do the neuter surgery before adoption to help control unwanted litter. But don't worry. We'll take good care of the little one until you pick him up."

Gwen's forehead furrowed. "He's not too young?"

Eliza shook her head. "Given his weight and size, he should tolerate the anesthesia just fine. This has become a pretty standard practice for shelters and rescues since, unfortunately, some adopters fail to follow through on their promise to spay/neuter. And don't even get me started on what a backyard breeder might try to do."

"Thank you for explaining—and for keeping watch over our pup," Gwen said, relaxing back as if a weight had been lifted. "That will give us time to get the right food, a little bed and some toys."

While Gwen, Florence and Eliza planned, the boys returned to playing with their puppy. Kindergartner Gus and toddler Mavis peeked around the corner, then saw the coast was clear and returned to play.

Doc Barnett leaned closer to Ian, asking softly, "How's your mom doing?"

Ian scrubbed the side of his neck, searching for the right words. "There are the normal forgetful moments, especially later in the day. But overall, she's into the Christmas routine. It's so familiar, I think that's helping her."

After the two nights he'd found her awake during the night, he'd discovered she was just admiring the Christmas lights. She'd confessed she was concerned about having enough gifts for her son, whom she seemed to be thinking of as a small child. The moment of confusion broke his heart as he glimpsed a window into the worries of her past returning to upset her even many years later. He'd gotten her safely back to bed, but right away the next day he'd added extra security alarms so he would know when exterior doors were opened.

"The holidays can go two ways," Nolan said, his tone measured and professional, engendering confidence in his words. "Some find the high level of activity agitating. I'm glad it went in the positive direction for your mom."

"Me too," Ian said with a sigh. He knew, though, whom to thank most for the positive results. "Gwen's really good with her."

She'd also been a comfort to Ian after he'd spoken to her about the night wandering. He was coming to appreciate so much more than just her help with his mom's care. He was grateful for her insights and her thoughtfulness.

"I hear you're great with the boys in turn." Nolan's gaze assessed over the rim of his ceramic mug.

"We help each other." The whole arrangement was so much smoother than he'd expected. He could see why there was gossip. "But I'm supposed to make sure everyone is clear, I should let you know that we are not engaged."

The doctor's mouth twitched. "I heard that rumor. But I figured it was just that…gossip. Otherwise my wife would have heard directly from Gwen. But you two *are* a couple?"

There was no denying the truth any longer. "Leaning that way."

Nolan propped a shoulder against the doorframe. "I imagine that's tough to juggle with your mother and the boys. Not much time left to be alone."

Talk about stating the obvious. "Responsibilities are important."

"And so is the support of those around you." Nolan

pinned him with that astute gaze. "I'm speaking from the perspective of a doctor and your friend in saying you and Gwen both have high-stress family setups. Your mom's Alzheimer's…" He held up one finger, then two. "And Gwen's young triplets. You need to guard against burnout."

"Sure." Where was the guy going with this? "I hear you. But it's easier said than done."

Nolan angled forward, motioning toward his wife. "Then let me and Eliza help. The kids are having a blast playing together and your mother can help us with Christmas baking. Let them stay for a few hours. Take Gwen out to dinner. Finish up holiday shopping. Do something as a couple."

As a couple?

After a December full of sleeping under the same roof with her, of yearning for her every night, he wanted nothing more than some "couple" time with Gwen. But where would it lead?

With thoughts of that shared kiss still igniting a fire in his veins, he couldn't help but wish for another chance to have her in his arms.

Chapter Twelve

Her arms were full of last-minute gifts for the boys, and the back seat of her minivan overflowed with pet gear after a shopping expedition with Ian. She intended to take the boys later to let each of them pick out a toy for their new puppy to put under the tree. But it was helpful not to have to corral her triplets while she and Ian shopped for the basics.

And truth be told, she hadn't been able to turn down the opportunity to go out with Ian. Alone.

It felt surreal to see him behind the wheel of her van, the sound of his humming caressing the air with husky holiday cheer. She'd asked Ian to drive while she cross-checked her list to see if she had anything left to accomplish. The sun was low in the sky, casting hazy beams through the bare branches as they made their way back to Ian's farmhouse.

She'd texted Eliza for updates on the boys every hour

and, apparently, all three were having a blast decorating gingerbread houses, followed by a snowball fight. Florence had helped bake cookies and now was putting together a Santa puzzle with Doc Barnett.

Her Top Dog friends were the best. She didn't know how she would have managed this past year without them.

And now Ian was a part of that system of support. But for how long? Even the thought of going their separate ways made her stomach knot with anxiety. How quickly their lives had become entwined.

She picked at the packaging on a new video game Gideon had been wanting. It was a bit more expensive than she'd hoped, but his words earlier worrying about his puppy being taken away really tugged at her. She wasn't sure yet how to approach the subject. And while a video game wouldn't undo all the loss he'd been through, at least she'd be able to give her son one small thing he wanted.

Sticking her booted feet farther under the heater blasting from the floorboards, she pushed aside worries for the moment and tucked her list back in her hobo purse. "I don't know how I would have finished up my errands without the Barnetts' generous offer."

These past weeks, there hadn't been much extra time left in the day after work.

Ian's humming came to a halt before he answered.

"Shopping for the puppy brought back a lot of memories of my childhood dog. His name was Domino because he had a white spot on his neck—just like the little fella they chose today." He steered off the two-lane highway, onto the gravel driveway leading to his house.

"Domino. I like that. I'll mention it to the boys." She turned her gaze from the snow-covered pine trees to shoot a quick look his way. "If it's okay by you that we snitch the name."

"I would like that. I think ole Domino would too." A sentimental smile notched the dimples into his cheeks. "This one time, when the power went out, I played hide-and-go-seek with Domino. No matter how well I hid, he always found me. Mom said it was a handy trick for whenever I wandered off."

The minivan jostled along the icy drive. Christmas tree lights twinkled in the bay window, reminding her of that special day decorating with the boys, surprising Ian. It was a holiday memory she would always treasure. Much like their day of picking out a puppy together, and so many other outings they'd shared these past weeks. She had to admit to looking forward to sharing Christmas with him and his mother.

He accelerated past the front gate to the side entrance, pulling the van as close to the kitchen door as possible. The vehicle's back hatch rose. After unbuckling her seat belt, Gwen threw open her door. A blast of cold air stole her breath as she jumped onto the fresh dusting of snow. Shivering, she hugged her coat tighter around herself and picked her way to the back.

Ian passed over two large bags before hefting the new wire kennel with an ease that launched a delicious shiver up her spine.

Blinking away temptation, she made fast tracks to the door, her boots crunching along the frozen ground. "You haven't told me what you want from Santa."

He set down the crate and pulled the key from his

jeans pocket. "The decorating you've done in the house has already been a great gift." Holding open the screen door with a shoulder, he unlocked the side entrance. "I'm long past the age of expecting something under the tree."

"The boys will be very disappointed if they can't pick out a present for you." She angled past him into the welcoming warmth of the mudroom, then to the kitchen. She slung the bags onto the scarred table and shrugged out of her parka. "Any hints to help me steer them?"

"Surprise me." He propped the folded wire kennel against the wall, underneath the faded yellow wall phone, then tossed his jacket over the chair and draped his scarf on top.

"Okay, then. But be warned," she said, pulling out two bowls with a paw print pattern and a neon tug rope, "when my sons' imaginations kick into overdrive, there's no telling what the results will look like."

"I'm counting on it." His smile launched warming golden flecks into his brown eyes.

Sampson padded into the room and lumbered straight over to the empty kennel, sniffing. Gwen tunneled deeper into the bag and pulled out the larger rope she'd purchased for the massive dog. Living with this furry gentle giant had gone a long way toward softening her heart on the subject of adding a dog to the family. "Will Sampson be riding on your float in the ranch's Christmas Eve parade?"

"Sure will. He'll be riding in the tractor with me as we pull our float of trees. I have a Frosty the Snowman suit for him. Well, just head gear and scarf, since the rest of his body pretty much already fits the bill."

"That's gonna be awesome. Perfect choice." She smiled at the image. "What about you? Will you be in costume?"

With a self-deprecating grin, he scratched the back of his neck. "Mom talked me into wearing a gnome costume. She thought it went with the whole forest theme. What about you?"

"The boys haven't already spilled the beans?" She laughed. "How about we let it be a surprise?"

"I look forward to the mystery reveal." Ian motioned toward the door leading to the fenced section of the yard and let Sampson out to run. He stood at the screened exit, keeping watch from the warmth of inside. "After we finish unloading, do you want to grab a bite to eat at the ranch?"

She glanced at the metallic clock on the wall, brass spikes radiating from the vintage 1970s device. It was a quarter past five. "Are you sure it's okay with the Barnetts that we stay out any longer? I wouldn't want to impose, especially at Christmas."

"Doc wasn't taking no for an answer," Ian reminded her. "And honestly, is there anyone else you can think of who's better equipped to look after my mom?"

"Good point. And they have our numbers. Your mom didn't seem fazed at all by our leaving. Neither did the boys. It would have been tough to peel them away from the puppy."

"He's a cute little fella." He stuffed his hands into his jeans pockets, well-washed denim encasing his long, muscular legs. "I have to admit, I'm disappointed we have to wait two days to pick him up."

She swallowed back the urge to drink in the sight of him. "I can't thank you enough for opening your home to a new puppy, as if my crew wasn't enough." Her cell phone buzzed, stopping her short. She held up a hand to Ian. "Hold on while I make sure this isn't about the boys or your mom."

As she pulled her cell from her hobo bag, he swept the door open again to admit Sampson. The furry white dog looked a bit like the abominable snowman, giving a massive shake and sending snow flying before ambling over to his water bowl.

She shifted her attention back to her phone, reading the message from Hollie. The couple in cabin 3C had to check out early for a family emergency. You and the boys can move in anytime and stay until your place is repaired. Call me in the morning for more details.

She could go.

Gwen read the message a second time, letting the information sink in. Her time at the farmhouse with Ian was finished. She should have been relieved to have a space of her own again, but she just felt…disappointed. Like someone had stolen the gifts from under her tree. She didn't want this magical time between them to end so soon.

"Gwen?" Ian called, drawing her attention back to the present, as he refilled Sampson's water bowl. "Are you ready to go to dinner?"

Startled, she gathered her scattered thoughts, her tangled emotions, until his request registered. He wanted to leave and go out to eat. It was a thoughtful gesture.

And the last thing she wanted.

No way would she waste what little time she had left alone under this roof with Ian. Perhaps her last chance to *be* with Ian before the real world and worries intruded again. She wanted—deserved—to have one wish come true just for herself.

Hollie's text had made one thing perfectly clear to her.

Right now, she knew exactly what she craved—what she wanted so much it took her breath away and made her question just how deep her feelings for Ian were growing. But she didn't question the impulse that suddenly felt imperative.

"How do you feel about leftovers from the fridge instead?" New purpose fueled her as she set aside her phone, putting the message out of her mind. She crossed to the counter, so close to Ian she could feel the heat of him radiating through denim. "After we make love. If you're in agreement."

Slowly, he turned from the sink, the sight of his powerful frame making her heart beat faster as she waited for his response.

He set aside the bowl, his hand gravitating to skim a lock of hair back from her face. "There's nothing in this world that I want more than to take you upstairs and peel every stitch of clothes off your beautiful body. But are you sure?"

She answered without hesitation, leaning into his touch until they stood chest to chest. "Absolutely," she said, grazing her lips over his, once, again. "I've dreamed of this since the first time I saw you."

His forehead tipped to hers, his voice deepening. "Is that so?"

Closing her eyes, she allowed herself to remember the moment. "You walked into the gift shop with your mother because she wanted a scoop of hard candy from the barrel. You were so patient and so unbelievably handsome. And when you turned those eyes of yours my way…" Opening her eyes, she breathed the words against his mouth, pushing away thoughts of other admissions, vows, whispering to be let loose. "Yes, I know exactly what I'm doing. Don't you think we've waited long enough?"

The golden flecks in his eyes turned molten an instant before he scooped her off her feet. He secured her against his chest. "I only have one more question."

She looped her arms around his neck, anticipation firing through every nerve inside her. "What would that be?"

"Your room or mine?"

Making love with Gwen had exceeded his every fantasy. And his fantasies had been mighty amazing.

Reclining against a pile of pillows in his brass bed, Ian smoothed his fingers down her bare arm as she curved against his side, one slim leg slung over his. Her head rested on his shoulder, the sheets and quilt draped over them to ward off the chill in the air. He wished he'd taken the time to light the logs in the fireplace, but they'd been in too much of a hurry, throwing off their clothes in a trail of impatience and desire.

The scent of her shampoo teased his senses. He wanted to make love to her again, then sleep tangled up together through the night. But they would have to leave soon, as they'd promised to pick up the boys and his mother by nine o'clock.

At least they would be under the same roof, able to steal intimate moments. Their time together had been so perfect these past weeks—other than the sexual frustration. And now that he knew how very compatible they were in bed...

Stolen encounters didn't feel like near enough.

He'd spent so much time planning for his previous engagement and it had backfired. Had he overcomplicated something that should have been more straightforward? From where he was sitting, nothing in his life made more practical sense than him and Gwen being together, helping and supporting each other.

He'd never considered himself an impulsive man, yet he couldn't stop himself from saying, "What do you think about making this official?"

Her answer meant more to him than it should, which only served to solidify his decision.

Gwen went still against him for four heavy heartbeats before tipping her head to look at him, her hair teasing along his skin. "What do you mean?"

The wariness in her eyes could be a good sign or a bad one. He couldn't tell what kind of response she wanted. But she hadn't run.

So he pressed on. "Let's move in together. Get engaged like my mother so brilliantly assumed. We can go ring shopping after Christmas." He held her hand, stroking a thumb along her finger. "Adding a rock there should quell the gossip."

His mind filled with images of telling the boys at Christmas. His mother would likely insist she'd known all along. Perhaps on some level she really had known.

Easing her hand away, Gwen tucked the sheet to her chest and sat up. "Quell the gossip?"

Not exactly the response he'd been hoping for. But then it hadn't exactly been the most romantic of offerings. Too late to go back and change that. All he could do was press forward and try to do a bit of damage control. Gwen was one of the calmest and most reasonable people he'd ever met. Surely she would get what he meant.

"That didn't come out right." He clasped her bare shoulders, caressing, wanting to go back to the connection of a few minutes ago, but time was running out. Not just because they had to leave to pick up the boys soon. He also knew Gwen's time under his roof was coming to an end after the holidays. "I just meant that it's obvious there's chemistry between us. We've both known that from the start. We enjoy each other and our families mesh so well together. Why shouldn't we make it official and continue to enjoy what we've found every day?"

She studied him through narrowed eyes.

"Chemistry," she echoed his word, but was that a hollow note he heard in her voice?

Clearing his throat, he tried again. "You can't deny it's been tugging at us both from day one. Why should we resist when we could forge a relationship based on shared needs. Helping one another."

Gwen hesitated for a moment before answering. "That sounds very...practical."

She blinked fast, holding herself utterly still.

It sure didn't seem like she understood.

He searched for the right words to win his point, only to come up short. "I'm not certain exactly what I meant. But I know what I want. And I want you." He linked fingers with her, tugging gently in an attempt to bring her closer and let the connection fire to life again. He angled to kiss her jaw, up to her ear. "Call Hollie and tell her you won't need a place to stay after all."

For an instant, she turned toward his mouth, their lips so close. The pulse in her neck beat faster... Then she shook her head and eased away. Worse than that, she stood and took the sheet with her. She stumbled as she almost stepped on Sampson sleeping on the floor by the bed.

Once she'd steadied herself, her solemn gaze met his dead on. "What would you say if I told you I'm moving out right away?"

Her words chilled him from the inside out. "To go where?"

Snatching up her clothes from the floor, she hurried about the room, throwing his jeans onto the bed with a haste that spoke of how very much she wanted to end this conversation. "The text that came in when we first got home—that was Hollie telling me a cabin has become available for the boys and me."

Her jeans, sweater and underwear clutched to her chest, she sidestepped Sampson and disappeared into his bathroom. The door closed behind her with a decisive click, shutting him out.

Gwen grabbed the edge of the bathroom sink and bit back a sob. Her clothes were on now, but her emotions still felt bare and raw.

Why couldn't they have just stayed in bed and kept quiet? Or showered, while staying silent? Or thrown their clothes on to get the boys and his mom? Instead, their time together had been ruined by his terrible, practical proposal that had stomped all over her growing feelings for him.

Was she sure about her decision to turn him down?

Of course not. She didn't want to leave. She wanted nothing more than to stay in this house with this amazing man and build a life together, to wake up every morning in his arms.

But she also knew his "proposal" hadn't come close to what it should have been if they were to stand a chance at a future. She couldn't settle for another loveless marriage. Her bruised heart couldn't take it.

Scrubbing her wrist under her nose, she stepped back from the sink and gathered her tattered pride. Pride that was as weary as the powder blue tile around her and the claw-foot tub with worn enamel.

She stepped back into the bedroom, careful to keep her eyes off the brass bed and tangled quilt where they'd shared such a beautiful connection just an hour ago. Ian stood in the open doorway leading to the hall, one shoulder braced against the frame.

He'd gotten dressed as well, flannel shirt, jeans and boots laced. "Are you ready?"

His simple words hurt more than if he'd pressed his point, doubling down on his stark offer that had been so devoid of emotion.

"In a minute." She drew in a ragged sigh, which, rather than bracing her, merely made her dizzy. "There's something I need to say first."

Something flickered in his chocolate eyes. Hope? Could this be hurting him as deeply?

He motioned for her to continue, keeping his vigil by the door. "I'm listening."

"I'm a person of my word, so even after I leave, I'll continue to help with your mother however I can." She would miss Florence with her dry wit and loving patience for the boys. She would miss Ian. "This isn't easy for me."

"Then don't go," he said curtly, still not offering anything in the way of a proposal for a real relationship.

She shook her head, willing herself to stay strong. "I just can't do that to my boys—or your mom. Because if—when—things fall apart, they will be the ones hurt most."

Although right now, she was hurting so much she wasn't sure how anything could be worse. Sampson whimpered and nudged against her leg. Her hand fell to rest on top of his big head, taking comfort as much as giving it.

Ian's mouth thinned before he said hoarsely, "And you don't think my mom and the boys will be hurt by the upheaval of you moving out right before Christmas? To have the promise of a big wonderful holiday here together ripped away because you can't wait to haul out of here?"

The image he painted made her blink in surprise. Why hadn't she considered how moving out would make the others feel? Leaving quickly, especially before Christmas, would be devastating for her sons and confusing for Florence. As much as she wanted to crawl under the covers and cry her way through to the New Year, she had responsibilities. She nodded sharply. "I can see your point. So I'll wait until December 26."

He quirked an eyebrow. "Well, there's no need to make staying sound like such a chore, even if it will be awkward to break up and stay under the same roof."

His harshness was like lemon juice poured over her already raw emotions. "We're not a couple," she reminded him firmly. "You just want a family after your fiancée dumped you. The boys and I would give you that. But do you actually want me?"

His teeth gritted in frustration, he gestured toward his bed with rumpled sheets. "Isn't it obvious?"

"I'm not talking about sex. I'm talking about wanting *me*, who I am." Stomping closer, she stifled the urge to shout at him. She wouldn't give him the satisfaction. Maybe she had some pride left after all. "Would you be proposing this if I didn't have the boys and your mother didn't need help?"

He grazed his knuckles tenderly across her cheek. "No amount of family needs would make me tie my life to someone I didn't respect and enjoy."

She flinched back from his touch. Respect? Enjoy? She wanted with every fiber of her being to ask why he hadn't mentioned love. But she feared he would only say the words to pacify her, as Dale had done.

So, instead, she said, "*Tie* your life to mine? Like you're being shackled?"

"Poor choice of words," he retorted quickly, defensively. "Tell me what you need to hear from me."

And there it was. What she'd feared most. That he would play on her emotions.

She knew exactly what she needed and deserved to hear, what she deserved to have. Never again would she let herself settle for less than a man's whole heart. Not even for her boys. In fact, what kind of example would she be setting for them if she entered a loveless union?

She shook her head, her heart splintering into pieces even as she held her ground. "If you have to ask, then that tells me everything I need to know. I mean it when I say that I'm grateful for your help. But on December 26, I'll be packing up the boys and our puppy to leave."

Chapter Thirteen

By Christmas Eve morning, Ian still didn't have a clue how to salvage the mess he'd made of things with Gwen.

As he watched the boys romp in the yard with their puppy and Sampson, he wondered if Gwen felt the loss of what had been growing between them as deeply as he did. He couldn't get a read off her. It was as if a curtain had gone down, hiding her emotions from him. Other than an attitude of overbright holiday cheer around the boys and his mom. But Gwen avoided even a moment alone with him. With the season's mayhem in full swing, that wasn't likely to change.

She'd left early for work. She would spend the morning in the shop before turning it over to her assistant to man during the parade. At least the boys didn't have to spend the morning away from the house and their new puppy. He'd offered to keep the triplets until time for the parade, and drop them off at her store on his way to his float, in a bid to show her, yet again, how seamlessly their lives could blend.

She'd looked ready to argue, but the boys' pleading for more time to play with their new dog had won the day. After all, who wanted to spend Christmas Eve hanging out in the play area at their mom's workplace? With pursed lips, she'd begrudgingly agreed.

Gloved hand pressed to an icy tree trunk, he watched the boys flop to the ground to make a trio of snow angels that were promptly smudged as they rolled around with the puppy. His chest went tight. He would miss them so much when they left.

How could he and Gwen have gone from such synchronicity to complete disconnect in the span of one evening? He'd gone from genuinely considering the idea of marriage to losing her altogether. In forty-eight hours, Gwen would be packing up her boys and her puppy, leaving his home—his life—for good. The pain of this impending loss eclipsed anything he'd felt over the breakup with Becky.

The sound of the screen door squeaking open had him pivoting hard and fast, hoping Gwen had somehow been drawn by his thoughts even though he knew she was gone. Instead, he found his mother walking down the porch steps and into the yard toward him. Bundled in her favorite coat, she'd wrapped a thick red scarf around her neck and over her ears. She wore insulated duck boots. Her quilted robe, visible beneath the coat, skimmed the top of the fur lining.

She passed him a large Yeti mug. "I brought you some coffee."

"Thanks, you're the best." He took the steaming mug of java and breathed in the bracing scent.

"You looked like you could use a pick-me-up." She studied him with wise eyes. "Is something troubling you?"

"Nope," he lied and washed down the fib with a sip of coffee.

Caleb and Timothy tossed sticks for Sampson while Gideon dangled the tug rope for the puppy. They were still debating names. Names in the running so far were Midnight. Jet. Smokey. And the sentimental favorite that tugged at his heart—Domino.

"Gwen looked just as grumpy as you when she tore out of here for work this morning." His mother's words puffed a white cloud into the cold morning air. "Not much holiday cheer coming off of either of you."

"It's a busy time of year." He dodged her not-too-subtle probing, hoping she would get the hint.

Kneeling, he scooped up a frozen tennis ball and tossed it to Timothy. The boy took off running, back in the game. Drawn by the activity, the puppy gave chase, big paws flopping as he ran. Privacy restored, Ian returned his attention to his mother.

Rocking back on her bootheels, she tugged her scarf more snuggly on her head, her familiar gray braid trailing down her back. "Son, I appreciate all you've done for me—and all you and Gwen are still doing." She pinned him with a gaze so clear, fully present. "But it's not fair to you or to that girl to string her along if you don't love her."

Her words hit him like a blast of winter air, stealing the oxygen from his lungs and icing him clean through. "I'm not stringing Gwen along."

Hadn't he proposed to her just two days ago only to have her toss the offer right back in his face?

His mom stuffed her gloved hands in her coat pockets. "I got the impression you two have entered some kind of engagement of convenience, except it got complicated. Unless you don't have any feelings for her at all."

"What makes you think I don't have real feelings for her?" he retorted quickly, the question rolling off his tongue a little too easily for his comfort.

"Oh, I believe you have feelings, but are you in love with her the way she deserves?" She paused, tapping her mouth in that way she always did when thinking. "Do you remember when you got that train set for Christmas when you were eight?"

That had been one of his top holiday memories. From the "reindeer hooves" on the roof to coming downstairs in the middle of the night and getting to play with the set until the sun came up. "Sure, it was shiny and red. I'd just heard from my best friend at school that Santa wasn't real and the gifts came from parents. Looking at that train, I realized how much overtime you had to work to buy it."

"And even as a kid, you knew it was a knockoff of the name-brand version you'd asked for," she said dryly.

He slid an arm around her shoulder. "I never said that."

"Your face did. For just a moment. Then you hid your feelings. You've always been good at that." She tucked an arm around his waist and hugged him back. "Just as you knew then the difference between the real deal and fake, I can tell that your relationship with Gwen has been a pale imitation. Or at least it was, until recently when something shifted between you two. So I'll ask again. Do you love her?"

He wavered between an automatic defensive feeling and intense gratitude for this moment with his mother seeing right through him. Clearly. His throat closed with emotions that were already churning from the tension with Gwen. Even as this conversation struck at his most raw spots, he hung on to the feeling of connection with his mom.

He studied the boys tossing snowballs for the dogs to chase, their laughter ringing on the wind, before he cleared his throat to reply. "I don't know how to answer that."

"Then you have to break things off with her," she said decisively. "It's only fair to both of you."

Her words made sense, but everything inside him shouted against the finality of that decree. Even though Gwen had rejected him, there was a part of him that had hoped he could wear her down if he just came up with a plan. But what his mother said about cutting ties forever? That ended all hope of a future with Gwen.

And the prospect of her out of his life permanently was untenable. Painful. His chest ached just at the thought of never seeing her again. "I can't push her away."

Smiling, his mother patted his cheek. "Then there's your answer. Now you just have to figure out how to win her over."

The cold whistled past his ears while his brain caught up to what she was saying. His heart felt like it was in slow motion since he'd grown accustomed to stuffing down everything he felt.

Because... Yes, he loved Gwen. He'd loved everything about her from the moment he'd first laid eyes on her. How could he not? His heart had just been too bruised to let her in.

But much like Gwen restored vintage toys, she had somehow restored his life to a bright and shiny state. And he'd rejected that, rejected her by denying his love for her.

And his mom was right. He had to correct the wrong he'd done to Gwen by shortchanging what he felt for her. Shortchanging *her*. He had to give Gwen the romance, devotion and love she deserved. "Mom, I need your help."

Gwen couldn't decide whether to be sad or relieved that the Santa Paws Parade was almost finished.

As the parade neared the end, she waved from her float to the bundled-up guests lining the ranch's main street. She'd so looked forward to this day, decorating the float with pride and anticipation. Now the approaching Christmas Day just left her feeling sad over her impending move. And yes, brokenhearted over leaving Ian, but she couldn't think about that right now or tears would blur her vision. Instead, she focused on the practical aspects of what she'd have to do in order to get through the upcoming days.

She knew she should have told the boys about the move, but she hadn't had the heart. They'd been so excited putting on their costumes this afternoon.

The flatbed trailer for her float was outlined as a vintage red wagon, filled with toys, a tower of ABC blocks and a massive beach ball in the middle. Gwen had chosen to dress up as Raggedy Ann, complete with a red yarn wig and a couple of layers of thermals under her costume. Even her red mittens were insulated.

Her boys soaked up the limelight, dressed as nut-cracker soldiers. The only fly in the ointment for them was that they'd had to leave the puppy at home. But she'd explained that little Domino had been through enough upheaval with being adopted and needed a nap.

Just her luck, they'd chosen the name of Ian's long-ago pup, Domino, at Florence's suggestion. And the fates kept right on flinging darts at Gwen's heart by placing her float directly behind Ian's. Perched beside him in the front seat of the tractor, Sampson wore his Frosty the Snowman costume with pride, his black top hat perched between two ears.

She pulled her attention off that tractor before her heart broke in two all over again. She shifted her focus beyond, to the front of the parade. Anything to distract herself in hopes of stopping tears.

Hollie and Jacob led the parade in a horse-drawn sleigh. They'd dressed as Mr. and Mrs. Claus, their four children as elves. Their dogs, a hodgepodge pack of Scottish terrier, beagle and border collie mix, wore reindeer antlers.

Behind them, Susanna and Micah Fuller rode in the back of a flatbed trailer with an elaborately constructed doghouse with bookshelves painted on the outside. Susanna was dressed up like a nineteenth-century schoolmarm, holding her shaggy pup, Atlas, while Micah sported a cowboy costume with a pony express and a leather mailbag slung over his shoulders. An inflatable Dalmatian with glasses waved at the crowd. Their little boy, Benji, sat with some of his classmates holding large books.

Some participants were on foot, like Eliza and her border collie Loki. She was herding four sheep and waving to her husband on the sidelines. Gus and Mavis jumped up and down, calling out her name.

Was everyone a part of a couple out here today? It sure felt like she was an outlier for flying solo in the relationship department. A tempting whisper in her mind taunted her, reminding her of Ian's offer. But she knew that kind of couplehood would only be a short-term solution, destined to lead to worse heartache down the road. She loved Ian, yes. But they couldn't have a relationship when he didn't love her in return.

Timothy tugged on the hem of her Raggedy Ann skirt. "When we get home, will you take a picture of me with my puppy and text it to our grandparents? Your mom and dad. And Daddy's mother and father?"

There were so many points in his question that made her heart squeeze, especially the parts about calling the farmhouse home and sending a photo to the Bishops.

She knelt down beside him, careful to grip the rail as the float finished the last few yards of the parade. "Of course I will."

"Thanks." He sat cross-legged on the Astroturf covering the metal floorings. "I was thinking that maybe if they see enough photos of us, then it will be easier to visit us in person. I don't want them to be sad."

More concerned about her son than any final moments of the parade, she took a seat beside him. "Why do you think they're upset?"

Frowning, he picked at the brass buttons on his costume. "What if telling you makes *you* upset? I don't want to make you cry."

"You can tell me anything." She tucked an arm around him as the trailer jolted then stopped as they waited for Ian's float ahead to turn the corner into a field for parking. "In fact, you should tell me whenever you're worried."

Timothy kept his gaze down, still plucking at his toy soldier costume, shifting from the brass buttons to the gold piping. "I think seeing us reminds them of Daddy."

"You're probably right," she said, choosing her words carefully. "But that's not your fault."

He waited so long to answer, she wondered if he was done talking. Then, finally, he looked up to meet her gaze. "Do you think of Daddy when you see us?"

She stifled a gasp, then hugged him tight, hating that he carried around such weighty concerns. "Sweetheart, of course I think of your father sometimes, but you three boys are a beautiful reminder of all the very best memories of our time with him."

He nodded against her, tiny arms wrapped around her waist. "Good. I was kinda worried about that."

"Even though I'll never forget your father..." she paused to cup his cheeks in her hands "...I also want you to know that when I look at you, I see you—my son *Timothy*. And I love you because you're you. Do you understand what I mean?"

"I think so. Kinda like how you can tell me and my brothers apart even though we look just alike." He chewed his bottom lip, but at least he'd stopped playing with his costume. "Maybe we can talk about it some more another time?"

"Absolutely," she said with relief, thankful he'd come to her. "I would like that very much."

He gave her a final squeeze, a hard one, before launching back to his feet. "Is the parade over? Mr. Ian promised we could look at the lights strung all over his tractor. Can we, Mom? Please, pretty please?"

Her heart beat faster at the prospect of time with Ian. She still wasn't sure what would happen after she and the boys left. How they would face accidental meets. Most importantly, how she would safeguard her emotions.

For now, she had to make sure her boys had the special Christmas she'd promised them. And she couldn't deny that Ian was a part of that.

"Yes, Timothy, we can." She eased off Timothy's tall soldier hat and pulled a knit hat over his head instead. "Hold on and I'll walk you and your brothers over."

One by one, she tugged caps on Caleb and Gideon, their chatter filling her ears. Some of it intelligible, other parts a jumble of their own special language. Their bond was so strong, yet Timothy was right. She could tell them apart, even with their haircut antics. Their DNA might be identical, but their personalities marked them as so very different, so individual.

She kept her hands on Gideon's and Timothy's shoulders, while Caleb held Gideon's hand, all connected and safe as she made her way through the throng to Ian's large green tractor. Multicolored lights were strung all around the vehicle. A wooden tree was attached to the roof. A wreath was affixed to the grill. And of course, the sides bore multiple Greer Family Tree Farm signs.

As she trailed her sons, her gaze met Ian's and held

for a moment that crackled with the ever-present awareness between them. Gulping, she released her boys and
let them charge ahead, peppering him with questions
and reports of their own ride through the parade.

He knelt down to their level, giving special attention
to each one of them. She couldn't miss the joy he ob-
viously took in spending time with her sons. The way
they made him laugh, the way he monitored Caleb's
interaction with Sampson while listening to Timothy's
long story about making cookies for Santa, and still
kept an eye on Gideon, who wanted to show off his
soldier moves.

The way they gathered around him made her think
of the early holidays with Dale, the way he'd played
with them after work each day, stacking blocks, listening to their babble.

But as quickly as the memory threaded through, she
realized how very different this moment was from the
past. Because Ian wasn't Dale. Not even close.

How simple, and yet how earthshaking that realization was at the same time.

Timothy had been so worried his grandparents
couldn't separate their love for Dale from their feelings for the boys. She'd reassured her son otherwise
and realized she needed to take her own advice. How
could she really see and appreciate one man while she
was still allowing the hurt from another to inform her
every reaction in a relationship.

She'd allowed her feelings for Dale to cloud the present, and that had been deeply unfair to the man in front
of her. A man who'd given unselfishly to her and her
sons, over and over again. Ian was his own person, a very

special man who'd shown her nothing but support—and yes, now that she really saw him clearly, love. Even if he couldn't say the words yet out of his own baggage from his previous relationship, she realized that she saw the depth of his emotions in his actions.

How could she blame him for holding back when she'd done the same? In fact, she suspected she'd pushed him away out of panic, fear of being hurt. The realizations snowballed, coming at her fast now that she'd opened her eyes to the way she was letting the past cloud her future. How foolish would she be to stay stuck in that hurt forever when a good man—a loving, kind and warmhearted man—stood right in front of her, offering to take a chance on a real relationship? He'd been brave to at least try it, while she'd been too afraid.

Well, she wasn't going to let fear rule her any longer. It was time to bravely take a risk on forever by laying it all on the line and telling Ian exactly how very much she loved him. And pray he could one day say the same.

Bundled against the cold, Ian stood in the twilight haze of Christmas morning moments from waking the family inside his farmhouse. And yes, he thought of them all as his family now—not just his mom, but Gwen and her boys too. Even the lanky puppy racing around the yard with Sampson, leaving big paw prints in the snow.

He'd been working on a plan to win Gwen. He just hoped it would be enough. And if it didn't win her over, then he would try again, and again, because he wasn't giving up on her, on them, on their future together.

As much as he'd wanted to scoop her into his arms

right away, he realized the timing was critical. If all went according to plan, this would be the most important moment of their lives. So he'd decided on Christmas morning to mark the start of their forever.

Besides, there hadn't been a free moment to talk. The children had been so wired the night before, they'd ended up staying up late, then falling dead asleep. His mom had wanted to be a part of setting up Santa gifts—new sleds for all three boys, plus stockings full of candy. Gwen had made sure the dogs had stockings as well, jammed with treats from the Top Dog's canine café. Throughout the Christmas prep, he'd caught Gwen studying him with a pensive look that gave him hope. Could she be regretting the way things shook out in their argument? Or was he just a victim of wishful thinking?

His hands clenched around a couple of small rocks mixed with pebbles. More were waiting at his feet. Just like his grandmother had done all those years ago, he tossed the stones onto the roof, a handful at a time. After lobbing the last of them, he called the dogs and jogged back up the side steps into the mudroom, then kitchen.

Gwen stood by the coffeepot, looking too beautiful in pink snowflake sleep pants and matching long-sleeve T-shirt. A hesitant smile teased at her mouth. "Merry Christmas. Did I happen to hear reindeer thuds on our roof?"

"Yes, ma'am, you most certainly did." He shrugged out of his coat while the dogs lapped up water.

Cupping her mug, she leaned back against the cabinet, her socked feet crossed at the ankle. "Do you have a minute to talk?"

He wanted to reach for her, to give her another mistletoe kiss and celebrate this day with her at his side… but he also didn't want to risk being interrupted. His mother was already in the living room with her morning tea. "I'd like that, very much. But the boys will probably be downstairs any minute."

Nodding, she said, "Shall I call the kids? Or would you rather?"

He looked toward the ceiling, sounds of little feet hitting the floor already signaling the early start of the Christmas celebration. "Let's do it together."

Would she understand his meaning behind the statement? He hoped so.

She pushed away from the cabinet and called, "Boys, we're downstairs. Come see what Santa left for you."

"Merry Christmas," he shouted, ditching his coat and striding into the living room with that special tree decorated by the boys. "Did you hear the reindeer on the roof?"

Footsteps thundered down the stairs, followed by young squeals.

Gideon dragged his ragged baby blanket behind him. "I did. I bet it was Rudolph making all that noise."

From the sofa, his mother drank her tea and shot him a knowing look. "It sounded like the whole herd up there."

The next two hours passed in a flurry of wrapping paper and breakfast casserole. A fire crackled in the hearth, and the boys were scattered through the room playing with their loot—a magic kit, books, grow your own aliens and more.

His mother had slipped off to her room to take a nap.

Gwen had given her a doll like one she'd had as a child, restored and placed in a stand. His mom had already set it in a spot of honor on the hallway entry table. Gwen had gotten him a custom-carved box, made from part of a tree on his farm, shaped by a Top Dog craftsman.

And a restored shiny red train set. Much like the one he'd had as a child. The gesture was so thoughtful it clogged his throat with sentimental memories.

He'd held back his present for her, not wanting her to feel pressured with a big show in front of everyone. "Would you mind taking a break and coming with me for a moment? I have a gift for you."

She looked up from helping Gideon inflate a sit-on bouncy ball. "But you already gave me something. I know you're the one who helped the boys pick out the necklace with the boys' birthstone crystal."

Caleb nodded vigorously. "He did help. He took us shopping when you thought we were sledding. Well, he took us after we went sledding. Do you like it?"

She slid an arm around her son. "I love it. It's perfect, just like you three."

The jewelry had been made from a crystal from the dude ranch's Sulis Springs Cave. "That's from the boys," Ian explained. "I have something for you as well—just from me."

Pushing to her feet, she smoothed her pajama pants. "It would be a good time for us to have that talk I wanted earlier."

Nerves knocked around inside his stomach, along with a mix of hope and fear that he might lose her regardless of his best efforts. "Would you like to go to the sunroom?"

More nerves kicked up a storm as he waited for her answer. He'd considered proposing outside with romantic twinkle lights, but the cold had been daunting. So, with his mom's help, he'd set up an alternative in his favorite place in the farmhouse.

Her nod sent a wave of relief washing over him. As he followed a step behind, he waited for her reaction.

Every bit of the space was decorated with the help of someone from the Top Dog Dude Ranch. When he'd approached his mother for help, she'd reminded him of the beautiful village of friends and support they had in that magical place. Was it any wonder she wandered over there so often?

And she hadn't been wrong. The ranch staff—their friends—had dived in full force to assist him in setting the romantic stage for a reconciliation with Gwen.

Candles on every surface were made from soy wax and scented with essential oils. Flower arrangements brightened the space with Christmas colors and more scents. Romantic love songs played softly, recorded by Raise the Woof. Chief contractor Micah had rigged tiny lights that were strung from corner to corner, while his wife, Susanna, attached tiny note cards with lines from love poetry that dangled down from overhead. A heart-shaped cake, from Hollie's bakery, was strategically placed on the coffee table.

And finally, a gift was placed beside it, chosen with Eliza's help. The room looked sort of magical, as far as Ian could tell. But would Gwen like it?

Smiling, she gasped, her fingers flying to her face and covering her lips for a moment before she whispered, "It's beautiful."

More relief swept through him. He steadied himself and walked past her, scooping up the tiny box tied with a ribbon. Just the right size for a ring. His heart slugged against his ribs now that the moment had come, but he didn't doubt his decision. Even if the answer was no again for now, he needed to do this the right way. Gwen deserved that.

Gwen deserved so much more.

Ian dropped to one knee in front of her and everything he'd scripted flew out of his mind. Instead, he spoke from his heart. "I want to make more beautiful memories with you for the rest of our lives. I want to build a family with you, yes, but also build a life together. Our life. As a couple."

Gwen pressed a trembling hand to her mouth, then opened her mouth to speak. He took her hand, squeezing.

"Hold that thought," he said, pressing the box into her palm and folding her fingers around it. "Before you say anything, I need to apologize for the way I let you down with my first proposal. It was shoddy. I was afraid of losing you. But also scared of acknowledging how much you mean to me. How much I love you. But I'm not afraid to embrace that love anymore, and I hope with all my heart that you will do me the great honor of being my wife."

She blinked fast, still clutching the box, not stepping away. "Are you just saying that because you don't want me to leave? Are you trying to tell me what you think I want to hear?"

His heart gave a rough squeeze at the worry threading through her voice. He'd put that anxiety there with his carelessness. He would fix that now.

Standing, he slid his hands up to clasp her arms, gently. "I'm also sorry that you even have to ask that of me. Gwen, you are my every dream come true—even the dreams I didn't dare entertain. You. Just you. Not because you come with those incredible boys of yours or because of how you celebrate my mom even on her worst days. Not because you're so enticing you turn my fantasies inside out. But because you are you. And I can't imagine spending the rest of my life with anyone but you."

She swayed ever so slightly closer. "Wow, that's..."

"Everything you wanted to hear?" he asked hopefully.

"Yes," she said hesitantly, "it is."

That hesitation gave him pause as well, but he needed to know. They needed honesty between them if they stood a chance at making this work. "But you're not sure if you trust me. Because of Dale."

Already, she was shaking her head, clasping the gift to her chest. He was grateful she still held it since it gave him hope she might slide the ring onto her finger. "You're not like Dale. I know that."

Her words rang with conviction.

"Good, because you deserve so much more than he ever gave you. And I intend to do my level best every day to make sure you have the love and support you deserve." He tapped the gift box lightly. "You don't have to answer today. I'll wait as long as it takes. I'm determined to prove that my love for you can be trusted."

She looked up at him with shining eyes. The hesitation had fled, replaced by a new certainty. "And I will do the same for you. Because I love you too, Ian. How could I not love you? You're the perfect man."

He wanted to be that—for her. He certainly intended to try his best for the rest of his days. "We both know I'm far from perfect. But thank you for thinking so."

She drew in a deep breath. "I'd like to open this now."

He should have felt nerves, but instead, he felt nothing but happiness, excitement and anticipation for their future as she tugged the ribbon. She creaked open the velvet box to reveal a vintage ring, a scrolled setting with diamonds and rubies, a fleck of emeralds, resembling a poinsettia in an understated way.

"I was going for a vintage and holiday vibe, like you strive for with your work. But if you prefer something more traditional…" he began.

"It's perfect, unique and perfect, just like our love." She threw her arms around his neck and kissed him, once, twice, lingering before she eased back, extending her hand. Joy filled his heart, spilling over, filling all of him.

He plucked the ring free from the box and slid it into place, sealing the placement with a kiss on her finger. Then moving up to her mouth. "Merry Christmas, my love."

"It is, isn't it?" she sighed, sinking into his arms.

"Thanks to you," he breathed against her lips, celebrating the best gift he'd ever received.

Their future together.

Epilogue

One year later

Timothy held the velvety ring bearer's pillow, certain this was the best Christmas night ever.

After a morning unwrapping their gifts and playing with all their toys from Santa, his mom was marrying Mr. Ian.

They'd decided to have the wedding at the Top Dog Dude Ranch in a huge barn, with lots of pine trees and twinkly lights and poinsettias. He and his brothers had even gone with Mr. Ian to cut down the trees because their family was all about team effort.

Except, since they were family, Timothy and his brothers didn't call him Mr. Ian anymore. They called him "Daddy Ian" now. They had a group talk about it because they didn't want to hurt anyone's feelings or be mean to their first father's memory. But it seemed weird to keep saying Mr. Ian when he was doing all the things a father did—playing ball games, helping with homework, training Domino together—and he said he loved them as much as a dad. They decided Daddy Dale and Daddy Ian made sense.

Timothy listened closely to the preacher, waiting for his cue to pass the rings. Caleb was the best man and Gideon had walked their mom down the aisle. But Timothy knew he had the most important job of all because it meant they trusted him not to lose Daddy Ian's silver ring and Mom's special band made of tiny diamonds and rubies. It matched the poinsettia ring she got a year ago on that special Christmas when Santa gave them the wish he hadn't even dared to dream could really happen.

And yet, here they were.

Mrs. Eliza sang a pretty song, her voice filling the whole barn. His mom was really beautiful in a lacy dress that looked old-fashioned. She also had a special cape with fur around the hood to wear later when they went on a sleigh ride to stay in the honeymoon cabin.

Daddy Ian wore a black suit that looked just like the one Timothy and his brothers wore. And they had matching red Christmas ties with a white snowflake pattern. Pinned on their jackets, they even had holly berries, greenery and a white rose that looked like Mom's big ole bouquet.

Everybody from the ranch was there, even the kids. Even the dogs. Domino had a place of honor close to the bride and groom, a white bow tie on his collar. He knew sit and stay so well that he got to be a part of the big day along with Sampson. But there were other dogs in a designated pet viewing area behind a little white fence. Mrs. Susanna and her dog, Atlas, monitored them. Top Dog wouldn't be Top Dog, after all, without them.

Raise the Woof was playing all the music. There would be a big Christmas supper party with dancing afterward.

But right now, for the wedding, Mrs. Florence was in the front row with both sets of grandparents. It made Timothy happy to see Grandma and Grandpa Bishop smiling. They said they liked Daddy Ian and that Daddy Dale would approve.

And what do ya know, all the grandparents were gonna stay together to help watch him and his brothers while Mom and Daddy Ian went on their honeymoon.

Mrs. Florence had been doing pretty good lately— actually, she asked them to call her "Granny" and they liked that. A lot. Doctor Barnett gave her some different medicines that made her a little better. Sure, she still forgot some stuff, and she and Daddy Ian had decided that it wasn't a good idea for her to be alone anymore. She had somebody who sat with her and helped her find her way around if she got lost while Mom and Ian were at work. It worked out good, though, since Granny said she enjoyed the company. They do puzzles and knit and go to the ranch sometimes. Granny even knitted little blankets to go with the dolls on Mom's online toy store.

Life was almost perfect. He had just one last wish. He'd explained it in his letter to Santa. By next Christmas, Timothy wanted a baby sister. And maybe, just maybe, if it wasn't too greedy to ask, could Santa bring three? Mom said it would be a miracle to have triplets again.

Timothy figured between Santa and Top Dog Dude Ranch magic, anything was possible.

* * * * *

Try these other great holiday romances, available now from Harlequin Special Edition:

Triplets Under the Tree
By Melissa Senate

The Rancher's Christmas Star
By Stella Bagwell

Holiday at Mistletoe Cottage
By Nancy Robards Thompson

SPECIAL EXCERPT FROM

HARLEQUIN
SPECIAL
EDITION

Divorced rancher Hutch Dawson has one heck of a
Christmas wish: find a nanny for his baby triplets.
And Savannah Walsh is his only applicant! Who
knew that his high school nemesis would be the
perfect solution to his very busy—and lonely—
holiday season…

Read on for a sneak preview of
Triplets Under the Tree
by Melissa Senate.

Chapter One

Hutch Dawson's new nanny stood in the doorway of his home office with his squirming, screeching baby daughter in her arms. "Sorry, but this just isn't working out," she said.

He inwardly sighed but completely understood. His triplets were *a lot*. But maybe if he didn't look up from his computer screen, she'd take pity on him and go back into the living room, where he could hear his other two babies crying. It was four thirty and her day ended at five. If he could just have this last half hour to deal with his to-do list.

He had three texts from his cowboys to return. Two important calls, including one from the vet with a steer's test results. And he was in the middle of responding to his brother's passive-aggressive email about the needs of the Dueling Dawsons Ranch.

The woman marched in, holding Chloe out with her

legs dangling as though she were a bomb about to explode. Given the sight of the baby's clenched fists and red face, she was about to let out one hell of a wail.

She did, grabbing on to the nanny's ear too.

Mrs. Philpot, with her disheveled bun and shirt full of spit-up stains, grimaced and pried tiny fingers from her ear. "I won't be back tomorrow." She stood at the side of his desk and held out the baby.

This wasn't a big surprise. The previous nanny had quit two days ago, also lasting two days. But Hutch had to have childcare. He had ten days to go before his ex-wife was due back from her honeymoon—he could still barely wrap his mind around the fact that they were divorced with six-month-old triplets and that she'd remarried practically five minutes later. With two of his cowboys away for the holidays, his prickly brother—and new business partner—constantly calling or texting or demanding a meeting, a fifteen-hundred-acre ranch to run and way too many things to think about, Hutch *needed* a nanny.

Chloe let out a whimper between her shrieks, and Hutch snapped to attention, her plaintive cry going straight to his heart. He stood and took his baby girl, Daddy's arms calming her some. The moment Mrs. Philpot was free, she turned and hurried from the room. By the time he'd shifted Chloe against him and gone after Mrs. Philpot to talk, use his powers of persuasion, to *beg*, she had on her coat and boots, her hand on the doorknob.

Noooo, he thought. *Wait!*

"I'll double your salary!" he called as she opened the door and raced out to her car in the gravel drive.

Then again, her salary, like the two nannies before

her, had already been doubled. The director of the nanny agency had assured him that Mrs. Philpot, who'd raised triplets of her own, wouldn't be scared off by a little crying in triplicate.

A little. Was there any such thing?

"They're just too much for me, dear," Mrs. Philpot called back. She smoothed a hanging swath of her silver hair back into the bun, rubbed her yanked-on ear, then got into her car and peeled away, leaving him staring at the red taillights disappearing down the long drive.

And hoping for a miracle. Like that she'd turn back. At least finish the day. Even that would be a big help.

He did not see the car returning.

The other two babies were screaming their little heads off in their swings in the living room. Hutch was lucky he was hundreds of acres and many miles away from his nearest neighbor in any direction. This morning, before his workday, before the nanny was due to arrive, he'd dared take the trio into town because he'd discovered he was out of coffee and needed some and fast. He'd taken them to Java House, and two of the babies started shrieking. Compassionate glances of commiseration from those sitting at the café tables with their lattes and treats turned into annoyed glares. One woman came up to him and said, "They could really benefit from pacifiers and so could we."

He'd been about to explain that his ex-wife had gotten him to agree to wean the triplets off their pacifiers now that they were six months old. He truly tried to adhere to Allison's lists and rules and schedules since she really was better at all of it than he was, than he'd been since day one. Even her new husband, a very nice, calm

optometrist named Ted, was better at caring for the triplets than Hutch was.

He shifted Chloe again, grateful that she, at least,
had stopped crying. Whether from being in her daddy's
arms or the blast of cold December air, flurries swirl-
ing, or both, he didn't know. She wore just cotton pj's,
so he stepped back inside and closed the door. In the
living room, Carson and Caleb were crying in their
swings, the gentle rocking motion, soft lullabies and
pastel mobile with little stuffed animals spinning having no effect. Little arms were raised, faces miserable.

What Hutch really needed was to turn into an oc-
topus. He could cuddle each baby, make a bottle and
down a huge mug of strong coffee all at the same time.
He might have been chased out of Java House but not
before he'd bought himself an espresso to go and two
pounds of Holiday Blend dark beans.

"Hang on, guys," he told the boys, and put Chloe
in her swing. She immediately started crying again,
which he should have seen coming. "Kiddos, let me
make a quick call. Then I'll be back and we'll see what
the schedule says."

He lived by the schedule. His ex-wife was a stickler
for it, and Hutch, truly no expert on how to care for triplet
babies, regarded it as a bible. Between the trio's general
disposition, which was crotchety, to use a favorite word
of his late mother, and the three-page schedule, complete with sticky notes and addendums, it was no wonder Hutch had gone through six nannies in six months.

And he really was no better at caring for his own
children than he was when they were born. He might
be making excuses, but he blamed his lack of skills

on the fact that he'd been relegated to part-time father from the moment they'd arrived into the world. His ex had left him for another man—her "soulmate"—when she was five months pregnant. He and Allison had joint fifty-fifty custody, so Hutch had the triplets three and a half days a week, which meant half the time to figure out how to care for them, to discover who they were becoming with each passing day, who liked and disliked what, what worked on which triplet. On his ex's custody days, he'd miss little firsts or milestones, and though just last week she'd Facetimed the trio trying their first taste of solids—jarred baby cereal—it wasn't the same as being there and experiencing it with them.

With his ex away for the next ten days, Hutch was actually very happy to have them to himself. The triplets were here, in his home, on his turf. Hutch's life might have been upended by the breakup of his marriage and the loss of his father just months ago and then everything going on with the ranch, but for the next week and a half his babies would be here when he woke up in the morning and here when he went to sleep. That made everything better, gave him peace, made all the other stuff going on trivial. Almost trivial.

He hurried into his office and grabbed his phone and pressed the contact button for the nanny agency, then went back into the living room, trying to gently shush the triplets, hoping his presence would calm them.

"I'm sorry, I can't hear you over the crying," the agency director said, her tone a bit strained. He had a feeling she'd already heard from Mrs. Philpot that she would not be back tomorrow. The woman had gotten *that* call four times before.

Hutch hurried back to his office, closing the door till it was just ajar. He explained his predicament. "I'll *triple* the salary of whoever can start tomorrow morning," he said. "I'll even double the salary of *two* nannies so that the big job isn't heaped on one person at such a busy time." Emergency times meant emergency measures.

"That's quite generous, Mr. Dawson, but I'm sorry to say that we're plumb out of nannies until after the New Year." His heart sank as he glanced at his computer, the blinking cursor on his half-finished email to his brother, his to-do list running in his head. "If I may make a suggestion," she added—kindly, Hutch thought, hope flaring.

"Please do," he said.

"You have quite a big family here in town—all those Dawsons with babies and young children and therefore tons of experience. Call in the cavalry."

Just what his cousins wanted to do when they had families, jobs and responsibilities of their own, and right in the middle of the holiday season. He'd leaned on the generosity and expertise of various Dawsons for the past six months. He needed a dedicated nanny—even part-time.

As he disconnected from the disappointing call with the agency and went back out into the living room, his gaze landed on the tilted, bare Christmas tree he'd ordered from a nearby farm the other day when one of those Dawson cousins noted there *was* no tree. Not a half hour after it was delivered, Hutch had accidentally backed into it while rocking Carson in one arm and trying to push Chloe in the triple stroller since that usually helped her stop crying. Two bare branches hung down pathetically. He'd meant to decorate the tree, but between running the ranch and caring for the triplets once the nanny left, the box of ornaments and garland remained in the basement.

He looked at his precious babies. He needed to do better—for them. No matter what else, it was Christmas. They deserved *better*.

Caleb was crying harder now. Chloe looked spitting mad. Carson just looked…sad. Very sad. *Please pick me up, Daddy*, his big blue tearful eyes and woeful frown said.

"All right, kiddos, I'm coming," he said, rallying himself. He went for very sad Carson, undid the harness and scooped him out. This time, just holding the little guy seemed to help. But no, it was just a momentary curiosity in the change of position because Carson started crying again. He carefully held the baby against him with one firm arm, then got Chloe out and gave them both a rocking bounce, which seemed to help for two seconds. Now Caleb was wailing harder.

Hutch needed a minute to think—what time it was, what the schedule said. He wasn't *off* schedule; he knew that. He put both babies in the playpen and turned on the lullaby player, then he consulted his phone for the schedule.

> *6:00 p.m.: Dinner. Offer a jar of vegetable baby food. Caleb and Chloe love sweet potatoes. Carson's favorite is string beans. Burp each baby. 6:30: Tummy time. 6:45: Baths, cornstarch and ointment as needed before diapers and pj's. 7:00 p.m.: Story time. 7:45: Bedtime.*

It was five forty-five. Clearly the babies needed something *now*. But what? Were they hungry a little early? Had soggy diapers? Tummy aches—gas? He tried to remember what he'd read in last night's chapter of *Your Baby's First Year* for month six. But Chloe had awakened at just after midnight as he'd been about to drift off with month six milestones in his head, and then everything went out of his brain as he'd gotten up to tend to her. The moment he'd laid her back down in her bassinet in the nursery, Caleb's eyes popped open. At least Carson had slept through.

The schedule went out of his head as he remembered he still had to return the texts from one of his cowboys and had mini fires to put out. He stood in the middle of his living room, his head about to explode. He had to get on top of everything—the triplets' needs and the to-do list.

Maybe someone would magically respond to his ongoing ad for a nanny in the *Bear Ridge Weekly*. Just days ago he'd updated the half-page boxed ad, which ran both online and in the print edition with an optional border of tiny Santas and candy canes to make the job seem more...festive. He quickly typed "*Bear Ridge Weekly* classifieds" into his phone's search bar to make sure his ad was indeed running. Yup. There it was. The holiday border did help, in his opinion.

Loving, patient nanny needed for six-month-old triplets from now till December 23. M–F, 8:00 a.m. to 5:00 p.m. Highly paid position, one hour for lunch, plus two half-hour breaks. See Hutch Dawson at the Dueling Dawsons Ranch.

He'd gotten several responses from the general ad over the past six months, but some candidates had seemed too rigid or unsmiling, and the few he'd tried out in between the agency nannies had also quit. One lasted three days. Now, everyone in town seemed to know not to respond to his ad. *It's those crotchety triplets!*

Caleb was suddenly shrieking so loud that Hutch was surprised the big round mirror over the console table by the front door didn't shatter. He quickly scooped up the baby boy and rubbed his back, which seemed to quiet him for a second. Chloe had her arms up again. Carson was still crying—but not wailing like Caleb. A small blessing there, at least.

The doorbell rang. Thank God, that had to be Mrs. Philpot with a change of heart because it was the Christmas season! Or maybe it was one of those wonderful Dawson cousins, any number of whom often stopped by with a lasagna—for him, not the babies—or outgrown baby items. They could strategize, make a nanny materialize out of thin, cold air. Mary Poppins, please.

He went to the door. It was neither Mrs. Philpot nor a Dawson.

It was someone he hadn't laid eyes on in seventeen years, since high school graduation. She was instantly recognizable. Very tall. The long red wavy hair. The sharp, assessing brown eyes. Plus there had always been something a little fancy about her. Like the cashmere emerald green coat and polished black cowboy boots she wore.

It was Savannah Walsh, his old high school nemesis—really, his enemy since kindergarten—standing there on his porch. In her hand was the updated ad from the *Bear Ridge Weekly*.

It might have been almost twenty years since he'd seen her, but he doubted she was anything like Mary Poppins.

"You might not remember me," Savannah said in a rush of words, her heart hammering away—so loud she was surprised he didn't hear it over all the wailing. "Savannah Walsh? We were in school together." *I had an intense crush on you since the first time I saw you—kindergarten. And every year I secretly loved you more...*

"I'd recognize you anywhere," he said, giving the baby in his arms a bounce. "Even without eyeglasses."

For a split second, Savannah was uncharacteristically speechless. She always had something to say. He *remembered* her. He even remembered that she wore glasses. She wasn't sure he would. Then again, she'd been the ole thorn in his side for years so she was probably unforgettable for that reason.

He looked surprised to see her—and dammit, as gorgeous as ever. The last time she'd seen him up close was seventeen years ago. But the warm blue eyes, almost black tousled hair, the slight cleft in his chin were all the same except for a few squint lines, a handsome maturity to his thirty-five-year-old face. He had to be six-two and was cowboy-muscular, his broad shoulders defined in a navy Henley, his slim hips and long legs in faded denim.

She'd seen him around town several times over the years, always at a distance, when she'd be back in Bear Ridge for the holidays or a family party, and any time she'd spot him on Main Street or in the grocery store or some shop, her stomach would get those little butterflies and she'd turn tail or hide behind a rack like a sixteen-year-old who couldn't yet handle her emotions.

Amazing. Savannah Walsh had never been afraid of anything in her life—except for how she'd always felt about this man.

His head tilted a bit, his gaze going to the ad in her hand. "You're here to apply for the nanny position?" He looked confused; he'd probably heard along the way that she was a manager of rodeo performers—even had a few famous clients.

She peered behind him, where the crying of two more babies could be heard. "Sort of," she said. "We may be able to help each other out."

His eyes lit up for a moment, and she knew right then and there that he was truly desperate for help. Then his gaze narrowed on her, as if he was trying to figure out what she could possibly mean by "sort of" or "help each other out." That had always been their thing back in school, really: both trying to read the other's mind and strategy, one-up and come out victorious.

They'd been rivals whether for class treasurer, the better grade in biology, or rodeo classes and competitions. They'd always been tied—she'd beat him at something, then he'd beat her. She'd had his grudging respect, if not his interest in her romantically. She'd been in his arms exactly once, for two and a half minutes at the senior prom, when she'd dared to ask him to dance and he'd said, *Okay*. A slow song by Beyoncé. But he'd stood back a bit, their bodies not touching, except for his hands at her waist and hers on his shoulders, and he'd barely looked at her except to awkwardly smile.

Savannah, five foot ten and gangly with frizzy red hair, oversized crystal-framed eyeglasses and a big personality, had been no one's type back then.

"Well, come on in," he said, stepping back and letting her enter.

The baby he held reached out and grabbed her hair, clutching a swath in his tiny fist. Ooh, that yank hurt. Rookie mistake, clearly.

She smiled at the little rascal and covered her eyes with her hands, then took them away. "Peekaboo!" she said. "Peekaboo, I see you!"

The baby stopped crying and stared at her, the tiny fist releasing her hair. Ah, much better. She took a step away.

He looked impressed. "You must have babies of your own to have handled that so well and fast."

For a moment she was stunned that she *had* done so well and she smiled, feeling a bit more confident about the reason she was here. But then the first part of what he'd said echoed in her head—about babies of her own.

"Actually, I don't. Not even one," she added, and wished she hadn't. *Do not call attention to your lack of experience.* Though, really, that was why she was here. To *gain* experience. "I have a three-year-old niece. Clara. She was a grabby one too. In fact, that's why I knew to put in my contact lenses to come see you. Clara taught me that babies love to grab glasses off my face and break the ear piece in the process."

He smiled. "Ah. I thought all my pint-sized relatives would have better prepared me for parenthood, but nope." Before she could respond, not that she knew what to even say since he looked crestfallen, he added, "So you said you're *sort of* here about the nanny job?"

Her explanation would take a while so she took off her coat, even though he didn't invite her to, and hung it on the wrought-iron coat rack. For a moment all the little snowsuits and fleece buntings and man-sized jackets on the various hooks mesmerized her. Then she realized Hutch was watching her, waiting for her to explain herself. Thing was, as she turned to face him, she really didn't want to explain herself. What was that saying, *all talk and no action*? Act, she told herself, like she had with the peekaboo game to free her hair from the itty fist. Then talk.

She turned her focus to the baby who'd resumed crying in Hutch's arms. Even red-faced and squawking, the little boy was beautiful. That very kind of observation was among the main reasons she was here. "Well, aren't you just the cutest," she said to the baby. "Hutch, why don't I take this little guy, and you go deal with the loudest of the other two and then we'll able to talk without shouting." She smiled so it would be clear she wasn't judging the triplets for being so noisy. Or him.

He still had that look of confusion, but he let her take his son from his arms. As she cuddled the baby the way her sister had taught her when Clara was born three years ago, rubbing his little back in gentle, wide circles, he calmed down a bit and gazed up at her with big blue eyes.

"You wanna hear a song?" she asked him. "I'm no singer, but here goes." She broke into "Santa Claus Is Coming to Town."

"He's making a list, he's checking it twice, he's gonna find out who's naughty and nice…"

Hutch paused from where he'd been about to pluck a baby in pink-and-purple-striped pj's from the swing area by the sliding glass doors and stared at her in a kind of puzzled wonder.

But she barely glanced at him. Instead, her attention was riveted by the sweet, solid weight in her arms, the blue eyes gazing up at her with curiosity. As the baby grabbed her pinky and held on with one heck of a grip, something stirred inside her. She almost gasped.

She'd been right to come here. Right to propose her outlandish idea. If she ever got around to it. She was stalling, she realized, afraid he'd shut her down and show her the door.

It was really her sister Morgan's idea. And it had taken Savannah a good two hours to agree it was a *good* one. She had no idea what Hutch would think.

She glanced at the baby she held, then at the other two. "Is it their dinner time?" she asked. "Maybe they're hungry?"

"Dinner is at six but I suppose they could eat ten minutes early." He paused. "That sounds really dumb— of course they should eat early if they're hungry. I'm just trying to follow the holy schedule."

Hmm, was that a swipe at the ex-wife she'd heard about from her sisters? "I know from my sister how important schedules are when it comes to children," she said with a nod. She'd once babysat Clara when she was turning one, and the list of what to do when was two pages long. "I'm happy to help out since I'm here."

His gaze shot to her, and he seemed about to say, *Why*

are *you here*, but what came out of his mouth was, "I appreciate that. Their high chairs are in the kitchen."

She followed him into the big, sunny room, a country kitchen but with modern appliances. A round wood table was by the window, three high chairs around it. She'd put her niece in a high chair a time or two, so she slid the baby in and did up the straps. The little guy must know the high chair meant food or Cheerios because he instantly got happier. "What's this cutie's name?" she asked.

With his free hand, Hutch gave himself a knock on the forehead. "I didn't even introduce them. That's Caleb. I have Chloe," he said, putting her in the middle chair. "And I'm about to go get Carson." In twenty seconds he was back with a squawking third baby, who also immediately calmed down once he was in the chair. Hutch went to the counter and opened a ceramic container and scooped out some Cheerios on each tray. The babies all picked one up and examined it before dropping it on their tongues.

"Are they on solids?" she asked, remembering that was a thing at some point.

He nodded. "Jarred baby food. Their schedule has their favorites." He pulled out his phone and held it so she could see the list, then went to the cabinet and got out three jars and then three spoons from the drawer.

"Bibs?" she asked, recalling seeing it on the schedule next to dinner: *Don't forget the bibs or their good pj's will get stained.*

"Oh right," he said, and pulled three bibs from a drawer. He handed her one and quickly put on the other two. "Since you've made buddies with Caleb, maybe you could feed him while I do double duty with these two."

She smiled and took the jar he handed her. Sweet potato. And the tiny purple spoon. He sat back down and opened up two other jars, a spoon in each hand, dipped, and into each little mouth they went at the same time.

The kitchen was suddenly remarkably quiet. No crying.

She quickly opened up the sweet potato and gave Caleb a spoonful. He gobbled it up and tried to grab the spoon. "Ooh, you like your dinner. Here's another bite." She could feel Hutch's gaze on her as she kept feeding Caleb.

"I definitely recall hearing somewhere that you're a manager of rodeo performers?" Hutch said, dabbing Chloe's mouth with her bib.

"Yes. I'm off till just after Christmas, taking a much-needed vacation. I'm staying with my sister Morgan while I'm in town."

"But you're sort of here about the nanny job?" he asked, pausing from feeding the babies. Chloe banged a hand on the tray, sending two Cheerios flying.

"I... Yes," she said. "I'll get this guy fed and burped and then I'll explain."

He nodded and turned his attention back to Chloe and Carson.

As she slipped another spoonful of sweet potato puree into the open tiny mouth, she wondered how to explain herself without revealing her most personal thoughts and questions that consumed her lately and kept her up at night.

She could just launch into the truth, how she'd been at her youngest sister's bridal shower earlier today, which she would have enjoyed immensely were it not for her least favorite cousin, Charlotte. Charlotte, also younger than Savannah and a mom of three, had peppered her with questions about being single—long divorced—at age thirty-five. *Don't you want a baby? And don't you want to give that baby a sibling? Aren't you afraid you'll run out of time?*

Savannah's middle sister, Morgan, happily married with a three-year-old and a baby on the way, had protectively and thankfully pulled Savannah away from their busybody cousin. And what Savannah had admitted, almost tearfully, and she was no crier, was that yes, she *was* afraid—because she didn't know what she wanted. She'd been divorced since she was twenty-five. Ten years was a long time to be on her own with every subsequent relationship not working out. She'd put her heart into her career and had long figured that maybe not every woman found their guy.

Over the years she'd wondered if she measured her feelings for her dates and relationships against the schoolgirl longing she'd felt for Hutch Dawson. No one had ever touched it, not even the man she'd been briefly married to. That longing, from grade school till she left Bear Ridge at eighteen, was part of the reason Morgan had shown her Hutch's ad in the *Bear Ridge Weekly*.

The other part, the main part, was about the babies. The family.

She just had to explain it all to Hutch in a way that wouldn't mortify her and would get him to say: *The job is yours.*

"I have a proposal for you," she said.

Chapter Two

Savannah held her breath as Hutch looked over at her, spoonfuls of applesauce and oatmeal midway to Chloe's and Carson's mouths.

"A proposal," he repeated, sliding a glance at her. "I'm listening."

Since no words were coming out of her mouth, he turned his attention back to the babies, giving them their final bites of dinner. Then he stood and lifted Chloe out of the high chair, cuddling her against him and gently patting her back. One good burp later, he did the same with Carson.

Maybe Hutch realized she could use a minute before she blurted out her innermost burning thoughts. She definitely did, so she focused on Caleb and his after-dinner needs. She'd never been able to get a good burp out of her niece when she was a baby. Savannah was on the road so often, traveling with her clients, or at home three hours away in Blue Smoke, where one of the biggest annual rodeos was held every summer, that she didn't really see Clara as much as she wanted. Savannah had a bit of experience at childcare. But it was just that. A bit. And when it came to babies, that experience was three years old.

She'd watched how Hutch had handled burp time, so she stood and took Caleb from the high chair, put him against her shoulder and gently patted his back. Nothing. She patted a little harder. Still nothing.

Her shoulders sagged. How could she expect Hutch to give her a job involving baby care when she couldn't even get a baby to burp!

"Caleb likes three fast pats dead center on his back," Hutch said. "Try that."

She did.

BURP!

Savannah grinned. "Yes!" The little boy then spit up on her fawn-colored cashmere sweater, which probably wasn't the best choice in a top for the occasion of coming to propose he let her be his nanny till Christmas. At least she wore her dark denim and cowboy boots, which seemed perfectly casual.

Hutch handed her a wet paper towel. "Sorry."

"No worries. That I don't mind is actually an important element of why I'm here."

"Right," he said. "The proposal." He stared at her for a moment. "Let's take these guys into the living room and let them crawl around. They're not actually crawling yet but they like to try. Then I want to hear all about this proposal of yours."

She had Caleb and he took both Carson and Chloe.

She followed him into the living room, and they sat down on the huge soft foam play mat decorated with letters and numbers. The babies were on their hands and knees and sort of rocked but didn't crawl. They were definitely content.

She sucked in a breath. *Okay*, she told herself. *Come out with it.* "I'm kind of at a crossroads, Hutch."

He glanced at her. "What kind of crossroads?"

"The kind where I'm not sure if I want to keep doing what I'm doing or…something else."

"Like what?" he asked, pushing a stuffed rattle in the shape of a candy cane closer to where Carson was rocking back and forth. The boy's big eyes stared at the toy.

Here goes, she thought. "I'm thirty-five and long divorced. Married life, motherhood, has all sort of passed me by. I have a great job and I'm suited to it. But lately, I've had these…feelings. Like maybe I do want a family. I'm not the least bit *sure* how I feel, what I truly want."

His head had tilted a bit, and he waited for her to continue.

Why was it so hard to say all this? "My sister happened to see your ad while she was looking for a date-night sitter in the local paper's help wanted section. She thought maybe I could get a little clarity, find out what family life is like by helping you out with the triplets till Christmas."

"I see," he said. And that was all he said. She held her breath again.

For a moment they just watched the babies, Carson batting the stuffed rattle on the mat, Chloe still rocking on her hands and knees, Caleb now on his back trying to chew his toe.

"I don't have any experience as a nanny," she rushed to say, the uncomfortable silence putting her a bit off balance. Clearly, since she wasn't exactly selling herself here. "I've cared for my niece, as I've said, here and there over the past three years. More there than here. I want to see what it feels like to care for a baby—babies. To be involved in a family."

"Like an experiment," he said.

"I guess so." Her heart sank. She was sure *experimenting* with his children wasn't going to be okay with him. Why had she thought he might consider this?

"And no need to pay me for the ten days, of course, since we'd be helping each other out." Savannah was very successful and didn't look at this as a temporary job; it was a chance to find out if motherhood really was what she wanted. For that, *she'd* pay. Her heart hammered again, and she took a fast breath to calm down a bit. "I'm sure you want to think it over." She hurried over to the coat rack and pulled her wallet from her coat pocket, taking out a business card. She walked back over and knelt down to hand it to him. "My contact info is on there."

He looked at it, then put it in his back pocket. "Can you start immediately?" he asked. "Like now?"

She felt her eyes widen—and hope soar. "I'm hired?" Had she heard him correctly?

"I can't do this alone," he said. "And I can't take off the next several days from the ranch. I need help. And here you are, Savannah Walsh. If there's one thing I remember about you it's that you get things done. And—" He cut himself off.

Well, now she had to know what that *and* was about. "And?" she prompted gently.

"And…okay, I'm just going to say it. I used to think, man, that Savannah Walsh is all business, works her tail off, but then I experienced firsthand that you have a big heart too. That combination qualifies you for the job. And like I said, the fact that you're here. Wanting the job. Many nannies have given up. I insist on paying you, though. And a lot."

She was still caught on the middle part of what he'd said. About his experiencing that she had a big heart. There could only be one instance he was referring to— that bad day at a rodeo competition when he'd come in third and his father had gone off on him, and she— who'd come in second—had tried to comfort him. She was surprised it had stuck with him all these years later, but she supposed those kinds of things did stick with people. When you were going through something awful and someone was in your corner.

"Of course, we were big-time rivals back then," he rushed to say. "So we might not get along even now."

She smiled. "I'm sure we won't, if it's like old times."

He smiled too. "Though we had a couple of moments, didn't we?"

She almost gasped. So he remembered the other incident too. The dance at the prom. All two and half minutes of it. Had *that* stuck with him?

"Plus it's been a long time," she said. They were different people now; they'd lived entire lives, full of ups and downs.

"A long time," he repeated.

"I can't promise I'll be great at the job," she said,

probably too honestly. "But I'll try hard. I'll be responsible. I'll put my heart and brains into everything I do when I'm with your children, Hutch."

"I appreciate that," he said. "And you have two hands. That's what I need most of all."

Happy, excited chills ran up and down her spine. "Well, then. You've got yourself your holiday season nanny."

A relief came over his expression, and she could see his shoulders relax. He was desperate. But in this case, it worked in her favor.

"Look, Savannah," he said. "Because I know you, I mean, we go way back, and this is a learning experience for you and a severe need for me, would you consider being live-in for the ten days? The triplets are pretty much sleeping through the night, if you consider midnight to five thirty 'the night.'"

Live-in. Even better. "That would certainly show me true family life with babies," she said. "So yes. I'll just get my bags from my sister's and be back in a half hour."

"Just in time for the bedtime routine," he said. "I'm pretty bad at that. And I have a lot of unfinished business from today that I still need to get to, so having your help will make it go much faster. I can't tell you how lucky I feel that you knocked on the door, Savannah."

Ha. We'll see if you're still feeling lucky tomorrow when it's clear I don't know a thing about babies. Times three.

She extended her hand. "And truly, I won't accept pay."

"How about this—I'll donate what I'd pay you to the town's holiday fundraiser for families who need help with meals and gifts and travel expenses."

She smiled. "Perfect."

He gave her hand a shake, holding on for a moment and then covering her hand with his other. "Thank you."

"And thank you," she said a little too breathlessly, too aware from the electric zap that went straight to her toes that her crush on Hutch Dawson was far from over.

"Well, guys," Hutch said to the triplets, each in their own little baby tub in the empty bathtub. "That is what's known as a Christmas miracle."

He still could barely believe he'd gotten so lucky—though lucky was of course relative. Savannah Walsh might not have experience with babies but she was here. Or would be in about ten minutes. To help. And oh man, did Hutch need help.

Carson banged his rubber duckie and Chloe chewed her waterproof book with the chewable edges as Hutch poured warm water over the shampoo on Caleb's head, careful not to let it get in his eyes. A minute ago, Chloe had dropped her head back at the moment Hutch had gone to rinse the shampoo from her hair, and water and suds had streamed down her face. She'd wailed for a good half minute until Hutch had distracted her with peekaboo—Savannah's earlier go-to. One of his cousins—Maisey, who ran the childcare center at the Dawson Family Guest Ranch—had given him five pairs of goofy glasses to make peekaboo work even faster. He'd grabbed the plastic glasses with their springy cartoon puppy cutouts, and Chloe was indeed transfixed and had stopped crying. He had a pair in practically every room in the house.

Carson batted his hands down, splashing lukewarm water all over his siblings, who giggled.

"All right, you little rug rats, bath time is over. Let's get you dry and changed."

He lifted each baby with one hand, drained their tub with the other, then wrapped them in their adorable hooded towels, a giraffe for Caleb, a lion for Chloe and a bear for Carson. He plopped them down in the portable playpen he'd bought just for this purpose—to get all three babies from the bathtub to the nursery at the same time. It was probably the baby item he used most often; he transported them all over the one-story ranch house with ease.

He got each baby into a fresh diaper and pj's, and now it was time for their bottles. Then it would be story time, then bedtime. Hopefully Savannah really would be back to help with that.

The doorbell rang. Perfect. She was back a little early and could help with bottles. He'd gotten okay at feeding two babies at once, but he didn't have *three* hands.

He wheeled the playpen to the door, but it wasn't Savannah after all. It was Daniel, his brother. Or his *half* brother, as Daniel always corrected him. Tall like Hutch, with light brown hair and the Dawson blue eyes, Daniel lived in town with Olivia, his wife of twenty years. When he and his brother inherited the ranch from their father three months ago, Daniel had surprised Hutch by taking down his CPA shingle in town and coming aboard full-time as chief financial officer, which Hutch had been initially glad about since it freed him up to focus on the day-to-day of managing the ranch. But his brother disagreed with a lot of Hutch's plans for the Dueling Dawsons Ranch—too apt a name, as always. Hutch had been the foreman for a decade—he knew the fifteen-hundred-acre ranch inside and out—but family feuds had plagued the Dawsons on this property since his great-grandfather and great-uncle had bought the land more than a century ago. He and Daniel did not break the pattern.

The one thing Daniel did not seem interested in was pursuing the list of "Unfinished Business" that Lincoln Dawson had left tacked up on his bulletin board. There were only two items, both doozies. But Hutch intended to cross them off by Christmas. Somehow, he thought his father would truly rest in peace that way. And Hutch by association. God knew, Daniel needed some peace.

"I'm leaving for the day," Daniel said, shoving his silver-framed square eyeglasses up on his nose. "And still no response to my email about your list of costly initiatives for the ranch," he added, shoving his hands into the pockets of his thick flannel barn coat. He wore a brown Stetson, flurries collecting on the top and the brim.

"I was actually in the middle of answering when disaster struck," Hutch said, stepping back so Daniel could come in out of the cold. "The new nanny quit on me."

"Another one?" Daniel raised an eyebrow, stopping on the doormat, which indicated he wasn't staying long—good thing. "Is it you or the triplets? Probably both," he said with a nod, answering that for himself.

Ah, Daniel. So supportive, as always.

"I was just about to make up their bottles," Hutch said, angling his head toward the playpen. "If you can feed one of the babies, I can do two and we can talk."

Daniel scowled. "I'm long done feeding a baby."

Hutch mentally shook his head. Daniel and Olivia were empty nesters; their eighteen-year-old son was in college two hours away near the Colorado border. "We'll talk in the morning. Or are you going to be trapped here with them and not out on the ranch, taking care of business?"

Keep your cool, hold your tongue. That was Hutch's motto when it came to dealing with his brother. His half brother.

"Trapped isn't the word I'd use," he said, narrowing a glare on Daniel. "And I have a new nanny already. She's starting tonight, as a matter of fact. She'll be a live-in through Christmas Eve."

"Good. Because you need to get your share of the work done."

Keep your cool, hold your tongue...

"I'll see you at 6:00 a.m. in the barn," Hutch said. "We can talk about the email and the sheep while taking on Mick's and Davis's chores."

"I don't see why cowboys had to get ten days off," Daniel groused.

Had Hutch ever met someone more begrudging than Daniel Dawson? "Because they've worked hard all year and get two weeks off. They both had the time coming to them."

"It's bad timing with our father being gone."

"Yeah," Hutch said, picturing Lincoln Dawson. He'd been sixty-two when an undiagnosed heart condition took him from them. Maybe he'd hidden the symptoms; Hutch wasn't sure, and Daniel had kept his distance from their dad as he had his entire life. Lincoln had worked hard, done the job of a cowboy half his age.

He'd hated administrative work and trusted few people so he'd offered Hutch the foreman job ten years ago, when Hutch had been fresh out of an MBA in agricultural business, about to take a high-paying job at a big cattle ranch across town. Hutch had shocked himself by saying yes to his father's offer at half the salary and fewer perks. *Maybe I'll finally figure you out, Lincoln Dawson*, he'd thought.

But he hadn't. And Daniel hated talking about their father, so he'd never been any help.

Daniel reached for the doorknob. "Six sharp."

"You could acknowledge your niece and nephews," Hutch said unexpectedly, surprised it had come out of his mouth. But he supposed it did bother him that his brother barely paid them any attention. He was their uncle.

"Don't make this something it's not," Daniel said, without a glance at the triplets, and left.

Hutch sighed and rolled his eyes. "Your uncle is something, huh, guys?" he directed to his children. "*A piece of work*, as your late grandmother would have said. Or as your late grandfather would have said succinctly, *difficult*."

His brother had always been that. When Daniel was four, Lincoln had walked away from his family to marry his mistress—Hutch's mother. A year after their marriage, Hutch was born, and Hutch could recall his brother spending every other Saturday at the ranch for years, until Daniel was twelve or thirteen and said he was done with that. Their dad hadn't insisted, which had still infuriated Daniel and also his mother; Hutch had known that from screaming phone calls and slammed doors between the exes.

What Hutch did know about his father was that he'd loved his second wife, Hutch's mom, deeply. The two of them had held hands while eating dinner at the dining table. They'd danced in the living room to weird eighties new wave music. They'd gotten dressed up and had gone out to a fancy meal every Saturday night without fail. The way his father had looked at his mother had always softened Hutch's ire at very-difficult-himself Lincoln Dawson; Hutch had given him something of a pass for what a hard case he'd been with Hutch and Daniel and anyone else besides his wife. Hutch's mother had died when he was eighteen, and in almost twenty years, Lincoln had never looked at another woman as far as Hutch knew. But the loss had turned his father even more gruff and impatient, and Hutch had threatened to quit, had quit, about ten times.

Your mother wouldn't like the way I handled things earlier, Lincoln would say by way of apology. *She'd want you to come back.*

Hutch always had. He loved the Dueling Dawsons Ranch. The land. The work. The livestock. And he'd loved his father. He'd been gone three months now, and sometimes his absence, the lack of his outsize presence on the ranch, gripped Hutch with an aching grief.

There were just some things that stayed with a person—the good and the bad. When Hutch's ex-wife had sat him down last year and tearfully told him she was leaving him for Ted, a distraught, confused, scared Hutch had packed a suitcase and turned up at the ranch. His father had taken one look at his face, at the suitcase, and had asked him what happened. Lincoln had called Allison a vile name that Hutch had tried to put out of his memory, then told his son he could stay at the ranch in his old room, take some time off work as the foreman if he needed, and went to make them spaghetti and garlic bread, which Hutch had barely been able to eat but appreciated. They'd sat at the table in near silence, also appreciated, except for his father twice putting his hand on Hutch's shoulder with a *You'll get through this*.

Whenever things with his dad had gotten rough, he'd remember that Lincoln Dawson had been there for him when it really mattered. He also liked how his father had bought the triplets a gift every Monday, the same for each, whether tiny cowboy hats or rattles or books, when Allison would drop them off. Lincoln would give her the death stare, then dote on the triplets, talking to them about ranch life. Then in another breath, he'd flip out on Hutch for how he handled something with a vendor or which pasture he'd moved the herd to.

He's never going to be any different, Daniel had said a few times the past couple of years when Lincoln must have started feeling sick or weakened but had refused to see a doctor and had brushed off questions about this health. *Stop chasing his approval already.*

Hutch often wanted to slug his brother, but never so much as during those times when he'd accuse Hutch of exactly that. Chasing his approval. He'd had it— his father had made him his foreman, hadn't he? Daniel would say it was more than that, deeper, but Hutch would shut that down fast.

Five minutes later, the doorbell rang again, and he shook off the memories, shook off his brother's visit and attitude. Savannah was back. His shoulders instantly unbunched. There was something calming about her presence, a quiet confidence, and he liked the way she looked at the triplets. With wonder and affection.

He liked the way she looked, period. Had she always been so pretty? He hadn't really thought of her that way back in school, given their rivalry. But he did remember being surprised by his reaction when she'd taken his hand in solidarity after that rodeo competition their senior year. A touch he'd felt *everywhere*. His father had screamed his head off at Hutch about a minor mistake he'd made that had cost him first and second place, and Savannah had heard the whole thing. She'd walked up to him and taken his hand and just held it and said, *You didn't deserve that. You were great out there as always.* The reverberation of that touch had distracted him for a moment, and he wanted to pull her to him and just hold her, his rival turned suddenly very attractive *friend*. But he'd been seventeen and humiliated by his father's tirade and wanted the ground to swallow him, so he'd run off without a word, shaking off her hand like it had meant nothing to him.

He wondered if she even remembered that. Probably not. It was a long time ago.

He went to the door and there she was, her long red hair twisted into a bun—smart move—her face scrubbed free of the glamorous makeup she'd worn earlier. She wore a down jacket over a T-shirt with a rodeo logo and faded low-slung jeans. He swallowed at the sight of her. Damn, she was beautiful.

"The doorbell reminded me that I need to give you a key," he said, reaching for her bags. He took her suitcase and duffel and set them down by the door, then reached into his pocket for his key ring and took off one of the extra house keys. "I'll give you a quick tour and show you your room, and then we can give the triplets their bottles."

She smiled and put the key on her own ring, looking past him for the triplets, first at their swings, then at the playpen, in which the three were sitting and contentedly playing with toys. "Let me at those adorable littles." She rushed over to the playpen and knelt down beside it, chatting away to the babies about how she was here to help take care of them.

As she stood and turned back to him, she seemed so truly happy, her face flushed with excitement, that he found himself touched. This was a completely different setup than he was used to; she wasn't working for him, he wasn't paying her. She was here to get experience, to have some questions answered for herself.

It occurred to him that they should probably talk about that setup—expectations on both sides, how she wanted to structure the "job," the hours he'd need to devote to the ranch, the triplets' schedule, details about each of them, such as their different personalities, likes and dislikes, what worked on which baby. They should also talk about nighttime wakings; at least one triplet woke up at least once a night and would likely wake her up. He wanted to ensure that he wouldn't be taking advantage of her being a live-in.

He suddenly envisioned Savannah coming out of her room at 2:00 a.m. to soothe a crier in nothing but a long T-shirt. He blinked to get the image out of his head. He seemed to be drawn to her—there was just something about her, something winsome, something both tough and vulnerable—and they did go back a ways, which made her seem more familiar than she actually was. But Hutch had had his entire world turned upside down and sideways and shaken—by the divorce, by being a father of three babies that he loved so much he thought he might burst sometimes, by his father's loss and the sudden onslaught of his brother. He couldn't imagine wanting anything to do with the opposite sex.

Or maybe I could, he amended as a flash of Savannah in just a long T-shirt floated into his mind again.

Nah, he thought. He really doubted that even sex could tempt him to step back into the romance ring. Not after what he'd been through.

Suuure, said a very low voice in the back of his mind where reality reigned.

Chapter Three

Savannah liked her room. It was a guest room next door to the nursery. There were two big windows, soothing off-white walls with an abstract watercolor of the Wyoming wilderness, a queen-size bed with a fluffy blue-and-white down comforter and lots of pillows, a dresser with a round mirror, a beautiful kilim rug, and a glider by the window. Perfect for taking a crying baby into her room in the middle of the night to soothe without waking up the other two.

Hutch, with the baby monitor in his back pocket, was putting her suitcase and duffel by the closet. Being in here, her room for the ten days, with him so close was doing funny things to her belly. "This was my room growing up. The furniture was different then, but that's the window I stared out every day, wondering where my life would take me." He walked over and looked out. He'd had a view of a stand of evergreens and the woods beyond and part of the fields.

"It took you right here," she said, thinking about that for a moment. Full circle. "Did you even consider that then? That you'd be the foreman on this ranch?"

"Absolutely not. My father wasn't the easiest man to get along with. But not long after I left for college to study agricultural business—with the intention of having my own ranch someday—I lost my mom. When my dad offered me the foreman's job, the idea of coming home called to me. She loved this ranch. I always did too."

"I grew up in town," she said. "But I've always wanted to live on a ranch. I'm a rodeo gal at heart."

"Well, for the next week and a half, you'll be woken up by a crowing rooster long before a crying baby or two or three, so that might get old fast. You should visit the barn. We have six beautiful horses."

She smiled. "I'll plan to. So what's on the schedule? I'm excited to jump right into my first official task as Christmas season nanny."

"It's time for their last bottles. Usually I feed two at once, then the third, but now we can split that up."

"I see what you mean about needing an extra set of hands," she said. "It must have been really hard these past six months, being on your own once the nannies were done for the day. I guess you had to figure it out as you went?"

"Yup, exactly. I'm a pretty good multitasker, though, something necessary to be a good ranch foreman. You know what the hardest part has been? When I don't know how to soothe one or two or all three, when they're crying like they were earlier when the former nanny quit on me. When I don't know how to make it better and nothing works. I feel like a failure as a dad." He frowned, and it was clear how deep the cuts could go with him.

"Oh, Hutch," she said, her heart flying out to him. "I'll bet it's like that for any parent of even just one baby. They don't talk, they can't tell you where it hurts or what they want, and you love them so much that it just kills you."

"Exactly," he said. "For someone who doesn't have experience with babies, you definitely get it."

She felt herself beam. She wasn't entirely sure how she "got it"; she supposed it was just human nature to feel that way about something so precious and dependent on you.

"Let's go feed them, and we can talk about how to arrange this," he said, wagging a finger between them. "How it'll all work. I really don't want to take advantage of you being here, living here, and the *reason* you're here. It's a tough job, Savannah."

"I'm a tough woman," she said. Except she didn't feel that way here in Hutch's house, in his presence. She felt...very vulnerable.

"You were a tough girl," he said. "Kept me on my toes."

She laughed. "Well, tough might have kept me from—" Ugh, she clammed up in the nick of time. Was she honestly about to tell Hutch Dawson that she was afraid her cousin Charlotte's assessment of her earlier at the bridal shower was right, that who Savannah was made her unappealing to men—*intimidating* and *too successful* were the actual words her cousin had used today.

Oh please, Savannah had thought, but she'd heard that her entire life. She'd been five foot ten since she was thirteen and no slouch, literally or figuratively, so she'd been standing tall a long time. And yes, she was straightforward and could be barky, and she was damned good at her job. It was true that she could make some people quake because of her stature in the industry at this point. But that was business, and her profession demanded *tough*. She'd never gotten very far with men, though. She'd get ghosted or told it just wasn't working out after a week or two of dating.

Or seven months of marriage. *I'm not one of your clients*, her new husband had said so many times that she'd started doubting herself—who she was, particularly. *You're trying to manage me*, he'd toss at her. *Maybe if you didn't work such long hours or travel so much, I wouldn't have cheated.*

With a friend, among others, no less. Savannah hadn't been sure he had been cheating until her "friend" had confirmed it and said the same thing her husband had: *If you devoted yourself to your marriage instead of your career...* At twenty-five she'd had an ex-husband, an ex-friend, and had dealt with her doubly broken heart by devoting herself even more to her career. She was in a male-dominated industry, but her voice, drive and determination had carried her to the top. She took reasonable risks, demanded the best of her clients and for them, but cared deeply about each one. Yeah, she was tough.

To a point, she reminded herself. Lately, she'd find

herself tearing up. She'd been in a grocery store a few days ago and the sight of a young family, a dad pushing the cart with a toddler in the seat, the mom walking beside him with a little girl on her shoulders and letting the child take items off the high shelves for her—Savannah had almost burst into tears in the bread aisle of Safeway.

Do I want that? she'd asked herself, perplexed by her reaction. Why else would she have been so affected? She'd written off remarriage and happily-ever-after, having lost her belief and faith in either, in the fairy tale. Her parents had had a wonderful, long marriage. One sister was happily married and the other was engaged and madly in love with her fiancé. Savannah knew there were good men out there, good marriages. But she'd always been…tough. And maybe meant to be on her own.

She didn't know how to be any different. It was her natural personality that put the fear of God into the men and women rodeo performers she managed, from up-and-comers with great potential to superstars, like her most famous client, a bull rider who'd quit fame and fortune to settle down with the woman he loved and the child he'd only recently discovered was his. She'd spent some time with the happy family the past few months, and Logan Winston's happiness, a joy she hadn't seen in him ever before, made her acknowledge a few hard truths about herself. That she was lonely. That she did have a serious hankering for something more—she just wasn't sure what, exactly. A change, but what change? She should talk to Logan about it while she was in town.

Hutch was leaving the room so she shook off her

thoughts and followed, excited to get started on her new role—for the time being, anyway. A life of babies and Hutch Dawson.

In the kitchen, she stood beside him as he made up the bottles, watching carefully how he went about it so she could do it herself. Back in the living room, he set the three bottles on the coffee table, then grabbed a bunch of bibs and burp cloths from the basket on the shelf under the table and, finally, wheeled the playpen over to the sofa.

"I'll watch you for a moment," she said, sitting down. "See how you hold the baby, hold the bottle, just so I know how to do it all properly."

"It's a cinch. Maybe the easiest part of all fatherhood— and the most relaxing, well, except for watching them sleep. There's just something about feeding a baby, giving him or her what they need, all in the grand comfort of your arms."

"I always felt that way when I watched my sister feed Clara," she said, recalling how truly cozy it looked, how content mama and baby had always appeared.

He picked up Carson and settled him slightly reclined along one arm, then reached for a bottle and tilted it into the little bow-shaped mouth. Carson put his hands on the bottle and suckled away, Hutch's gaze loving on his son.

"Got it," she said. "Should I grab another baby for you?"

"Sure, take your pick."

"I'll save Chloe for myself since I got time with Caleb earlier." She scooped the little guy from the playpen and settled him on Hutch's right side. When he shifted

Caleb just right, she handed him a bottle. In no time, he was feeding both babies.

My turn! She picked up Chloe, who stared at her with huge blue eyes. *Oh, aren't you precious*, she thought, putting Chloe along her arm and grabbing the third bottle. "Hungry?" she asked. She slipped the nipple into the baby's mouth, and it was so satisfying as Chloe started drinking, her little hands on the sides of the bottle. Savannah gazed down at her, mesmerized. When she glanced up, she realized Hutch was watching her. Her. Not how she was holding Chloe or the bottle. *Her.*

Could he be interested? Hutch Dawson, guy of her dreams since she was five, star of her fantasies since middle school? He was the one thing she'd ever wanted that she hadn't gone for, her fear—of rejection and how bad it would hurt—and lack of confidence when it came to personal relationships making her anything but tough.

"This is great," he said with a warm smile. "Having the extra two hands."

Oh. That was what the look of wonder was about. How helpful she was. He wasn't suddenly attracted to her. It wasn't like she'd changed all that much physically since high school, and he'd never given her a second glance back then.

"Having you here for the bedtime routine will be a huge help," he added. "I've really never been good at it. One of the triplets always fights their drooping eyes and fusses, then another fusses, then one starts crying... What takes Allison and Ted fifteen minutes takes me an hour."

"Allison and Ted?" she asked, glancing at him. She

darn well knew who Allison was—his ex-wife. Savannah remembered her from school. Petite, pretty, strawberry blonde and blue-eyed. A cheerleader. Hutch Dawson's type. They'd dated on and off but had always been more off as Savannah recalled. She knew a little bit about the divorce from her sister. Apparently Allison had reconnected with an old flame from college on Facebook. And actually walked away from her marriage at five months pregnant. According to Morgan, Allison had been shunned by some and lauded by others—*How could you?* vs *Life is too short not to follow your heart.*

All Savannah could think was how absolutely awful it must have been for Hutch.

"My ex-wife," he said. "And her new husband. You might remember Allison Windham from school. Then she was Allison Dawson for three years but now she'll be Allison Russo. Sometimes I can't wait until the triplets are old enough for people to stop gossiping about how I'm divorced with babies. Some folks know the sob story but most assume *I* left, even though my ex is the one living in my former house with another man. You should see some of the stare downs I get in the grocery store."

"Ugh, that's terrible," she said. "How unfair. To have your life turned upside down and to get the blame."

He shot her something of a smile. "Small town, big gossip."

"Yeah, I remember. It's one of the reasons why I was excited to leave for bigger pastures. I do love Bear Ridge, though."

"Yeah, me too." They glanced at each other for a

moment, and she felt so connected to him. They came from the same place, had the same beginning history in terms of school and downtown and the Santa hut on the town green. She'd passed it several times since she'd arrived, her heart warmed by the sight of the majestic holiday tree all decorated and lit up in the center of the small park, the red Santa hut with the big candy cane chimney, the families lined up so that the kids could give Santa their lists.

She wondered if Hutch had envisioned himself standing with his family in line, the triplets in the choo choo train of a stroller she'd seen by the door, his wife beside him. Had he been blindsided by her affair? In any case, he must have been devastated when his ex had told him she was leaving.

She glanced down at Chloe, just a tiny bit left in her bottle, and then the baby turned her head slightly.

"That means she's done," Hutch said. "You can burp her and set her in the playpen, and then grab Carson—he's done too."

Savannah stood and held Chloe up vertically against her, about to pat her back.

"I'd set a burp cloth on your shoulder and chest," he said. "You don't want spit-up all over that cool shirt."

She glanced down at her *Blue Smoke Summer Rodeo 2019* jersey. Years old and soft and faded. She'd worn it specifically for the job—no worries in getting dirty and grabbed and pulled out of shape. But she'd still prefer spit-up on the burp cloth and not her. She shifted Chloe and bent a little to pick up a cloth, arranging it on her shoulder, hanging down on her chest.

She gave Chloe's back a good three pats and a big

burp came out. "Success!" Savannah said. "What a great baby you are," she whispered to Chloe. "An excellent burper."

She set Chloe in the playpen and reached for Carson. Was it her imagination or did Hutch's gaze go to the sliver of belly exposed by her shirt lifting up as she leaned over? He handed over Carson and she repeated what she'd just done, but getting a burp out of this guy was taking longer.

How many times had she told her clients—and in talks to various groups and schools—not to think one great performance meant another? You had to work for it—always. She adjusted Carson in her arms and gave up two more pats with a bit more force, and out came a big, satisfying burp.

"I've got this!" she said, unable to contain her excitement. "I was afraid you'd regret taking me on as a student nanny, but I'm feeling a lot more confident."

He smiled. "Good. Because you're doing great."

"You hear that, Carson?" she said, running a finger down the baby's impossibly soft cheek. "I'm doing great!"

Once all three babies were in the playpen, Hutch stood. "If you'll keep watch over them, I could use a solid twenty minutes to finish up today's work—just some administrative stuff, texts and calls and emails."

"Sure thing," she said.

As he left the room, she felt the lack of him immediately.

My crush on your daddy will never go away, I guess, she said silently to the triplets as she wheeled the playpen over to the sliding glass door. There was a pretty pathetic Christmas tree with one strand of garland hanging down along with two branches. The entire tree was tilted as though someone had backed into it. She had a feeling that someone was Hutch with two babies in his arms. She'd help him get the tree decked out. Since the babies weren't crawling, there were no worries about safety-proofing for Christmas yet.

"Well, guys," she said. "How am I doing so far? Not too bad, right?"

Carson gave her a big gummy smile, two tiny teeth poking up.

I sure do like you three, she thought, giving Caleb's soft hair a caress. She'd been here, on the job, for barely an hour and she was falling in serious like with everything to do with the triplets. And Hutch Dawson all over again.

Hutch sat at his desk in his home office, half expecting Savannah to appear in the doorway with a crying baby with a firm grip on her hair or ear and say, *Sorry, but I've already realized that this isn't the life for me, buh-bye*—and go running out the door.

But he'd gotten through three calls, returned all the texts and had made himself mental notes for tomorrow's early-morning meeting with his brother in the barn—and no appearance in the doorway. No quitting. No *crying*.

Blessed silence.

His office door was ajar and every now and then he could hear Savannah's running commentary. She'd wheeled the babies in the playpen into the nursery and changed them one by one, choosing fresh pj's, which he knew because she was chatting away. *Stripes for you, Caleb. Polka dots for Chloe, and tiny bears for Carson. Ooh, another rookie mistake, guys, Caleb almost sprayed me!* She'd laughed and then continued her commentary all the way back down the hall to the living room.

Now she was talking to the triplets about the Christmas tree and how she and her sisters used to make a lot of their ornaments when they were little as family tradition. From what he could tell, she'd wheeled the playpen over by the tree and was picking up each triplet to give them turns at being held and seeing the lonely, bare branches.

"Ooh, that's what I get for letting you get too close to my ear," he heard her say on a laugh to one of the triplets. "Strong girl," she added. "Peekaboo! I see you!"

He smiled as he envisioned her playing peekaboo with one hand to get her ear back. He'd have to tell her about the goofy glasses.

"Okay, now it's Carson's turn," she said.

This was going to work out just fine, he thought, turning his attention back to his brother's email. Ten minutes later, he was done, turned off his desk lamp and went to find Savannah and the babies.

They were sitting on the play mat, and she was telling them a story about a fir tree named Branchy who no one picked for their home at Christmastime.

"Buh!" Caleb said, batting his thigh.

Carson shook his stuffed rattle in the shape of a bunny.

Chloe was giggling her big baby laugh that always made Hutch laugh too.

Savannah turned and grinned. "They like me! Babies like me!"

He realized just then how nervous she'd probably been about how they'd respond to her. They'd managed to chase off professional nannies, including one who'd raised her own triplets. So he understood why a woman who'd never spent much time around babies would worry how she'd fare with three "crotchety" six-month-olds. She'd probably expected them to cry constantly and bat at her nose.

They did do a lot of that kind of thing. But they were also like this. Sitting contentedly, giggling, shaking rattles. If not exactly listening to her story, hearing it around them, enjoying her melodic voice.

"I'd say so," he confirmed, and she beamed, her delight going straight to his heart. "It's bedtime for these guys."

As if on cue, Carson started rubbing his eyes.

Then Caleb did.

Chloe's face crumpled and she let out a loud shriek, then started crying.

Savannah picked up Chloe and held her against her chest, rubbing her back, which helped calm the baby.

Hutch picked up both boys, Carson leaning his head against his father's neck, one of Hutch's favorite things in the world, and Caleb rubbed his eyes.

Savannah's phone rang, and she shifted Chloe to pull it from her back pocket. She glanced at the screen. "Ugh, business," she said, continuing to rub Chloe's back as she bounced her a little. "Savannah Walsh," she said into the phone. "Ah, I've been waiting for your call…No, those terms are *not* acceptable…That's right. No again…

Oh well, no deal then. Have a nice night…What's that? You'll come up the five thousand?…Wonderful. I'll expect the contract by end of business tomorrow." Click.

He watched her turn the ringer off and then chuck the phone on the sofa.

"Sorry," she said. "I just realized I shouldn't have taken that call. I'm on duty here."

"Of course you should have taken it. Your life off this ranch still exists. You do what you need to. And that was very impressive to listen to. Hopefully you'll rub off on me and I'll be tougher when it comes to negotiating at cattle and equipment auctions."

She eyed him. "Were you always a nice guy? I don't remember that."

Hutch laughed. "Nice enough. But competitive with you. Now, I'm just relieved we're both Team Triplets."

She grinned. "Team Triplets. I like it. And I don't want my life to interfere with my time here. In fact, I just realized that for certain. I'll have my assistant, who already has a few clients of her own and is ready to be an agent in her right, handle that contract. I want to focus on the reason I'm here."

Chloe rubbed her eyes and her face started scrunching.

Savannah cuddled Chloe closer. "You better watch out, you better not cry," she sang softly. "You better not pout I'm telling you why. Though, that is what babies do, isn't it, you little dumpling. But Santa Claus *is* coming to town, and he's making a list."

Chloe made a little sound, like "ba," her gaze sweet on Savannah's face, then her eyes drooped. She let out a tiny sigh and her eyes closed, her little chest rising and falling.

"Aww, she fell asleep!" Savannah said. "Huh. I'm not too shabby at this after all. They're all changed and ready for their bassinets."

"You really are a Christmas miracle," he said.

Her face, already lit up, sparkled even more. He led the way into the large, airy nursery with its silver walls decorated with tiny moons and stars, a big round rug on the polished wood floor, the bookcase full of children's titles, two gliders by the window. His father had ordered the three sleigh-shaped wooden bassinets, each baby's name stenciled and painted on it. Every time he looked at the bassinets, at the names, he'd forget all the crud that Daniel kept bringing up and he'd miss his dad, his grief catching him by surprise. People were never just one thing.

Savannah was a good example of that. If he'd seen her walking down Main Street yesterday in her cashmere coat, barking a negotiation into her cell phone, he'd never imagine her as someone who'd sing Christmas carols to a crying baby, whose eyes would light up at a crabby little girl falling asleep in her arms. People could always surprise you, he knew.

"I'm praying for my own Christmas miracle that I can transfer Chloe to her crib without waking her," she said. "What are my odds?"

"She's iffy," he said. "You just never know. Carson's more a sure bet—heavy sleeper. Caleb always wakes up the minute his head touches a mattress. At my house, anyway."

Savannah glanced at him for a moment, seeming to

latch on to that part about "his house." She started quietly singing "Santa Claus Is Coming to Town" again, then carefully lowered Chloe down, gently swaying just a bit. The baby's lower lip quirked, and when she was on the mattress, she simply turned her head and lifted a fist up to her ear, eyes closed, chest rising and falling.

"I did it!" Savannah whispered.

But then Chloe's eyes popped open and she started fussing.

"Scratch that. I didn't do it." Savannah's shoulders sagged.

"Told you she's iffy," he said. "She likes having her forehead caressed from the eyebrows up toward her hairline. And she likes your song. You could try both."

Savannah brightened and reached down to caress Chloe's forehead, singing the carol, and the baby girl's eyes drooped, drooped some more, and then she was asleep. "Phew," she whispered.

A half hour later, both boys were finally asleep in their bassinets, Caleb indeed taking longer than Carson. Hutch had the urge to pull Savannah into his arms for a celebratory hug, but a fist bump seemed more appropriate.

"Our work here is done," he said, holding up his palm. "I could use coffee. You?"

She grinned and did give him a fist bump. "Definitely. And we can talk about the grand plan for my time here."

As they tiptoed out of the nursery, the urge for that embrace only got stronger. Because they were Team Triplets, and it felt so good to have someone on his side, someone who wouldn't quit on him, someone he could talk to?

Or was it all of the above *and* because he was attracted to Savannah Walsh?

It was choice B that made her just as scary as she'd been seventeen years ago.

Don't miss

Triplets Under the Tree *by Melissa Senate,*
available November 2023 wherever
Harlequin® Special Edition
books and ebooks are sold.

www.Harlequin.com

#3019 A MAVERICK'S HOLIDAY HOMECOMING
Montana Mavericks: Lassoing Love • by Brenda Harlen

'Tis the season...for a holiday reunion? Rancher Billy Abernathy has no interest in romance; Charlotte Taylor's career keeps her far away from Montana. But when the recently divorced father of three crosses paths with his runaway bride from long ago, a little bit of mistletoe works magic...

#3020 HER BEST FRIEND'S WEDDING
Bravo Family Ties • by Christine Rimmer

Through the years Sadie McBride and Ty Bravo have been rivals, then enemies—and in recent years, buddies. But when a Vegas wedding party leads to a steamy no-holds-barred kiss, will they risk their perfectly good friendship with something as dangerous as love?

#3021 MARRY & BRIGHT
Love, Unveiled • by Teri Wilson

Editor Addison England is more than ready for a much-earned promotion. The problem? So is Carter Payne, her boss's annoyingly charming nephew. Competition, attraction and marriage mayhem collide when these two powerhouse pros vie for *Veil Magazine*'s top job!

#3022 ONCE UPON A CHARMING BOOKSHOP
Charming, Texas • by Heatherly Bell

Twyla Thompson has kept Noah Cahill in the friend zone for years, crushing instead on his older brother. But when a bookstore costume contest unites them as Mr. Darcy and Elizabeth Bennet—and brings unrealized attraction to light—Twyla wonders if Noah may be her greatest love after all.

#3023 A FAMILY-FIRST CHRISTMAS
Sierra's Web • by Tara Taylor Quinn

Sarah Williams will do anything to locate her baby sister—even go undercover at renowned investigation firm Sierra's Web. She knows her by-the-book boss, Winchester Holmes, would fire her if he knew the truth. So falling for each other is not an option—*right*?

#3024 MARRIED BY MISTAKE
Sutton's Place • By Shannon Stacey

For Chelsea Grey, the only thing worse than working next door to John Fletcher is waking up in Vegas married to him. And worse still? Their petition for annulment is denied! They'll keep fighting to fix their marriage mistake—unless knee-weakening kisses and undeniable attraction change their minds first!

HSECNM1023

HARLEQUIN
PLUS

Try the best multimedia subscription service for romance readers like you!

Read, Watch and Play.

Experience the easiest way to get the romance content you crave.

Start your **FREE TRIAL** at
<u>www.harlequinplus.com/freetrial</u>.